AWAKENING FIRE
THE DIVINE TREE GUARDIAN SERIES

Marsha, Happy Reading! ♡

LARISSA EMERALD

Larissa Emerald

Awakening Fire
The Divine Tree Guardian Series Novel

Copyright © 2015 Larissa Emerald
Castle Oak Publishing LLC

ISBN-10: 1-942139-06-3
ISBN-13: 978-1-942139-06-5

http://www.larissaemerald.com

Published in the United States of America.

BOOKS BY LARISSA EMERALD

Contemporary Romantic Suspense
WINTER HEAT

Paranormal Romance
AWAKENING FIRE

For

My mom, Joyce Mair Wallace,

because had you not taught

me the value of perseverance

this book never would have been written.

AWAKENING FIRE

PROLOGUE

Isle of Skye, Scotland
1120 AD

The crusty old man with long ropes of coal-black hair didn't look like an angel, but he had earned the attention of Venn and his eleven brothers. With a flick of the wrist, the angel plucked an enormous boulder into the air and dropped it on the snarling barghest, plastering the demon onto the ground.

"Guid God, that was close." Minutes ago, he'd thought he and his brothers would all be dead as, in force, they'd fought against the barghest that had attacked them from out of nowhere. Then that angel had joined their ranks and outdone them all. With heaving breaths, Venn crouched near the fire pit and thrust his sword into the flames. As the beast's thick, yellow blood sizzled on the metal, Venn's brothers gathered in a loose semicircle: Njorth, Ian, Euler, Rurik, Aidan, Brandt, Colby, Graham, Dustin, Tristan, and Lachlan. All alive. Bruised, bloodied, clothing clawed and shredded. But alive. Thanks be to God.

Seth, as the angel called himself, perched atop the sandstone rock, apparently fishing dirt from under his fingernails. Beneath him, the boulder flattened the malicious barghest facedown into the dirt, limbs and head protruding, far larger than the biggest dog Venn had ever seen. A foul odor of rotten eggs permeated the air as the thing fought mightily against the stone's weight. The barghest scored the earth with four-inch claws, flashed fangs the length of swords, and snarled, its black fur quivering.

Venn coughed at the stench, then winced as a biting pain seized his rib.

"Finish off the monster," Njorth, the eldest brother, demanded.

"Nay." Seth breathed deeply. His wings expanded and retracted in time with each inhalation. "Io will not die this day. My brother is cast into a net by his own feet." With one hand reaching skyward, he summoned a somewhat smaller boulder at cliff's edge, which he dropped on the barghest's protruding head. "That may silence him for a while."

The rasp in the angel's voice brought to mind wheels catching on rough ground. "'Tis said that each man's future is written before it occurs." Seth passed his perceptive gaze over the brothers. When he came to Venn, his expression darkened, his eyes narrowed. "And 'tis true. Well, partially so. Occasional exceptions have been known to alter one's course. Brothers, you have been chosen."

Venn stood, met the angel's piercing blue stare, and sheathed his sword. A biting wind scurried along the embankment at his back, then shot out over the cliff to meet the riotous waves, enhancing the swirl and shift of the late-morning fog.

The brothers were border guards, protecting their kin against skirmishes and raiding. Venn had been the last invited to this gathering, most likely due to his fierce disbelief in angels.

Not anymore.

"The two prime virtues ascribed to Highlanders are fidelity and courage. This day thou art offered a great challenge to draw on both of these merits. " Seth glanced to the enormous tree several rods from the brothers as he circled his hand upward in a dramatic flourish.

The undercurrent in the air changed, foretelling an approaching storm. The ground shook with an intensity that sent Venn tumbling to the dirt. He rolled sideways to avoid the fire but still fell close enough to it to singe his hair. The pungent burned smell pinched his nose. He staggered to his feet.

As he got his bearings and raised his head, a tremendous sound akin to a ship splitting in half thundered painfully through his ears and chest. The tree rose, uprooted like God himself had reached down and plucked it from the earth. Soil and rocks dropped away, and Venn shifted his stance, muscles tensed, as his fight-or-flight instinct warred within.

Suspended in midair a furlong overhead, the tree began to rotate. Agonizingly slow, at first, then faster and faster, gaining momentum. Clumps of earth flew from the roots as a rain of rock and mud pelted the ground. Within the space of a few breaths, the oak created a whirl of limbs and branches, and leaves peeled away. Venn recoiled, shielding his eyes, as a burst of white light and a deafening boom pummeled them all. He glanced up in time to glimpse the trunk splintering apart, chunks of tree launching skyward and soaring across the land in every direction.

And then it was gone.

The maelstrom was over as quickly as it had begun, and twelve forked sticks dropped at Seth's feet. Venn cursed under his breath and palmed his bearded face. What had they just witnessed?

He sprinted toward Njorth and clasped his elder brother's arm, ready to drag him away from the alleged angel.

Seth shot him a reproachful glare, then knelt to retrieve the sticks. "Peace!" He tossed one to each of the twelve brothers, saving Venn for last.

Venn had not intended to comply with the angel's bidding, but he caught the stick instinctively. As soon as his hand closed around the rough wood, an odd burning sensation spread under his skin, followed by pain slicing through him from neck to groin.

What had the angel done?

A pleased, knowing smile broke across Seth's face as spasms continued twisting in Venn's chest. He groaned, hearing his brothers do the same. He turned to find their heads thrown back, their arms spread wide, all seeming to be experiencing the same horror he was.

The sequence coursed through Venn three agonizing times. When the fit subsided, he gasped airless pants as if he'd raced across several deep furrows.

Seth's smile vanished. "For every honest man bent to the purpose of noble deeds, there are thousands driven by greed, lust, revenge, and power. Hundreds vying for the secrets of youth, the secrets of the universe, the secrets to manipulating time and space. Men whose misplaced allegiance increases evil."

Venn balanced the stick in his palm and tested its weight, curiosity replacing his agony. Oddly heavy, it felt like part of him, an extension of his arm.

"The Divine Tree has splintered and will take root in new domains. Thou hast been given a divining rod to direct you to your tree. As Immortal Guardians, you are to protect that tree and its secrets with your life. But most importantly . . . do not allow the Dark Realm entry into the tree. And if your tree dies, so shall you. And all of humanity will suffer the consequences for the loss of its knowledge. Go, and be well."

As if that explained everything, Seth disintegrated into

shimmering particles that faded to nothing.

"Wait," Venn called. Immortal Guardians? Tales of Odin and Yggdrasill and the Christian uprising vied in a mist of confusion.

Why would Venn and his brothers be called to guard anything? Seth must be mad.

Venn tossed the divining rod aside. "Firewood," he scoffed.

When he looked up, he met his brothers' disapproving stares as they gathered their belongings. Njorth prodded his injured thigh, where an ugly gash oozed red. He grimaced, raised and lowered his leg. Then the wound dried up and closed.

His eyes widened. "Look at that. Healed." He turned to his brothers, each of them looking in turn to see the cut now gone. He gave a small chuckle. "Oh, but it aches like hell."

"Stop complaining," their brother Ian grumbled.

Njorth gave Venn a hearty clap on the shoulder, a wallop meant to suffice for a long time. "This ain't half-bad."

They were *immortal?* No, it wasn't possible.

Part of him wanted to ignore Seth's directives as nonsense and head home, but he stole another glance at Njorth's healed thigh. He eyed his other brothers, packed and ready, each fisting their shares of the tree. He swallowed, pulling a sheepskin pouch over his shoulder as his heartbeat escalated with indecision, then slowed in resignation.

Ah, hell, brothers fought side by side. He trod toward the fire pit to retrieve his divining rod from where he'd thrown it. As he fisted the wood, a prickling force pulsed up into his arm and shoulder, the rod seeming to yank him to the east. He shook off the feeling, his attention was forced back to the barghest, whose menacing paws thrashed from beneath the boulders, announcing that its wild nature had revived.

"I can't stand that beast," Euler declared. He raised his sword, stepping closer to Io. "Let's take his head and be done with him while we can."

"No." Seth's booming voice crashed over them like a rolling wave.

"Hope he stays under there 'til he rots," Njorth grumbled.

Venn backed cautiously away, a hand on his sword hilt, allowing a wide berth for the beast's vicious claws. "Let's go. I suggest we figure out the game rules somewhere else. Before we hav'ta yield more of our blood."

. 1 .

At the subterranean entrance to the Divine Tree sanctuary, Venn Hearst halted and raised his eyes to the etchings of a wolf and hawk emblazoned in the aged wood above the door, a nod to his alternate forms. Venn extended his tattooed wrist, positioning the elaborately inked tree, and the pulsing artery beneath it, below a glistening twisted root for the anointing ritual. An amber-colored drop of sap spilled over the image, then pooled and bubbled before it was absorbed into his skin, sending a sharp zing to each of his neurons before settling within the larger matching tat on his back.

The language of the universe rustled through the air. The Secrets men died to know, Guardians swore to protect, and the Dark Realms were determined to steal or destroy were housed within this sacred place.

His Divine Tree was one of the original dozen hidden around the globe. There were eleven left after the Divine Tree Guardians had lost his brother Tristan along with the Divine Tree in Germany in the mid-nineteen hundreds. The tree's demise had caused the earth to shift on its axis ever so slightly, bringing them one step closer to Armageddon with an escalation of malevolent forces. Evil had blossomed with Hitler taking millions of lives before balance could be restored. It had been an uphill battle ever since.

Venn opened and closed his fist, considering the tattoo on his wrist. Not even one more tree could be lost.

"Benison," the oak whispered.

"Blessings," Venn returned. "My strength and loyalty are yours."

With his vow, the door to the tree creaked opened, and he strode through the massive entry. He looked around the comfortable aboveground chambers and kept walking. Keeping watch wasn't his intention this night. No, he sought the tombs within the root structure below and hoped the tree would communicate to him if something out of the ordinary was happening.

He grabbed a nearby flashlight from the alcove next to the door, flipped it on, and started along the narrow tunneled path, down a staircase that had been fashioned by twisted knots of wood and roots fused together over centuries. It wound deep into the layers of knowledge, to the catacomb of interconnected scripts, like a true, living computer.

Once in the belly, he ran a hand over an electrical switch. Battery powered lights illuminate the cave-like room in a pale glow. Venn glanced about and drew an awed breath. *Holy shit. The place had grown.*

With careful steps, he moved from the tunnel into a cavern, where rough splinters jutted out of smooth swirls in the timber's pattern, creating a golden wooden cave. He used to come down here often in the beginning, during the early years of loneliness, always expecting to discover something exceptional. Which he usually did.

He'd learned that if he pricked himself on this special wood, a series of images would fire though his brain, teaching him something new, its lessons sharper and more thorough than those of any history or science channel on TV.

Centuries ago, he'd stumbled on this cavern and its amazing phenomenon quite by accident. The power the tree gave him had become an obsession, the data exchange an addiction. He knew better than to come back again after that. But this time he had no choice, his duty demanded he use every means available to him. He was well aware of the risks and didn't intend to overstep his limits.

Something was off-kilter in the universe, and he needed to know why. The odd weather pattern—winter when it should be spring—was an ominous sign, Venn knew, even if humans simply took it as a fluke of nature. Just as humans showed symptoms of illness, so too did the machinations of the universe. And a shift between good and evil often triggered such nasty weather patterns.

He needed to be on high alert. "Custos," he spoke quietly to the ancient tree. "Do you know what's going on?"

There was no answer.

Taking a seat in a worn cradle of wood, he felt the need to connect with the Divine Tree . . . and to his brothers. He squeezed the back of his neck. Perhaps that's what the problem was. Not outside at all, but within him.

He felt as isolated from everything as this tree was. What was it like to house all humanity but not feel humanity?

The groan and creak of the tree, as if it were caught by a strong gust of wind, caused Venn to lift his head. Seth stood framed in the tunnel doorway. "I didn't think you'd be down here," the angel said, walking into the chamber.

Now Venn *knew* there was trouble brewing. The angel rarely dropped in just to say hello. "What's happenin'?" Venn asked in way of greeting.

Seth shrugged, his wings lifting and falling with the movement. "I'm not sure. But you must feel it also if you're down here."

"Indeed. Have a seat," Venn motioned to another curve of wood.

Seth sat and crossed his legs, resting his back and folded wings against the smooth inner walls of the tree. "I dunno. On one hand the off weather pattern seems like a trivial thing, but coupled with all the unrest in the world—with ISIS beheading people in the Middle East and people protesting over police in the US—I think we need to pay close attention."

"I agree. The planet is digressing into a state of anarchy and I'd bet my right arm that the Dark Realm is behind it all," Venn proclaimed.

"No doubt."

"I think you'd better hang around," Venn suggested.

"Fine. You got a room to spare?" Seth asked, firing a glance from beneath heavy eyelids without lifting his head.

"No."

Seth shrugged. "Then I can't help you."

Venn chuckled, knowing full well he'd just gained a house guest. "It's hard to think back to when this guardianship began." He rested his head back and closed his eyes, trying to see that far into the past. "You know you could have given us a little more information when you set us on this task."

"What for? You figured it out."

"Huh. It took me forever to learn to control my shifting. The hawk being able to manipulate time and space, and the wolf's incredible strength. Shit, I was a mess in those days."

"You're still a mess," said with exaggerated disdain.

Venn straightened. "Hey, I didn't ask for this gig. You can head back up anytime."

——————————

Emma sympathized with anyone who had to make transatlantic flights on a regular basis. The trip from Paris to Atlanta's Hartsfield–Jackson airport had left her weary as a rag doll. Two hours later, she was still stifling yawns as she surveyed the snow-covered park where her mélange-metal statue would reside.

"I'm sorry. I shouldn't have made you stop here on the way from the airport. You must be exhausted." Grams tugged the zipper of her trendy black leather jacket higher before passing the leash attached to her little, aging Yorkshire terrier, Izzy, from one hand to the other. The pup scooted around her legs. "It was thoughtless of me. I'm just so excited."

Emma shrugged. "I'm fine," she assured her grandmother, then twisted to face the trunk of the enormous tree they stood beneath when the next yawn came. A whisper of energy coiled around her, heat seeming to seep out of the bark itself. She pursed her mouth and clasped her arms around her rib cage. As if the move offered any protection. Fatigue always made her paranoid. She even sometimes saw visions, though she didn't like to admit it, even to herself.

She sighed. No use in worrying about something she couldn't control, and she'd long since learned she wasn't in the driver's seat where her visions were concerned. Instead, she engaged in her most prevalent form of evasion, her art.

Nothing wrong with burying problems in a little work.

She studied the space again. Which metals would capture the hues of oyster shells in the sky? What subject would best fit the colors? Emma jotted down some mental notes for her next project. She watched the changing colors of dusk descend on the park as clouds loomed, back-lit in an eerie coppery shimmer. The diffused light made the snow appear almost warm, the rocks somehow spongy, and the trees . . . They were mystical.

Her apprehension escalated as the walkway in front of her blurred. Her knees grew weak.

No. Not this time.

She sucked in a deep breath and tensed, resisting. But she knew with sickening certainty that the vision was coming. There was no controlling it . . .

An arrow shaft protruded from her chest, and air wheezed through her stagnant lungs. In the wake of the brutal, radiating pain, time slowed. Her heart stopped.

Oh God.

An image of a huge gray wolf materialized, howling a cry of grief alongside her lifeless body, and it lingered, dimming slowly to a sepia shadow. Had she . . . died here?

Emma blinked, disoriented, as the brief manifestation faded, reality setting back in. Exhaling hard, she shifted her feet, peering down at her strappy, crystal-embellished, leopard-print sandals and seeking solid ground. Izzy licked at her toes where they peeked from her shoes, as if trying to console her as best he could.

Her gaze swept up her own body, and she settled shaky fingers over her beating heart. No blood. No arrow. Definitely alive.

Still, the suffocating sensation of a collapsed lung remained, causing her stomach to churn. How she even knew what one felt like alarmed her.

Stop thinking about it.

With determined strength, Emma overcame the pervasive mental intrusion, forcing her attention back to the grossly neglected Georgia park where she stood trembling, to the place her sculpture would call home. She'd had these dreams and visions her whole life, and when she'd researched the phenomenon, she'd discovered they were each giving her a glimpse of one of her past lives. If one believed in that sort of thing. Which she did. But knowing that didn't make it any less disturbing.

Emma's breath swirled in a misty cloud as she focused

on her surroundings. Cold, damp air patted her cheeks. The massive oak before her released a sad moan. Or was that just her active imagination at work? Whatever it was triggered a familiar warmth that spread into her limbs, and reminded her she possessed . . . talents beyond her visions. Heat radiated through her right arm, and she glanced down, opening her blazing hot fist to discover she'd inadvertently melted her grandmother's butterfly key fob beyond recognition.

Some *talents*. More like she'd been cursed.

With an unsteady sigh, she pushed her hair away from her face. Geez, her life hadn't changed one iota. Since she was a toddler, she'd been molding metal with her bare hands as if it were clay, both intentionally and accidentally. It was the latter that caused her grief. The episode with a neighborhood boy and his squished red Hot Wheels car came to mind. It always did. Her dad had been so angry with her.

"Are you okay?"

Her grandmother's question snapped her back to the present. Would Grams know if she lied? She'd discovered when she'd moved to New York that the visions and dreams had lessened with the distance. She'd run all the way to Paris to avoid them. And they must have let go, too, because she hadn't thought of them for a long, long while.

"Sure. But I can't say the same for this." She dangled the key chain in the air.

Her grandmother gave a chuckle. "I should have nicknamed you Hot Hands."

Emma managed to summon a smile, but it faltered as her gaze shifted back to that tree. Its spindly canopy of branches seemed to reach out. The hair on her arms prickled. Something in the fractures of time yanked free and another ripple of unease washed over her.

Good and evil used this place as a playground. At the moment, evil acted the bully. She felt a bizarre tug-of-war for dominance, the power of it making her sway.

Leave. Me. Alone.

This evening's vision was beyond vivid—a seven-point-five on the Richter scale, and it wasn't passing as it normally did. She flailed her arms, trying to shake off her frustration. She usually had an easier time coming out of it. An erratic pulse thumped in her neck, bringing her circulation back. Her temples ached with the awakening.

She shook her head. *Ignore. Regroup. Move on.*

Thank goodness her grandmother, who tarried a few steps behind, wouldn't know the depth of Emma's latest episode, since time distorted or elongated only within her mind. What she needed was an anchor, physically and mentally. There was no way she'd allow her father to be right about her differences making her crazy. She didn't have a psychotic disorder as he'd suggested when she was young. No, she would control the visions, but, darn, this bout threatened her common sense. She'd never seen herself die before.

Besides, wasn't that supposed to kill you or something?

Or was that just in dreams, not visions? She gave a mental shrug, figuring it didn't matter because she had both.

Focus. She was here on a job. The park.

It was spring in Tyler, Georgia, yet the late-season snow masked the evidence. Weeds and yellow wildflowers nudged aside a layer of snow, and fresh green growth attempted to unfurl on branches. The square must have been lovely at one time, especially when everything began to bloom, but not now. A battered, rotten wood bench lay on the ground sideways, collapsed. The sidewalk that wound through the center of the park resembled a war zone, with chunks of concrete broken and upended. The branches of the old oak swept the earth. Clearly ignored for many, many years, the mammoth tree looked as if it had never been pruned or shaped.

The untamed tree was so out-of-character for prim-

and-proper Georgia. Just like her. Her dad had always proclaimed that her overactive imagination would lead to trouble. If he only knew the whole truth.

A hand slid across Emma's back and bony fingers grasped her shoulder. She almost jumped out of her grandmother's hug.

"Just think, a Grant getting the honor of creating a statue for the old town square. I can hardly believe it." Grams heaved one of her exaggerated, bursting-with-pride sighs, the way she did when the family dinner table was landscaped to perfection.

"You drive a hard bargain, Grams. The committee couldn't say no." And neither could Emma. Her grandmother had requested a sculpture of a confederate soldier on a rearing horse. Not very original, but Emma had obliged, thankful for both the much-needed income and the chance to build her portfolio. She gradually relaxed into the woman's solid embrace, somewhat grounded again.

She touched her head to her grandmother's salon-teased auburn one, in the same let's-stick-together way she'd done since she was six, when she'd spent every summer vacation here after her family had moved to New York.

"Thanks for your help," Emma said. Nothing like getting paid to visit her favorite relative. Since the city had commissioned her sculpture for the park renovation project, she'd be hanging out for the next few weeks to supervise its placement and participate in the dedication ceremony.

Grams nodded. "Anytime. Paris is too darn far away, if you ask me." She picked Izzy up and tucked him beneath her arm.

Actually, the greater distance meant fewer visions, so it wasn't even far enough. Emma wasn't sure why, but they seemed to be worse, more frequent, when she returned to her Georgia birthplace. Bonus points for Paris.

"We talk and Skype all the time," Emma pointed out.

"That's not the same as seeing your smiling face." Her grandmother slid a hand down Emma's arm and back up over her shoulder. "Look at you. You're shivering."

Ominous gray clouds were moving in, and the sky was growing darker. Emma felt more than saw the clump of wet red clay that oozed into her Sam Edelman sandals. She tamped her foot against a rock to clear it. "What an awful spring. Can't believe it snowed on Easter."

"Yes. The pecan blooms froze. The crop'll be ruined." A smile lit Grams's eyes, and she tsked, seeming to dismiss the unfortunate prediction that might steal her pocket money. "But give it a few days. It'll warm up."

"I'll hold you to that."

Tree branches whipped one way, then the other, generating an eerie whistling. Emma shuddered, then tugged the neckline of her suddenly constricting turtleneck sweater as she turned to explore a staked-out plot of ground. "It looks like this is where they plan to put the statue."

Her gaze swept along the snow-patched ground, up the broken walkway, to the side of the park where fluorescent-orange construction fencing sectioned off individual trees, marking them for protection. Landscaping equipment near the road formed a neat line, ready to be put to use.

A tiny ping caught in her gut, and her internal compass gravitated to the old oak standing center stage. Its trunk stretched out to the size of a small house, as if several trees had grown together. She frowned as intense golden eyes seemed to peer at her from the grained bark. A figment of her imagination? With her history, it had to be.

When the eyes vanished, she angled her head, unable to shake the weird drag on her heart. As if she should know something important, yet couldn't bring it forth. The feeling didn't seem like a remnant of her vision but felt like it originated from an entirely different source. More like an unfathomable power or presence. She scanned the park and rubbed her chilled arms, but she didn't see a single soul.

———————

Io slipped behind the downed bulldozer bucket, in predator mode, his eyes fixed on his target: Emma Grant. The machine inched to the side as his back jammed against a metal support. In his eagerness, he hadn't sufficiently controlled his brute strength. He grumbled at the oversight but kept tuned to the young woman. While in human form, as he was now, his senses were faulty. It was a weak form, practically useless, with few special powers.

He'd known the moment Emma Grant had set foot on Georgia soil.

Not such a difficult task, really. He'd been expecting her.

Now, he was curious about the reason she'd stopped at the park on her way from the airport. Was the Divine Tree's power already blooming in Emma? Had the old tree spoken to her?

He'd met her quite by accident years ago when she was a little girl of five. They were in an ice cream shop, and he'd accidently dropped a handful of coins on the floor—as fine motor skills was another issue he had with the human form. But it turned into a fortunate event for him, really, for Emma gathered the coins up off the floor. And to her great embarrassment, when she handed them back to him the lot was fused together in a solid clump of metal.

He knew then and there that she was gifted. And he made it his business to discover why. Eavesdropping in on her dreams at night gave him the connection to her past. Even over the years after she moved from Tyler, he managed to keep track of her. He was damned proud of himself for discovering the reason behind her metal-altering ability.

Well, it wasn't precisely *his* discovery, but he would take credit for it nonetheless.

When he'd killed Emma in her past life and she'd lain on the grassy ground with his arrow jutting out of her chest, her blood had seeped into this magical oak's roots. Who knew such a simple act would create the catalyst to destroy a Divine Tree? He certainly hadn't. Not until the High Counsel of Devils had recently congratulated him for it, that is. And he wasn't disappointed.

That arrow, her blood, and her reincarnation had caused a shift, something even he couldn't grasp the implications of. It had taken him shitloads of long, painful, boring hours of watching before he discovered how he could use her newborn alchemist powers to his advantage. He deserved this boon, and the recognition from the counsel. He'd show his brother, Seth, that he was equally as favored by his superiors.

Now if only he could overcome the free will part of the equation. He couldn't force her into using her alchemist powers on the metal as he wanted her to. At least not physically.

But there were other ways to get the results he desired.

With a mental shake, he glared at Emma.

Did she realize the connection she shared with the tree? If so, he'd have to move much more quickly than he'd thought. No, no, he wouldn't allow things to get out of hand. He swiped a restless hand along his jaw.

He tried to quiet the nervous energy that continually tugged him in conflicting directions. One moment he was certain of his mission's success, the next of its failure. His gaze darted from Emma to Mrs. Busybody, listening intently. He plunged his hands into his pockets, withdrew them, then clasped them behind him.

The best he could determine, Emma was simply cold, not agitated or suspicious.

And Mrs. Grant took credit for arranging the commission of the statue her granddaughter had arrived to install.

Yes, it was better that Emma thought her grandmother was the instigator. Better she not discover the significance of the invitation to the installation ceremony. At least not until the ruination of the tree was complete or Emma and the Guardian were dead. Either outcome would give him great pleasure.

After all, he'd discovered firsthand that the best way to make someone suffer was to destroy the one thing that someone most loved. Yes, revenge would be his. About time.

Seth, Mr. Goodie-Goodie, would soon have his world turned upside down. And Venn and the Divine Tree along with him. He could barely contain his excitement. Three for the price of one. Brilliant.

Excited and restless, Io tugged on his shirt sleeve, then sought focus by touching the picture of a burned tree he kept tucked in his pocket. It represented his brother's failure. His channeled hatred grew, and his smokescreen, the shield he'd put in place so the tree wouldn't detect his presence, disintegrated. Damn.

The stupid dog in the old lady's arms barked and growled.

A deep moan resounded within the catacomb. *Custos?* Venn straightened from his relaxed position. Immediately, his attention shot upward—above him, outside—and he stood.

What *was* that?

An irresistible tug made him palm his chest. He

proceeded through the cavern entrance, back up the knotted stairs and angled tunnel, the pull intensifying with each step. If he were human, he'd be wondering if he were having a heart attack.

He hadn't felt this collision of energy in two centuries.

Inside the sprawling tree, he climbed rough-hewn stairs to the watch room at ground level. He ignored the enormous circular space and its new modular furnishings as he fixed his attention on the highly polished wooden wall, where the force ran strongest. The bark itself had sight, a transparency by which he could see through the layers of wood to the world beyond, at will. He looked out, as he had done so many thousands of times in the past.

Outside, two females engaged in conversation. He immediately recognized Claire Grant. The old lady had been bragging everywhere she went about how her granddaughter, Emma, had designed a sculpture for Tyler's historic town square and oldest park.

Venn's park, not the town's.

But he'd lost that battle a long time ago, and until recently, he had managed to direct the city officials' attentions elsewhere. Damn their renewed interest. The tree had been marked for preservation purposes, which was a good thing, yet it also attracted unwanted attention. There were others who had an inclination of the riches the tree held, not in monetary value but in what they could do with the knowledge contained within.

The presumed granddaughter turned.

Venn advanced to the barrier, curious. He wanted to be closer to her, wanted nothing between them, not this tree, not this space. With his extraordinary sight and hearing, he could make her out perfectly, but it wasn't enough. There was something about her . . . yet he couldn't fathom why he'd be drawn to Claire Grant's granddaughter. How odd.

With a sweeping glance, the young woman arched her brows and strolled toward the tree. She seemed to stare right at him. Thick auburn hair draped over her shoulders, and she tilted her head, his equilibrium shattering. A roar took up residence inside his skull. Thunder vibrated through his chest, and explosive desire made him hard and ready.

His breath hitched. His inner beasts stirred without the customary summons, fighting each other, wolf and hawk vying for a glimpse of her.

She inched forward.

Yes, move closer.

She spoke, and he vaguely caught her whispered French phrase. *"Coeur de mon coeur."*

Heart of my heart.

He swallowed, hard.

She placed a delicate palm on the trunk, and Venn growled as a surge of energy—her very essence—flowed into the tree, filled him as much as earthy air filled his lungs.

"I . . . feel something," Emma said with opened-mouth awe. "The oak has been here for hundreds of years."

When recognition hit Venn, it was with the force of an 18-wheeler rear-ending a car waiting at a traffic light. Every muscle in his body tensed as he saw flashes of her in a past life, of their limbs entwined, of her lips warm on his, of her vibrant laugh . . . of her dying.

Could it truly be Amelia? Had she returned to him in this woman, this Emma Grant?

Venn closed his eyes and summoned energy in all its manifested forms—heat, light, sound, magnetism, gravity, and all of life's functions—reaching out to her, touching deep into her soul to test the theory. Her initial response was a lazy yawn, but then her mystical imprint danced, the spirit unique to her, proclaimed, *Yes!*

She. Was. His.

A heaviness slammed against his chest, followed by whiplash, pain, confusion. He'd been robbed of time, his woman, his love.

Ah, Amelia. Brought back to him after so long.

A spark flared in his chest, and his pulse sped up. Unwilling to move lest this sudden feel-good moment disappeared, he held his breath.

She glanced over her shoulder at her grandmother. "I have the strangest feeling of déjà vu."

Overwhelmed, he wished he could vault through the barrier and take her in his arms. Instead, he braced both hands on thick chair arms as he slowly lowered himself into the seat, not taking his eyes off the woman with fiery hair and golden skin. Every fiber in his body stretched out to embrace her. She was his.

They'd been lovers in 1809. Companions. Promised journey mates. A favor from God.

His throat tightened at the memory, and he tried to drink in the air. She was the one woman gifted with the powers to complement his. He hadn't known until too late how much he needed to share his life with someone. And his enemy had murdered her.

She must be the reason the tree summoned him.

He narrowed his eyes, scrutinizing the grounds for yet another assassin. But the only ones there were the Grants.

Uncertain what to expect, he watched, fisting his hand with a vow.

This time he would protect her. This time he would fulfill the promise of a lifetime mate. This time she would be his. Forever.

Emma's brow furrowed as her hand swept along the bark of the tree. *His* tree. "Did I come here as a girl?" she asked. "I seem to know this place."

"I don't think so, child. Your father didn't wander much south of the ravine. Claimed he got bad vibes here. Always afraid, that boy. Not enough faith. Of course, there were all kinds of stories bantered about back then. Some about a man being killed out here, tales about witches and ghosts, you name it. The place became run-down. But with the city rejuvenation and cleanup, well . . . As you can see, things are different now."

Indeed, things had changed, Venn mused. His mansion lay south of the park, far enough away so as to not attract visitors. A strategic plan he'd sanctioned to assure his privacy. Back in the day, he'd met with wealthy plantation owners and connected politicians on his own terms. Otherwise, he'd avoided them. As time passed and with the never-ending urbanization, he didn't care for the coziness.

When Emma pulled her hand away from the bark, it was like part of him flickered, then snuffed out. He got a mild case of shakes, and his temperature plummeted.

"It's getting late. You must be tired," Mrs. Grant said.

"Nah. I'm a night person, remember? How about if we stop by Aunt Fay's Coffee Shop on the way home? I've been dreaming about one of her famous cinnamon buns all the way here."

"Okay. You drive." Grams hitched the small dog she held higher under her arm.

They were leaving. With a leap, Venn stood, banging his knee on the side table. He winced and beat back a wave of anxiety. He'd been given a second chance, and he'd be damned if he'd let her out of his sight this time. At least, not for long.

Keenly aware that she wouldn't know him in this life, he needed to initiate a meeting. This minute. However, walking up out of nowhere in a shabby park might scare her.

He wished they could simply pick up where they'd left off.

He envisioned her smiling at him with recognition and running into his opened arms.

But as she got closer to the car and farther from him, the vision scattered.

Aunt Fay's. That was it.

He could use a jolt of caffeine.

———————

As Venn pelted across Aunt Fay's parking lot, loose pebbles crunched beneath his feet. The Tyler streets were fairly deserted, with most people in bed by nine on a workday like today.

He paused to watch Emma through the store window, noting that Mrs. Grant had chosen to wait in the car with her dog. His anticipation mounted.

When he entered the shop, her scent grabbed him— plumeria and cinnamon—an instant turn-on. Even the heady aroma of coffee couldn't rob him of her sweet, luscious fragrance, a perfume he'd profoundly missed. He drew a deep breath as he stepped behind her in line and enjoyed the sound of her voice while she spoke into a cell phone.

Instantly, she seemed to sense him as she stopped mid-sentence and turned.

He smiled and couldn't help but flirt with her. "Something with whipped cream?"

She narrowed her eyes and angled her cell away from her ear with an incredulous nod. "Excuse me?"

"To drink."

"Oh." Her cheeks flushed a pretty pink. "Yes. Umm, and your recommendation is?" She cleared her throat, her green eyes now glinting with pale fire, and then her brows pinched as if she were trying to recall something.

Was it possible she recalled *him*? That would make things so much easier. He was already finding it difficult to behave as though he didn't know her.

"Anything with chocolate," he answered as his lupine senses went into overdrive. Her fragrance intensified, warmed, indicating to him that her body knew what her mind did not.

Her subconscious recognized him.

She gave her head a shake, confusion painted on her face. "Sorry. I . . ." She paused a beat, steeling her features, and then pointed to her phone.

Her voice drove him to the brink of desperation. He wanted to get her alone. He needed her to remember what they'd shared.

And his beasts concurred with a beat of wings and hammer of paws.

"Miss. What would you like?" the clerk behind the counter asked.

She faced forward again, leaving him to stare at her long, sleek, shimmering hair. He'd kill to slide his fingers through those rich strands.

"For some reason I'm craving something I haven't had before." Her voice was soft and sweet. "A mocha latte. And forget the calories. Add on some extra whipped cream. Also a cinnamon bun, to go."

He swallowed. He had cravings, too, ones he hadn't given in to for a very long time. "Good choice," he said to her back.

Now to convince her of a few other things . . .

Hell, she'd fallen for him before, she would again.

Remarkably, she seemed eerily the same as the woman he'd known all too briefly. Just modernize the setting and dress—her red-tinted hair, the perfect, to-his-shoulder height, her lovely mouth. He wondered if she'd see the resemblance given the chance.

With the briefest glance at him, Emma stepped to the pick-up line. Venn swiftly placed his order, telling the clerk he'd have the same.

As he came up behind her again, she broke off her phone conversation. "Todd, sorry, I'll call you back. I have to get my order."

Todd? Jealousy surged through his inner wolf, the idea of her even chatting with another male unbearable. His hawk flexed and curled his sharp talons. Fighting to keep control of his body, Venn rolled his shoulders.

While he got it together, the all too efficient waiter handed over Emma's drink and to-go bag. She removed the lid, dropped it in the trash, and sampled the fluffy white cream. A died-and-gone-to-heaven expression lit her face.

Venn suppressed a groan. Then the sway of her hips as she walked toward the door came, nearly driving him wild.

Oh hell. This wasn't going as he'd imagined.

He stepped out of line. "Excuse me! Emma?" he called after her.

She paused and glanced back.

"Sir, wait. Your drink," the man behind the counter said.

Venn could care less about the joe, but he grabbed his order, thanking the guy, and caught up to her.

Her brows pushed together harder. "Do I know you?"

"No. But I know you. You're the sculptor." He smiled at her, trying to put her at ease.

"Yes," she said, pride resonating from the single word.

Aw, that voice. The glue that held him together melted as if put to a blowtorch. A long-ago picture of her naked, full body pressed against him flickered through his mind. The temperature in the room spiked. The latte she held frothed and boiled over.

"My God," she gasped.

Her exclamation hit a tripwire that made him regain focus. He grabbed the cup from her hand, noting in his peripheral vision that the other patrons were experiencing identical problems.

"I've heard of this. A sudden rise in barometric pressure," he lied, knowing full well exactly why the tables closest to him encountered the worst of the damage. The means of discharging excess energy that had built up inside of him just from being near her had explosively discharged.

Surprise lit her face. "How did you . . .? Man, you moved fast."

He shrugged. Hell, being near her messed with his powers and made them hard to control.

Steam rose from the coffee cup, and he swirled the remaining liquid, then set his drink aside. He snatched a napkin from a table nearby and dried the outside of hers. "Here," he said, handing it back. "This should be fine now. Maybe a bit hotter, so take care."

"Thank you." Her body tilted slightly closer to him.

"You're welcome. Now, in exchange for saving you from having coffee all over your clothes, will you have dinner with me tomorrow night?"

Her eyes widened, and then she glanced down.

"Forgive me if I'm overstepping," he quickly added. "It's just that I don't like to dismiss opportunities when they arise." And he had a major rise happening down south.

She looked down, sunk her teeth into her lower lip, and lifted her shoulders.

Damn. She was going to refuse. He held his breath, waiting for her response and feeling like the world balanced on the tip of her finger.

. 2 .

Emma stared into the cup, hiding a guarded smile. *Oh. My. God.* This man radiated raw sex appeal. And the hint of a Scottish accent made her absolutely melt.

She swallowed nervously, realizing he expected an answer. "I'm here on business, so I won't be in town long. But thank you anyway."

For the first time in her life, she understood the way her Paris friends went crazy over a particular male. A violent wave of attraction consumed her body, making her feel flushed and wanting to strip off her clothes.

Oh, the thought of being naked was the wrong direction to go.

She groaned inwardly, looking up at his rugged, sculpted face. He inhaled a deep breath, his nostrils flaring. She'd never noticed a man do that before. It was as if he thoroughly absorbed a scent.

The coffee? No. *Her*, she sensed. Heat suffused her cheeks. She needed to get out of here.

She blinked, chafing at her imagination, as something inside her protested with an excited high-pitched, *No, no, no. Don't. Miss. This. Opportunity.* But she wasn't the quick pickup sort. She didn't even accept dates in bars, let alone coffee shops. All those years growing up in New York had taught her to go slow.

Yet today, the fast track appealed to her. More than it should, considering she'd been dating Todd exclusively for a while. But was dating across the Atlantic really *dating*? She in Paris, Todd in NYC. And here this hunky guy—with his hard, muscular, good looks—was asking her out.

And her body screamed, *Yes!*

No. Way, her voice of reason chimed in.

She gave him a tight smile and turned toward the exit. With incredible speed, he somehow blocked her path. Her knuckles grazed his broad chest, and she numbly watched coffee slosh in her cup. Then her eyes focused on the buttons of his shirt before sliding to an up-close-and-personal view of his chest. The guy worked out, if the well-defined fit of the shirt over hard pecs was any indication.

"You like wolves," he said, smiling, indicating her T-shirt with the sweep of his gaze.

"Yes, I like wolves. They're beautiful creatures. I love to sculpt them."

"See, we already have something in common."

"Sculpting?" she teased.

He raised a single brow and tipped his head in that sexy way that made her heart flutter. "Wolves."

She sipped her drink, and couldn't look away from him.

"Come on, trust your instincts. I can be very persuasive," he said, with a warm, yet challenging voice.

I bet you can. How did he read her so well?

She tipped back her head to look into the most unique hazel eyes she'd ever seen. Hues of copper, gold, and mahogany blended in a kaleidoscope of motion, and she licked her lips. He watched, not seeming to miss a thing as he took in every detail of the sweep of her tongue, making her feel self-conscious. His expression struck her as hungry. Sensual. Infatuated.

Emma scoured her brain. His features were familiar.

Maybe from TV or a movie? But she couldn't recall the who, how, or where.

Her heartbeat quickened. "I don't even know your name."

"Venn." He hesitated, then added smoothly, "Venn Hearst."

"Well, Venn." She stepped back, putting distance between them and taking a tentative sip of her latte, stalling. "I just arrived in town and plan to spend time with my grandmother. I'm not—"

"Nonsense," Grams said as she popped out from behind Venn's large frame, startling the bejesus out of Emma. "We'll have plenty of time together. Go on, dear."

Emma stared at her in disbelief. She'd been so enthralled with Wolfman that she'd missed the chime of the door.

Grams leaned in close to Emma and whispered behind her raised hand. "Gotta go to the little girl's room. I'll be right back." Her voice turned serious for an instant. "He has a noble aura, dear." Then she had the audacity to wink at Venn. A flush of blood migrated to Emma's cheeks again.

She gazed hard at the man to unearth what her grandmother saw. *Noble aura?* Her grandmother embraced on-the-edge beliefs—auras, chakras, mercury retrogrades, and all that. She was a Christian, make no mistake, but it seemed she had privileged knowledge at the same time. That's why she was the one person Emma could talk to about her visions, although she rarely did.

"There you have it." The corners of his mouth lifted, and his enticing eyes locked on hers. "We have your grandmother's blessing."

She didn't realize she'd followed him to the exit until his palm splayed against the glass door. His hand looked as strong as the rest of him. Then she noticed the ring that graced the ring finger of his right hand. Comprised of a weave of gold, silver, and platinum with interlocking circles and a cluster of stones—a ruby, emerald, and diamond—in the center, she couldn't stop staring at it. She needed to get a closer look. Something felt familiar about it, like she'd seen one like it before.

She blinked. Maybe she should accept his offer of dinner.

But no . . . This wasn't her.

Emma nibbled the inside of her cheek, glancing in the direction of the bathroom to make certain the woman wasn't sneaking up on her again.

"I'll come by your grandmother's tomorrow night at six-thirty," he said.

When she snapped her head around, ready to decline the date for a second time, he was gone. Vanished. She blinked and peered out the window. In the parking lot, a set of bright red taillights flashed.

Oh crap.

As the tension and heat dissolved from her body, she grew tired and, irrationally disappointed. She sighed, clutching her latte with both hands. What had she just done? For a brief second, she wondered how he'd even know where to pick her up, but then she realized she was in Tyler, where everyone knew everyone. She glanced at the coffee cup, knowing that he'd held it in his firm hands and feeling the ghost of his touch still imprinted on the cup somehow.

No, what she felt resided within her. She was being ridiculous for so many reasons. Good heavens, she'd been *attracted* to him. Incredibly so. The thought of having dinner with the man made her heart patter and her knees weaken. But this date was definitely not a good idea.

It was well past midnight, and Venn couldn't sleep. He

stood naked, sipping Jim Beam at the floor-to-ceiling window of his master suite, staring out at the moon-dappled forest that surrounded his estate. The feverish attraction he'd felt when Emma was near had not dissipated, her presence lingering on his senses. Her floral scent had set up camp in his sinuses. The image of her autumn-red hair and sweet body hid behind his eyelids. And he hadn't missed the wolf T-shirt she wore, stretched over her delectable breasts.

He inhaled several long, controlled breaths. *Get it together, man. She's just a woman.* But he knew that wasn't true. She was more. She was his mate. Now that he'd seen her, smelled her, touched her, she was like the worst craving *ever*. He was desperate to have her with him once again.

And he would. Soon. Very soon.

As coherent thought returned, worry replaced desire. Emma, like Amelia, could be in grave danger. His enemy was a killer and had proved long ago he'd do anything to get at Venn. Fear for her safety tore at his gut.

His inner wolf howled at him to guard her doorstep. Yes, an excellent idea.

He tipped back the glass and drained it. Indeed, waiting until tomorrow was too risky. He would go to her place and keep watch. As he set his glass down, the tree sent out a distress signal for a second time in twelve hours, hitting him square in the chest.

Now what?

Not demonic thieves, this time. No, it seemed a different source of energy.

He reached out with his senses. The tree tattoo on his back grew feverishly hot, and he grimaced. He pressed a hand to the matching mark on his wrist, acknowledging the warning.

The oak remained quiet, yet desperate. And desperation had an unpleasant, moldy odor. He wrinkled his nose as the smell segued to one of fear.

Never a good sign.

He headed for the closet and dressed in jeans and a loose sweatshirt. Then he decisively made his way to the study and behind the massive desk to the expensive handmade bookshelf, where he traced a finger along a wormhole in the wood. The precise slide and pressure over the irregular indentations triggered a concealed panel to open off to the left. A section of wall trundled upward, one solid hunk of cloaked steel, a guillotine set to descend on an unsuspecting intruder.

He advanced into an eighteen-by-eighteen square secret room and eyed an arsenal fit for a ruler. Behind armored glass, a selection of deadly weaponry from ancient to state-of-the-art avant-garde lined an entire wall. A collector's dream, a defender's necessity.

The safe room was built of four-inch steel, had a dual-ventilation system, and housed all the high-tech cameras and equipment any Guardian could want. His gaze skimmed over the blade Njorth had found in India and sent to him as a gift. From the middle shelf in the center cabinet, he selected the five-inch, perfectly weighted knife, as well as a Glock and an appropriate custom holster that he strapped to his waist.

Minutes later, he exited through a second door in the back that took him down a steep set of stairs, fifty feet into the Earth. He jogged through an underground tunnel a couple of miles long, heading from his estate to the ancient oak.

At the subterranean entrance to the sanctuary, he stopped to listen. A sense of urgency prompted him to bypass the anointing ritual. He climbed the staircase two steps at a time as it led into the heart of the grand oak. Entering the watch room and looking out through the tree's magic walls, every muscle in his body tightened, on alert.

This time was the real deal.

Io opened and closed his fingers around his knife, then

thrust it into branch and sliced away a hunk of bark. Next, the spiteful hand reached for a sprig of budding leaves. Cut it free.

What the hell was he up to?

Usually, Io slunk around with the change of seasons, checking on Venn, probably hoping that he no longer breathed. But this attack was definitely out of character, even for him, more brazen.

Knowing it would do Venn little good to face Io man-to-man—they each had pronounced limitations in that form—Venn summoned his hawk. His ability to manipulate time and space in that form would serve as a powerful weapon in a time like this. With ease, the molecules of his body and clothes came alight with energy, like electricity flickering inside a plasma ball. The flow settled as he adopted a new sleek body, all bird and feathers.

He exited the tree through an invisible porthole and perched on a branch.

Io spotted him. "Guardian, you know she has returned."

Tapping into an evil mind was draining. "What's your point?"

"Don't get attached. She will die once again."

Venn gripped the branch harder with his talons and felt the veins in his neck swell.

Wouldn't you know Io couldn't resist hurling that threat? Not an ounce of humility within those ugly bones. It was damned difficult to reconcile that the demon was Seth's brother.

One of these days, though, that wouldn't matter.

If there was a way for Venn to kill him on the spot, he would. But the Alter Realms didn't work like that. Fuck it, neither of them could do away with the other unless by doing so through an intermediary. Part of the immortal plan of checks and balances.

Which totally annihilated the enjoyment of seeing Io

fry.

Well, perhaps not totally.

If it were up to him, Io would die, nonetheless. But there would be hefty consequences for such a death. The universe always demanded consequences. Venn had realized long ago that dealing with Io was like playing chess. He must actively work to keep his enemy off-balance and create counterplay to distract him from his offense.

Emma's life might depend on it.

He could at least slow Io down, send him a warning.

Venn swooped into a steep dive aimed at Io's head. He unfurled a talon and slashed a gash in his enemy's neck. Io hissed and clamped a hand to his jugular to stop the spurts of blood. Immediately, the wound began healing.

An aggressive hawk's shriek split the air as Venn fired a warning into the demon's mind. *She's mine, Io. I'm ready. My hands are not tied this time.*

Io seethed with anger, and the demon changed into his long-fanged barghest once more, burst into flames and vanished.

Spurred on by his enemy's foul stench, Venn navigated the contours of the land as a hawk, heading directly for the Grant property. Io would soon find his way to Emma's doorstep, and when he did, Venn would be waiting.

With wings sheathed in silence, he flew over strip malls and restaurants, a chain of small farms and a state-protected forest, until he arrived at the Grant orchard of moon-glistening, frost-covered pecan trees. He descended to a stately maple several yards from the house, then perched on the highest sturdy bough. On the horizon, the sky radiated a soft glow of lavender. With his hawk's increased visual acuity, he assessed the area and waited out the remainder of the night.

Shortly before dawn, a light flicked on in the ground level of the house. Minutes later, in an upstairs window, curtains were thrown wide. Emma stood in a fuzzy white robe, a cup clutched between her hands as she peered out.

The window faced east. She was waiting for sunrise.

A morning person, like Amelia. Foolishly, that pleased him. He'd love to guard her through the night, be there when she awoke, and enjoy those quiet moments with her.

With an ache as wide as a valley in his chest, Venn longed to return to his human form and go to her.

The sun was peaking above the trees when Emma finished eating breakfast, and she took a few scraps of bread onto the front porch for the birds.

"Don't leave," she said to the regal hawk she'd been watching all morning. She slipped inside the house to fetch her camera. With a quick stop at the dishwasher, she disposed of the plate that she'd left on the table. She ducked her head into the connected laundry room where water gushed into the washing machine while Grams sorted clothes. Izzy trotted around her feet, sat, and waved both paws in front of him, begging to be picked up. Grams lifted him and placed him inside a basket on the dryer.

Emma smiled, tipping her head farther past the threshold. "It's a beautiful day, Grams. Come sit outside and see this hawk I've been watching."

"After a while, dear. You go on."

Emma nodded and turned to leave.

"Umm, wait."

Emma paused, halfway in the doorway, halfway out, and looked back.

Grams turned a red shirt inside out. Emma wondered

why her father's old college sweatshirt was in the laundry. She shrugged it off, but Gram's keen gaze must have caught her questioning glimpse for she explained, "I thought you might like to wear it if you didn't bring enough warm cloths." She paused, then asked, "How long has it been since you've spoken to your dad?"

As anxious as she was to click pics of the hawk, and as much as she disliked the subject, she wouldn't dodge her grandmother's question. She leaned a shoulder against the doorframe for support. Would it hurt Grams less if she lied?

"More than six months," she said truthfully. "All men want to do is control you, my father especially."

"He's a proud man, just like your grandfather." Grams closed the lid on the washer.

"Yeah. I know." Emma lifted a hand loosely, palm up in a "Who cares?" gesture. "But it doesn't excuse him."

"You just have to keep trying to get past his stubbornness."

"And you, when did you talk to him?" Emma straightened.

"Last week. I told him you were coming."

Emma sighed. At least they were speaking. That was a good sign, wasn't it? Better than she was doing, anyway. She and her dad hadn't gotten along since her early teens when she'd refused to hide her metal bending abilities. Not in public, of course, but at home, she didn't sneak off to work on her sculpting any longer. And her coming out, so to speak, created a huge rift between them. He wanted her to be like all the other girls. She wanted him to accept her for who she was.

"Maybe he'll come to the statue unveiling," Grams said, the age lines around her eyes turning up.

A lump formed in Emma's throat. "Sure." She straightened. "Meet me out front when you're done."

Knowing her grandmother wouldn't stop working until she was good and ready, Emma traipsed up the stairs to her room. She snatched her camera bag from where she'd deposited it on a floral damask chair, and dashed back to the porch, fearing the bird would be gone.

The hawk remained perched on an old, fat tree stump. The bird tracked her as she took her Nikon D40 from its case, attached a zoom lens, and adjusted the settings. With breathtaking maneuverability and speed, the bird took flight. She held her breath as it flew, and she snapped a few action shots. Then the hawk dipped closer, landing on the porch rail.

His eyes, the color of blood, glowed like burning embers as he considered her.

"Now you're too close," she said, lifting the camera to remove the zoom she'd just put on.

He was exquisite, gun-smoke gray with a sloped head and gripping talons tipped with daggers. Suddenly, he launched into the air, giving a cry—a brittle high-pitched lament, like the screech of metal on metal.

Then the sound of gravel crunching beneath tires caught her ear. She squinted and looked down the drive. "That's why you took off. Hmm?"

She checked her watch. Ten o'clock, already? She sighed. That'd be the guy about the sculpture mounting, here to show her the final park plans. *Time to get to work.*

She wondered what the man was like who'd engineered the project. He was paying her a visit as a courtesy since he didn't have an actual office, acting as the volunteer he was. Evidently, the polite Southern gentleman still existed.

She slung the camera strap around her neck, traveled down the walk, and stopped a few yards from a Suburban. A tall man with messy spiked blond hair exited the SUV and approached. He wore a light blue business shirt and expensive navy twill pants.

"Hello. You must be Emma Grant. I'm Jacob Price. We spoke over the phone." He moved forward, hand extended.

"Glad to meet you," she said, reaching out to shake it. Then she paused, narrowing her eyes, puzzled. "Have we met before? You seem familiar."

"When you were young, you went to First Baptist Church with your grandmother, didn't you? Perhaps we met there." He extended his hand a bit further. But before their fingers touched, the hawk swooped from above, executing a sleek dive, streaking forward like an arrow. Then something fell to the ground, landing between her and Jacob.

A snake. Scaly. Lethal. Squirming.

She leaped back, her heart slamming in her chest. The thing slithered away.

Jacob tracked the hawk, his lips pressed in a thin line. "You bugger," he mumbled.

"Pardon?" Emma said, breathless, as she tried to calm her shaking nerves. Of all the creatures in the world, she hated snakes with a passion.

She glanced at the beautiful hawk circling overhead, her unease slowly melting away.

Jacob's cheeks puffed out as if he were ready to blow. But maybe she was misreading him and he was covering up a similar fear. Macho-man stuff.

She followed his gaze. "I've been watching him all morning. He seems to like me, friendly even. When animals present you what they consider *food*, it's a sort of gift." She turned to smile at him. "Even if a disgusting one," she added with a forced laugh.

"Huh. Until he sinks his talons into you," Jacob Price said with hatred in his eyes. She was shocked at how his almost handsome features turned hard, the creases framing his mouth cutting lines into his face.

Clearing her throat, she indicated the roll in his left hand. "So, are those the mounting drawings?"

"Yes. Shall we?" He directed her toward the house with a palm up, lead-the-way gesture.

The hawk gave another raspy cry as she guided the odd

man inside and closed the door.

Jacob Price, my ass. Her contact for the park was none other than Io using a fictitious name. Venn circled the house. He needed to get inside, and he tried, but every damned door and window was closed tight. Not a crack big enough for a mouse, let alone a hawk.

Immensely frustrated, he settled on the porch rail, where he had an imperfect view of the dining room. He could see the table and part of the hutch. That was it.

TNT with a short fuse. That was what he felt like.

Io, Emma, and Mrs. Grant were chatting inside as if at an after-church social—all smiles and handshakes. The smug bastard even pulled out a chair for Emma to sit down. Venn's foraged breakfast threatened to come up.

"Would you like a glass of sweet tea or lemonade, Mr. Price?" Emma's grandmother asked.

"Why, yes, that would be refreshing. Tea, with extra sugar. And, please, call me Jacob."

The elderly woman nodded, then asked, "Emma, would you care for anything?"

"No, thank you."

Venn's blood boiled as Mrs. Grant left the room. Emma was now alone with a beast. He dug his talons deeply into the rail, gouging the wood. Instinct demanded he march in and remove his mate from danger, to handle the situation like the warrior he was born to be. By God, it had been far too long since he'd wielded his sword. Since he'd burned Io's evil blood from the blade almost nine hundred years ago. Since this all began and he'd accepted the responsibility of Guardian.

Was he truly expected to let this monster live this time? He could not. And he would tell Seth as much when next they met.

Expelling a harsh breath, he plastered his wings against his body. Io and Emma were sitting at the end and side of the table, respectively. She rolled out the plans, and Io reached over to help her. His hand brushed hers.

About to explode, Venn winged brutally in a circle and landed on the sill, drawing Io's attention. He looked over his shoulder to sneer at Venn, seeming to gloat, to taunt.

And there lay Venn's saving grace, the one thread of sanity he held on to—he could bank on the fact that it was early in the game for Io. His enemy would want to drag out the suffering. At least that gave Venn time to stop the monster before he hurt Emma. But Venn's options to do so at this point were few, and they both knew it. Sure, if he changed into human form, he could counter Io face-to-face, but it would gain him nothing. They were both immortal and couldn't kill each other by normal means.

Except there was pleasure to be had in fighting Io. *Ah, wouldn't that feel good.*

Venn tried to focus on the task at hand, pushing his violent urges away. The first obstacle he had to overcome was Emma's memory. How could he protect her if she was clueless about her past life and didn't realize the danger Io posed? She'd just as likely kick Venn to the curb as admit she had feelings for him.

Mrs. Grant came buzzing back into the room, the perfect hostess with a tray full of goodies. The little lapdog yipped at her heels but immediately started to backpedal when it caught sight of Io. The animal sensed the evil in the room in a way the women could not.

The dog bared its small sharp teeth and growled. *Nice going, pup.*

"Izzy, hush." Mrs. Grant looked apologetically at Io. "I'm sorry. He's unusually vocal today."

Io's face pulled into a strained smile. He stretched his neck, then he took a long drink of tea. The next thing

Venn knew, Io and Emma were bent over the drawings again. Too close. Io pointed to a few locations, spoke of a commemorative plate that would label the statue.

"Excellent," Emma said, her eyes alight with excitement. "The granite base will set off the sculpture magnificently. You've done a terrific job."

"It all sounds perfect. Just perfect," Mrs. Grant agreed, beaming, and then Izzy unleashed a mean bark in Io's direction.

Bite his ass.

The older woman flipped her hand by her leg and shushed the animal. "Will you excuse me? I'm going to let him outside."

It was the opening Venn had been waiting for.

He beat his wings and headed for the side entrance. By the door, the elder Grant scolded the dog for its bad behavior and walked away from the house, leaving the door open wide.

Venn flew into the mudroom and cloaked himself in invisibility. The shadow would hide him for a short while. Ready to rip apart whatever got in his way, he executed several short elegant glides, first to the washing machine, then to the refrigerator, and finally into the dining room to a rich, old mahogany hutch. Statue still, he perched, observing. Holding on to his invisibility took every ounce of control he had as Io and Emma continued to lean over the drawings. Again, far too close.

He couldn't tolerate Io's game a second longer. Couldn't stand the beast within touching distance of Emma. Emotion after emotion fired through him— possessive devotion, feverish hatred, wretched regret. He was to blame; he was the connection to Io.

Io rested his hand on her arm, and this time the touch ignited the fuse.

With his mind, Venn quickly willed Emma into sleep. She didn't need to witness what could be a gory fight. Venn felt, rather than saw, when she went limp and slumped onto the table because his focus was trained on Io. He shed his cloak and shrieked a cry into Io's mind, vaguely aware that Mrs. Grant could return at any moment.

Shocked, Io jerked up his head, and Venn descended, flying between them. Wings spread, flapping ever so slightly, he nipped and ripped at Io's face with the sharp hook of his beak, then readied for another pass.

The man pulled lips back from teeth as he froze with his hands fisted. "You fool. It isn't time. From nothing it's formed, light-shadow catching ridges or hollow, surfaces, texture, proportion, depth, shape, mass, space, three-dimensional, all-intentional, enduring."

Riddles. Not a surprise. Anger raged through Venn, and he grew in size, his wings beat the walls, his crown struck the ceiling, and he angled forward over Io.

Wide-eyed, Io jumped backward. He continued to retreat, knocking over a chair.

Change, Venn mentally ordered Io. "Change into the monster you are, so that—" A door creaked open. *The grandmother . . .*

Io laughed in a way only Venn could hear. He moved to intercept Mrs. Grant. "Excuse me. I believe something is wrong with Emma. I think she fainted," he said sounding concerned.

Venn flew to the far side of the room and hid behind a chair.

"Oh my," Grams exclaimed. She patted Emma's cheeks. "Let me get a cool cloth."

"I'll just leave and let you tend to her. Obviously she's ill. We can go over this another time." Io traveled to the door and let himself out. He half stumbled down the steps, then stomped full speed to the car as Venn watched through the window.

If it weren't for Emma, unconscious with her head down on the table, Venn would have given chase. But he was worried. As he turned, he gathered as much quiet energy as he could and surrounded himself with it until his blood began to settle. Not an easy task to accomplish, given the circumstances. He drew his shadow-cloak around him once again.

Emma moaned as she came awake, and his chest ached. What he wouldn't give to be in human form right now and hold her.

Like she'd allow that.

"Emma?" Mrs. Grant called from somewhere outside the dining room.

Emma groaned louder, rolling her head from side to side.

Venn glanced at the doorway where the old woman would probably appear any second and took off in the opposite direction. He beat his wings, clipping one of them on the light fixture overhead. His strained emotions made him woozy. He changed direction and flew out the still-open front door, following the path Io had taken moments earlier.

"Oh my goodness!" He heard Emma's grandmother's ruffled exclamation as he fled.

It was a knife to his heart not to be there to comfort Emma when she awoke.

Once outside, he circled back to the window, perched on the sill, and peered in again. He could see Emma pushing herself to her feet and listing sideways as she assured her grandmother she was fine. She explained that she couldn't remember what had happened—one minute she was talking with Io and the next, she awoke on the table.

Both Emma and Mrs. Grant glanced about.

"Well, where is he?" Emma asked.

"I . . . I don't know. Wait, he said something about getting together another time," her grandmother said. "I wasn't really paying attention, dear."

Venn heaved a relieved sigh. Now that he knew Emma was safe, his sense of panic and fear calmed. Emma seemed to come out of the mind-wash with ease, her movements growing more fluid with each moment. He regretted having to do it to her, but she didn't need to see the ugly side of things, yet. Let her remember their past first. Let her join him in thwarting the evil beast. Then she'd be more likely to accept their relationship. In the meantime, he had to push Io away, keep the demon at a distance. Having him out of the picture meant Emma would live another day.

All at once, his vision clouded with wavy spots and his stomach gave a nauseous churn. Venn knew he was about to unwillingly change. On occasion, when his emotions became too involved, his control went haywire. The glitch happened most often when he was with Amelia—now his Emma. He'd forgotten that hiccup from their previous life.

He flapped to the edge of the porch when the transformation began. His body burned with energy, a flickering sort of feeling. In human form, he crouched near the railing, the molecules that would make up his clothing starting to settle into place.

Three things kicked through his brain as his senses acclimated. One, he sure as hell didn't want Emma to catch him. Two, Io was gone, along with the SUV. And finally, his cell phone was in his pocket, so he could at least call Henry to pick him up. Good deal.

A phone rang then, but it wasn't his. He listened carefully as Emma answered from inside the house. "Hello?"

Just the sound of her voice made him feel better. He breathed in a fresh sip of pine, earth, and flowers that filled in the air. She was okay.

"I'm sorry. I'm so embarrassed I passed out. I don't know what happened. I don't even recall you leaving," she said, her voice climbing to a higher pitch.

Io. Again. His exceptional hearing even caught the demon's jeering response on the other end of the phone. Standing beyond the scope of the window, he grabbed the porch rail, fighting the urge to snap the wood and wishing it was his enemy's neck.

Protect. The mantra dominated his thoughts as he tried to keep his cool. Going ballistic like he did moments earlier couldn't happen again.

In order to keep her safe, he would have to earn her trust. And damn, what'd he do? Put her to sleep. Wasn't that smooth.

The front door squeaked and started to open. He vaulted over the railing, landed in a bed of snow-covered pink and yellow flowers, then booked it around the building, where he got cozy with the clapboard siding.

He heard the scrape of Emma's feet on porch planks and the change of rhythm that sounded when she traveled down the front steps. Holding his breath, he glanced around the corner. With her back to him, her long auburn hair fell to her waist as she glanced up, searching the sky and trees. She was looking for something.

The hawk?

His jaw ached from the grin he was holding back. From over her shoulder, he glimpsed the twirl of a feather she held with the tips of her fingers. Evidence he'd somehow left behind. She may not remember what happened in the dining room, but she obviously recalled the rest of the morning.

She turned, her expressive brows furrowed as she palmed the phone closed, then ran the feather across her cheek and lips.

Venn swallowed hard.

She patted her hip, then shoulder. "My camera."

He ducked as she glanced around, and his phone chimed "Everybody Dance Now." He grimaced, reached for his pocket and hit the "mute" key. Shit. His practical joker of a friend, Kianso, would pay dearly for changing his ringtone. But that wasn't even the worst of his problems right now.

What would she think if she found him snooping around? That would require one helluva explanation.

"Jacob?" Her feet smacked the deck in a rush, getting louder as they approached him.

Venn moved faster. With superhuman speed, he sprinted for the dense shadows of the forest fifty yards away and folded his large body behind an immense tree.

"Jacob? Is that you?"

Like an animal camouflaged in the brush, he peered out between the branches. Emma stood with her fists on her hips, searching the area he'd just left. He could hear her shaky exhalation as she crossed her arms over her chest and shook her head. He could smell her confusion, mixed with a hint of fear.

Not a bad outcome if she turned suspicious of Io, make that Jacob. He needed to remember the fabricated name. Yes, he hoped to capitalize on her ray of doubt.

"Well, damn." She spun on her heel and walked into the house.

As she retreated, the image of her sexy swaying hips was seared into his mind. Time couldn't pass fast enough until their date that evening, when he'd get a chance to make her remember the past life he'd never put out of his mind.

Reconsidering his original inclination of having Henry pick him up, he instead texted Henry with instructions to have a meal prepared. He would need to eat to keep up his strength. With his feet as heavy as cinderblocks, he trudged off the roadway and into the woods, changing into wolf. He felt emotionally drained, but worse, hoofing it gave him way too much time to think . . . and agonize over what to do.

He needed a plan that enabled him to be with Emma all day and night.

. 3 .

That evening, Venn parked his Harley in the Grants' driveway and cut the engine. He was eager to feel Emma pressed to his back, her arms wrapped around him. But a red flag flashed in his brain, telling him to slow down and not push a physical relationship. It wasn't easy to control the beasts within, though, especially when he knew time wasn't on his side.

He set the kickstand, removed his helmet, then strode to the front door. He knocked, and Mrs. Grant swung open the door wide.

"Oh my. What time is it? I'm sorry. We both lost track of time."

"I take it she's not ready?" he asked with a chuckle.

Emma's grandmother angled her head to the side. "She's in the garage, working." Her voice beamed with pride.

"Thanks." Venn nodded to the older woman, and she pointed him toward the garage, which was detached and set to the back of the house. He passed the area where he'd hidden earlier this morning as he approached, the blast of a blowtorch growing louder with each step closer to the garage.

He paused at the door to absorb the picture. Emma

wore heavy work gloves and a tinted face shield. She wound barbed wire into place as the heated metal glowed red. Even with the project in an early stage, he could easily make out the form of a tree and branches. *The Divine Tree?*

She tilted her head, concentrating, dabbed some solder, then stepped away to assess her progress. He enjoyed watching her, studying her.

He waited and watched, admiring the fit of her blue jeans over her curved hips and the pattern of a lacy bra beneath her T-shirt. Of all the powers he possessed, x-ray vision wasn't one of them, unfortunately.

He swallowed hard, then spoke. "Hi there."

She jumped at his voice and shot him a glare.

"Sorry," he said. "I didn't mean to startle you."

She sighed heavily. "Well, you did." She looked down at his feet, perhaps wondering how she'd missed the scrape of gravel. After removing a glove, she cut the torch and yanked off the face shield. "I didn't hear you."

"You wouldn't with that thing going."

She opened her mouth to say something, then closed it quickly. She shook her head. "Never mind."

"So, are we going to dinner?"

She bit her bottom lip. "Oh, uh, I got lost in my work. I'm not ready."

"I'll be glad to wait while you change."

She hesitated, her eyes searching his, and he sensed she was about to object.

"Come on." He held out a hand.

She set her equipment aside. "Okay."

Emma avoided his touch, moving just beyond his reach, teasing his senses. Venn followed her out and helped her ease the massive garage door to the ground. She set the pace as they walked briskly around the house.

A gazillion sounds competed for his attention. Birds chirped and flapped wings, a squirrel scurried across leaves, car tires squealed on the interstate miles away, a dog barked in the distance. But the soft throb of Emma's heart surpassed everything else; it held the power of her love. Finding her again transformed him: New expectations erupted, new plans formed, life had meaning again.

They bypassed the side entrance, which indicated he was clearly still company. And he wondered how long it would take for her to remember their past together. He clasped a hand to the base of his neck and stretched tired muscles. What if she didn't?

When Emma rounded the porch and caught sight of the motorcycle, she hesitated. She peered over her shoulder at him. "You can't possibly expect me to ride that."

He suppressed a chuckle. Most of the women in town seemed to *like* the bike. "Racy, huh?"

She shook her head. "I don't even know you, and you expect me to ride with you on a motorcycle?"

Her brows pinched as she scurried up the porch steps. To his surprise, her heart rate increased. Again, he could smell her anxiety.

"Wait," he said. She stopped and politely turned, but he could tell she'd made a decision. "Please. I'll run home and get the car if it bothers you that much."

Her jaw dropped, and then a flush suffused her cheeks. She exhaled sharply. "Really, we can do this another time."

Not on your life. "You need to change clothes, and I don't live far."

She searched his eyes, and her mouth curved into a little grin.

"Ah, you're smiling."

She glanced again at the bike, perhaps reconsidering.

"Trust me. It's your call. But I'm a very good rider."

———————

Emma tried to ignore his gorgeous, persuasive eyes. She couldn't think when she looked at him. Which was ridiculous.

She paused with her hand on the doorknob, deliberating. She abhorred timid, lackluster characteristics. Just look at her mother. Perhaps it was time to live a little wild.

My life. My terms. My mistakes.

Without glancing back at Venn, she straightened her spine and said, "I've changed my mind. We can take the motorcycle."

"You sure?" he asked. Was that a smile in his voice?

She rotated the knob and walked in, allowing him to catch the door behind her. Remembering her manners, she asked, "Would you like something to drink while you wait?"

"No, thanks."

"I won't be long."

"No rush."

In the living room, Izzy greeted them, and as soon as he saw Venn, the pup scooted over and nudged against his leg, asking for attention.

Emma jogged up the stairs, the clap of her feet echoing off the wall. Part of her couldn't get away from him fast enough, yet another part was fascinated by his dark, mysterious presence. He was all scruff and bicep but tied up in an elegant package. And she loved a good mystery.

In the small bedroom she always stayed in when visiting—it had the best view of the sunrise and it *hadn't* belonged to her father—she quickly flipped through her clothes, selecting black jeans and a long-sleeved, green V-neck sweater. Hands loaded with clothing and toiletries, she tucked her hairbrush between her arm and chest and dashed across the hall to the bathroom.

Dropping everything to the floor, she twisted the faucet, adjusted the temperature, and shed her work clothes. She grabbed a fresh bar of soap from her bag and stepped beneath the spray of water. As the water cascaded over her skin, the awareness that Venn waited downstairs made her as uncomfortable as much as it turned her on. Which was *so* not cool.

She began to wash, an image of Venn— *naked*— invading her mind. His muscular arms and chest . . . Firm, ripped abs . . . A scar over one hip bone.

Man, was her imagination vivid. She was even giving him fake war wounds.

She straightened, staring at the aqua-colored tile.

Yeah, definitely not cool. She barely knew the guy, and he made her hot in a way Todd never had. Guilt seeped through her. Why was she going out with a stranger? He has an honorable aura, Grams had said.

She flipped on the shower radio, grateful for any distraction, and rolled her eyes at the selection. Elvis night. *Yep, definitely back in Georgia.* Reaching for her back, she scrubbed herself clean.

As the final guitar chord of "Ain't Nothing But a Hound Dog" twanged, she blinked at the soap. The last remnants melted across her open palm. How? Was she beginning to heat up everything she touched? It had always just happened with metal before. Panic began to rise in her chest. What was going on with her now?

She drew a calming breath. *It's only nerves*, she told herself. *This date is just a bad idea, and my body is reacting.*

She knew it, yet, she couldn't resist. Didn't even truly *want* to resist.

After dressing and quickly doing her hair, she declared herself ready. She patted her cheeks and applied a dab of lip gloss. She wasn't aiming to impress him anyway, right?

As she descended the stairs, he came into view—ankles to narrow hips, hips to solid chest, chest to roguish grin. She nearly missed a step, she was so distracted. She fought to control her racing heart in the same way she controlled her sculptures, a little at a time. A picture in her mind that she brought to life. Only—

Oh, God. How was she going to get through this date when lovely pictures of him kept bombarding her?

This was not the reason she came back to Tyler. But he

was already here, and she'd already agreed. One dinner, she decided, and then she'd avoid him for the next few days until the statue project was done and she was on her way home to Paris.

———————————

It took every ounce of strength Venn had for him to stay put at the bottom of the stairs. She looked fabulous. Her hair was draping in silky waves over her shoulders, her green eyes flashing. Her chin eased a tad higher, going for a confident declaration even though she'd said earlier that she didn't like motorcycles, and he'd felt her nervousness.

That was his strong Amelia.

No, Emma.

"I hope you weren't too bored," she said to him, eyeing her grandmother as she approached.

"What? No faith in me," Mrs. Grant retorted.

"I know you, remember," Emma shot back playfully.

Venn chuckled. "I've just gotten a little history lesson." But he decided not to add, *About you.*

She slipped on her jacket. "As I feared, bored to death."

"Never." He opened the door, allowing Emma to exit first, saying to Mrs. Grant, "I'll take good care of her."

. 4 .

Minutes later, Emma stood beside the bike and shifted from one foot to the other as Venn fastened the helmet clasp under her chin. She swallowed, causing her neck to brush ever so slightly against his fingers. A pleasant shiver coursed down her spine. Then her brain kicked in.

She was going to die.

Not because they might get into an accident, but because an odd sensation grew from deep within her, a hot volcanic sensation threatening to explode, and the knowledge that Venn was somehow responsible made her anxiety inch higher. He was so close. So powerful. So appealing.

For no apparent reason, the episode at Aunt Fay's flashed in her memory. *So hot.*

"There. Ready?" he asked as he strapped on his own helmet.

She forced bravado into her voice. "Whenever you are."

He straddled the seat. "Hop on."

She did. She stared at his wide, muscular shoulders. She didn't quite know where to place her hands. This was their first date. Revision—their *only* date. The required intimacy of her chest pressed against his back, well . . . it had all come about too fast.

He gunned the throttle, and she tensed.

"Here we go," he said over the roar of the engine.

The cycle took off, shifted gear. Emma clapped her arms around Venn's waist, holding on as if she were dangling over a cliff with a five-thousand-foot drop.

Oh, no.

She was going to be ill.

"You okay?" he asked as they exited the drive and veered onto the road.

"Yeah." It was a lie, and her tummy knew it. She swallowed hard, ignoring a spasm.

Get over it, Emma. Breathing deeply, she tried to focus on other things. The wind whipping her clothes. The trees and scenery flashing by. Venn breathing in and out.

He felt solid and warm and in control.

They hit a bump in the road, and she gasped.

"Piece of cake, huh?" he said.

"Uh, yeah, right." Her grip on him tightened. And she found herself smiling at what she found.

His muscles contracted beneath her arms—fine, strong, capable muscles—and his ribs expanded as he inhaled. On a groan, she pressed her face into his jacket. He smelled fabulous. A spicy musk. Woodsy.

Suddenly, images began bombarding her brain. The pictures appeared and disappeared in a confusing, rhythmic tempo. She saw herself riding a horse, which was crazy. She'd never ridden. Yet the loping sensation felt natural, familiar.

In her mind's eye, fall foliage clipped past, frame by frame. If she didn't know better, she'd think she was in an old-time movie. Her breath caught in her throat as she realized these were a new type of vision, and mere snippets. Her visions were usually more fully formed and focused on some sort of danger. But that didn't seem the case now. *Strange.*

Then as if her previous thought prompted it, the scene switched and she saw fire. Raging fire. A building burned. She inhaled a sharp breath. There was no rhyme or reason as far as she could tell. What on earth was the deal?

It wasn't difficult to return to the here-and-now since she was traveling forty miles an hour along a winding road. The situation took care of that for her. And she went with it. She'd have plenty of time to think about her visions later.

Venn navigated a curve with ease, as she leaned into him. As scared as she was, and despite her stupid visions, she felt wonderful.

Before she knew it, he slowed the bike, stopped, and cut the ignition. The silence was cold and disorienting, a stark contrast to her Paris home. She didn't want to, but she raised her head. Taking in as much oxygen as she could, she breathed.

"Was it too bad?" he asked over his shoulder.

"No," she answered. However, in her mind his question and her response weren't about the same subject. Holding on to him for dear life hadn't been bad at all.

But she still felt like she was moving and remained unsettled.

With unbelievable grace, he kicked one leg over the handle bar and landed with both feet on the ground in a smooth twist, the picture of a martial-arts pro.

He was so fast, she flinched. "Oh."

Holding out one large hand to help her, he asked, "Hungry?"

She placed her palm in his. "I will be as soon as my stomach recovers." Unlike his, her dismount wasn't pretty. Her leg had caught on the seat awkwardly, and after a lot of shifting, she'd finally managed to stand up.

To her relief, he didn't seem to notice her clumsiness. Or at least he was polite about it. She stared at her feet, feeling the firm ground beneath her soles, and inconspicuously tugged her jeans down at the side seams.

"Where are we going?" she asked.

"To my cottage."

It occurred to her that being in the middle of nowhere with a stranger should elicit fear. But that's not what she felt. No, she was drawn to this man in a way she couldn't explain.

"I hope you don't mind, but I arranged a very private dinner," he said, his voice a husky rasp.

She jerked up her head. Glancing around, she took in the water, a pontoon boat, and lots and lots of forest. Where *was* his cottage?

"Is this the Savannah River?"

"Yes, there's a small island there that's been in my family for generations. It allows me to get away from it all."

She raised an eyebrow. "Your job must be demanding."

"That depends. If you mean how I make money, that's a pretty easy job, actually. I'm an investor."

"Must be nice." She swallowed, wondering where her brain had gone as a hint of perspiration made her bra cling to her skin, even though it was cold outside. Any other time she'd adjust the thing. The constricting pressure grew worse as her stomach tensed. Was she actually going to hop on a boat with a man she'd just met?

Grams knew him, she reasoned. That made it okay, didn't it?

She stepped onto the boat, and the floor tilted under her weight, dipping and rocking even more when Venn came aboard and sat beside her.

In the form of a great horned owl, Io had tracked the motorcycle along winding roads. He stayed well out of sight, employing his keen eye and acute hearing to spy on his prey. When they'd stopped and boarded the boat, he knew exactly where Venn was taking her and winged ahead to the cottage.

Leave it to Venn to take Emma to his private lakeside retreat.

Cozy.

And dangerous to Io's mission.

After all, Venn's and Emma's souls were connected. If Venn swayed Emma and convinced her not to follow Io's commands during the statue-raising ceremony, well, the tree would live. Venn would live. And the Guardian's world would remain intact.

Not going to happen.

Emma held the power to cause the tree's demise. Io had the ambition to use it. The instructions from Satan had cost him a heavy price. It required her to hold the statue's anchor stakes in her bare hands, using her inner heat to change the chemistry of the metal, making it toxic to Venn's precious tree. As long as she moved forward and nothing messed up his plan, that was.

No, he wouldn't dwell on that. He would focus on the victory to come. By the time Venn figured it out, it would be far too late.

Still, he mustn't get cocky. It was imperative to keep them off guard.

Harsh yellow light angled between oaks and maples as he flew ahead to the cottage. He carefully chose his landing spot high in a dense oak for optimum cover, a good spot to watch the show. Below, a servant fine-tuned the atmosphere, complete with gleaming china and linens. How elegant. Tea lights floated in a crystal bowl. How romantic. Expensive wine ready to pour. How predictable.

And best of all, in his opinion, a hot glowing fire pit.

Io swallowed. Taking down a Divine Tree and its Guardian would earn a huge trophy in the form of well-deserved recognition from the Dark One himself. Only one scion had ever achieved such a thing.

His heart smiled wickedly.

It was his turn now and much overdue.

Broken shadows elongated between trees as the sun dipped low on the horizon. Venn guided Emma off the boat and along the flagstone walk leading to the three-hundred-year-old stone cottage. He'd made a few upgrades, but the place was basically the same as it had been when he'd brought her here two centuries ago. Only then she was Amelia.

Would the familiar environment jump-start her memory?

"Venn, this is adorable," she said while eyeing the house.

"I'm pleased you like it." The cottage sat on a thumb-sized island, and every window offered a waterfront view. Perfect isolation. Easy to monitor.

"Like it? I love it. But if I were a sane person, I'd be—"

She didn't finish, her hesitation clear. "Demanding that I take you back to civilization," he murmured in a lighthearted yet soothing tone.

She rewarded him with a laugh. "You read my mind." With a shake of her head, she met his eyes. "I don't really know you at all, though."

"You know me better than you think. I'll convince you otherwise," he said, only half-kidding, prepared to do precisely that and more.

Instead of leading her through the house, they followed the path around to the back deck. He wanted the first thing she saw to be the glowing fire pit and deck overlooking the river. They would go inside and sit and chat later. Maybe she'd even remember their past by then. A gentle breeze rolled off the water and reminded him that it was a bit cold. Yesterday's snow had melted showing patches of earth, but the chill remained.

She stopped when the prepared table and roaring fire

came into view. She inhaled sharply. "Oh, my God. This is sooo beyond first-date material."

"It's a sin to do things half-assed." He cleared his throat and extended his hand. "Shall we?"

He led her to the table, where he pulled out her chair. His fingers brushed her shoulder as she sat, and he sucked air into his lungs. Jesus, the surge of desire that coursed through him would boil liquid again, if he didn't control himself.

He straightened, a feeling of unease suddenly nudging him. At the faint whoosh of wings, the muscles in his arms and back tightened. *Shit. Not. Now.* He glanced around, reining in his anger, scanning the foliage and trees. Sure as Satan, Io was here.

Venn didn't have days, didn't have hours, didn't have *minutes* to convince Emma her life was in jeopardy. However, such a claim wasn't something blurted out to a stranger. He couldn't just say, *Jacob Price is out to kill you.*

"On second thought, let's move inside. It's too cold out here," he said. Yes, the stone cottage equaled armor.

"Nonsense. This is delightful. The fire pit gives off plenty of warmth."

Of course she'd refuse his suggestion. Emma shook out her napkin and placed it in her lap. All he wanted was to wrap her in his arms and protect her. But he couldn't very well toss her to the ground in the name of safety.

She flashed a smile that hit his heart, and his gaze shot from tree to tree, surveying the area. At the moment, the one good thing was that Io couldn't fire an arrow, or truly harm her, while in his owl form.

If only she'd remember, then she'd believe him. But he still needed to progress slowly, dammit. Earn her trust and pray for the stars to line up to speed her memory along.

Using his mind, he roared at Io. *Leave her be. You'll not harm her again. Hell will not be far enough to run off to and hide this time.*

Ah, why did you not come after me?

Venn didn't reply. "Wine?" he asked Emma, ignoring Io's taunt.

She nodded.

He filled a glass and handed it to her, allowing his fingers to stroke hers as she took it. He loved the way her touch made him feel alive. It had been so long since he'd experienced that glow of warmth deep inside him. The sensation extended to his beasts, and they rolled inside of him as he felt them stretching for the caress. All those years of loneliness and isolation, they'd been part of that, too.

Her eyes flared as she looked at his hand. "Your ring is beautiful. So unusual. I noticed it at the coffee shop." She set down her glass. "May I have a closer look?"

He leaned into the table and reached his hand across for her inspection. "Sure. But it doesn't come off my finger easily."

She took his hand in hers, and the delicacy of her touch made his heart bang against his ribs as wild, driving desire coursed through his body. He studied her face, wishing again that they could just pick up where they'd left off in her previous life.

"It has a Celtic look." Her brows pinched. "And so meaningful, the tree set in circles, a wolf and a hawk guarding each side. The stones are gorgeous. The metals are blended together so expertly. I'm jealous."

"An old friend gave it to me," he murmured.

Oh, how sweet, Io shot at Venn with a snort, half contempt, half laughter.

Venn tensed, trying to erect walls to keep Io out of his head. If Emma knew the danger he'd put her in, she'd run for the high hills, back across the ocean to Paris. And maybe that was the best way to protect her. To let her go.

If it were that easy, he'd put her on the next plane.

"Your friend has excellent taste," she said with another smile and released his hand.

With perfect timing, Henry brought out their meals. A

medium steak—done to a perfect pink, just the way Amelia had liked it—crusted asparagus, and garlic mashed potatoes.

As Emma picked up her utensils, she made a face. Almost imperceptible but he caught it. "Is something wrong?"

She blushed. "I prefer my meat a bit more well-done. But that's okay."

Shock zinged through him, making him sit straighter. He thought the two women would be the same. That he could draw on the past to affect her now. Suddenly it occurred to him that winning Emma might not be so simple.

"No. It will take but a moment for Henry to cook it more." He stood, retrieved both their plates and began to head for the kitchen when he recalled Io and thought better of leaving her. "Henry," he spoke from the door. When Henry arrived he explained the situation in low tones, then returned to the table and refreshed their wine.

"I'm sorry," she said. "You've gone to too much trouble."

"Not at all."

She giggled. Like the sound of a perfectly tuned wind chime.

"What?" he asked, pleased that she'd relaxed.

"You don't talk much, do you?"

He grinned lazily over his wineglass. "I talk enough."

She rolled her eyes.

"So tell me about your project for the square."

She cleared her throat daintily. "It's a statue of a soldier on horseback. I'm sure there are similar ones around, though."

"Not using the techniques you use. Have you always worked in barbed wire?"

"I forget the medium seems unusual to people. Bronze or poured metals are more traditional. Barbed wire is made of steel, but it's not that hard to work with once you get used to it. I like working with the old or 'black' wire. It's soft yet durable."

"I enjoyed watching you work earlier," he murmured.

"Really?" Her shoulder rose and fell. "I didn't think it would be that interesting to someone who isn't emotionally involved in the work."

"Is that what happens when you craft a project? You get attached or something?"

"Yes. It's like having a child, I suppose. I create and shape it, then let it go."

Henry returned for a second time with their meals and then quietly exited.

"How long do you expect your project to take?" he asked as they dug in.

"I'm scheduled to be here for a week." She paused to eat some asparagus, closing her eyes briefly as if the morsel were melting in her mouth. Gently stabbing her fork into more, she continued. "Mmm, this is heavenly . . . Anyway, the park is in far worse condition than I had imagined. Had I known, I would have delayed my trip."

"I suppose I should opt for full disclosure and tell you that technically I own the park, or at least the land it sits on. A skirmish during the Civil War forced my ancestors to relinquish usage rights to the town."

Her mouth slackened. "How could you allow it to fall into such disrepair?" Her cell phone purred. "Oh, I'm sorry. I should have turned it off."

"That's okay. Go ahead and take the call."

"Only if it's my grandmother," she said as she fished around in her small shoulder bag. In quick succession, she withdrew a pair of sunglasses and a misshapen spoon and set them on the table, then she pulled out the phone. Her back straightened as she read the screen. "Oh darn. It's Paris. I really should . . ."

Venn gestured her to go on, then turned his attention to the distorted spoon. Certainly an odd thing to carry. It was smooth, with the handle kind of misshaped in a stretched-out sort of way, like the metal had been heated and cooled. He was itching for a closer look.

After a cursory hello, she switched to French, angling her body away from him.

Well, at least it isn't Io.

His gaze swept from her to across to where the river joined the lake, where a full moon peeked above the trees and then to the dancing fire. He kept his eyes on the flame despite the way her tone abruptly grew pressing. As hard as he tried to distract himself, he couldn't help overhearing both sides of the conversation. It was a friend with bad news. His gaze slid to hers.

"Incendie? Mon appartement?" she repeated, her eyes round.

He frowned and leaned toward her. He stopped pretending he was just looking off into the night.

She hung up, closing her eyes.

"Is everything okay?"

"Not really. There was a fire in my apartment."

"Bad?"

"Not burned to the ground, but bad enough."

Venn absorbed the implications. The timing of the act concerned him. He wondered if Io had anything to do with the incident. Perhaps he was trying to force her back to here, or distract her, or just cause her grief in general.

He reached over the table and rested his hand on her forearm. "I'm sorry."

She shrugged. "Thank you. It's just difficult being this far away."

"And your belongings?"

"Yes, I'll have to deal with that when I return. Until then, my roommate is there." Her words came out rushed, somewhat distracted.

He backed off and picked up his fork and knife once more. Then added, "If you need anything—"

"Thank you." She returned her array of items to her bag.

"Your food must be cold," he said. "Would you like it warmed?"

"No. My appetite seems to have deserted me." She smiled awkwardly. "It was excellent, though."

He nodded. She was putting on a brave face, but he suspected she was feeling otherwise. And he was helpless to make it better. He was going to find out through Ian what actually happened in Paris. His brother had extensive connections throughout France and should be able to offer an accurate report of the situation. Possibly it was merely a coincidence. But no, he didn't believe that. He longed to talk with her about it, share everything with her the way they used to. He couldn't push her, but it was hell to act like they didn't have a bond.

5

A cold breeze rolled off the water as the temperature plummeted. Emma polished off the last of her wine, hoping to ease the ache in her chest, then stared into the empty glass at the tiny crimson pool that remained. Frustration flamed in her gut.

What was she to do? She couldn't simply hop on a plane and tear back home to Paris. Her grandmother had gone through a lot of trouble on her behalf. She couldn't abandon the project. So no matter what happened at home, she had to stay here. And maybe . . . maybe it was time to investigate the meaning behind her visions. The one in the park yesterday had left an incredible mark. And earlier, she'd seen the fire and now it was coming true. She inhaled and exhaled slowly. *What's going on…and why are my visions changing?*

She felt Venn's eyes on her, and an intoxicating awareness bubbled to the surface, pressing aside her troubling thoughts. And it wasn't the wine. Her desire to stay intensified because of him. This striking masculine man sitting across from her made her insides turn giddy and messed with her head. A dangerous combination. An overwhelming sensation she hadn't felt since she was a sophomore in high school, when she'd tried to smoke a cigarette in order to fit in with her senior boyfriend.

As she attempted to recall that teenaged moment in more detail, she found she couldn't. Venn dominated her thoughts. She turned her head and met his eyes.

Silence fell between them, a long interval of what should have been an uncomfortable lack of exchange. But it wasn't. The encounter was like a pause that came between whipping gusts of wind, comfortable and treasured. He seemed to be giving her space, and she appreciated that consideration. It was more than she was accustomed to with her father, who was always pressuring her, trying to make her into the normal pretty little rich girl he wanted her to be. And in the midst of her emotions she wondered . . . who did Venn want her to be?

Oh no, that was her father's influence talking, she scolded herself, then set her wineglass on the table.

Avoiding Venn's powerful gaze this time, she said, "I think I should go. I have a busy schedule tomorrow."

"Of course." His brow creased in displeasure before he expertly hid it. "You must also be tired from traveling."

"A little." *A lie*, she muttered to herself. *Stay.*

Go. Stay. Go. Stay. What was wrong with her?

Venn stood and came around the table. "Let's walk through the cottage this time. It will warm you before the ride home."

"I'm not cold." Her core temperature rose the closer he got. He helped her with her chair, and beads of perspiration dotted between her breasts. "The fire's, uh, been quite toasty. Thank you."

She heard him draw an extended breath. "My pleasure."

His long fingers flexed, as if he were dying to touch her and had to forcibly hold himself back. If he only knew how her body longed to embrace him in return. She glanced away, lightly touching her face and lips as more images stole her thoughts, creating a pang in her heart. Hands, powerful yet gentle, stroking along her collarbone, over her shoulders, down her back as she was drawn into a kiss.

"Would you like to go inside?"

She blinked rapidly, startled by Venn's words as they slowly dragged her from more fragments of the vision. "Yes. I'd love to see the cottage. It's so quaint."

They walked side by side toward the entrance, and he motioned for her to enter first. Past the threshold, warm air cocooned her, the drastic temperature change overpowering. If she stayed in here long, she'd have to shed some clothing.

Moving to the center of the room, she took in the decor, awed. It was masculine and pleasing, dark leather and wood. But everything in the room changed her opinion of the cottage. This was far from quaint. A floor-to-ceiling bookcase lined one wall. A river rock fireplace centered another. What surprised her most was the abundance of artwork. Expensive pieces, too. Some works she recognized from a Christie's auction. A gorgeous nickel-coated brass sculpture of a tree dominated a collection of animals and beer steins on the coffee table.

"You've done some serious shopping." She peered at him, intrigued and impressed. "Hmm, superb taste in food *and* art. I'm going to have to keep my eye on you."

"I'll count on that," he said with a hint of flirtation.

"Mind if I look around a moment before we leave?"

He smiled. "Take your time. I'm going to speak with Henry. I'll be right back."

Either she was too absorbed or he was damned quiet because she didn't hear him leave the room. Unable to resist, she circled the seating area to examine each piece more closely. The art was a mixture of American and European artists, ancient and modern, originals and high-end replica work. One thing was clear, Venn Hearst had money. Lots of money.

But she knew firsthand that money didn't buy happiness.

She barely breathed as she moved from picture to picture, ending on *The Violin* by Juan Gris. The last she'd heard the painting sold at a Christie's auction in Paris featuring Yves Saint Laurent's private art collection. Holy moly. Venn had connections, too.

She moved into a hall and lingered engrossed in an original from American artist Bev Doolittle, *The Forest Has Eyes*. She looked at the faces hidden in the scene. She sensed rather than heard him as he came up behind her. "As a child I had a book of Doolittle's pieces," she murmured.

He placed a hand at the small of her back, and she let the moment roll over her. A few other art forms were tucked into display boxes and featured on shelves. One in particular caught her attention, and she moved closer to the wolf standing on a rock. She stared at the piece, rubbing her fingers over her brow. It was one of her early sculptures. She recalled entering it in a local art show the summer of her junior year in college. "This is one of mine. I'm surprised you have it."

"I never realized." He scratched along his firm jawline apparently in genuine surprise. "I've always felt a connection to wolves."

She lifted the wolf from its stand and held it in her hands. More images and sensations fired through her mind—soft, thick fur so long her fingers disappeared into it, golden eyes, howling. Wolves had been in her dreams many times, and in her visions, too.

She passed the sculpture to Venn—his warm fingers brushed over hers as he took it, making her even more aware of him, if that was possible. In this light, his eyes shone amber. She looked away, then back, and leaned in closer as her cheeks heated.

He balanced the piece on his large, opened palm. "Huh. You created this. No wonder I was drawn to it." A sexy smile eased across his face. "It's coming home with me tonight."

All of a sudden, she wished she were going home with him, too.

His eyes lingered on her face, his gaze flickering to her lips. She moistened them with a sweep of her tongue, wondering what it would be like if he kissed her. With his free hand, he touched her face, sliding his fingers over her cheek. He tipped up her chin and ran a thumb over her lower lip. Her knees grew weak. Oh, geez. If he kissed her this moment, she'd let him.

"Ready?" he whispered.

She took a deep breath and stepped back. "Yes."

Pulling her jacket closer around her, she suppressed a sigh, not worried at all about the return motorcycle ride home as she should have been. Instead, this time her stomach churned because of the growing connection she felt for Venn.

During the boat trip back to the motorcycle, Emma longingly stared past his shoulder at the receding cottage. The place touched her in a way she couldn't express. She'd always known her visions and dreams were more enthusiastic when she was in Tyler, but now she realized they were undeniably increasing in frequency and intensity.

She chewed on her lip and watched Venn from beneath lowered lashes, again in comfortable silence until they reached the shore. The motorcycle ride home was exhilarating this time, and Emma relaxed into Venn while letting go of inhibitions as she became one with the cold wind, the balancing motion of the bike, and the firm male form she had her arms around.

She knew in that short ride she wanted to see him again. Venn was so different from Todd. His mature and sophisticated manner attracted her beyond measure, his appreciation of art touched her soul, and he made her heart race like no one else ever had.

Oh, my. She had some decisions to make.

The walk to the front door of Grams's house made her heart skip with a burst of panic, almost afraid to let him out of her sight. Afraid she wouldn't get to see him again.

He gently pulled her into his arms, forcing her to look up at him. "The evening was too short," he said. "Can I see you tomorrow?"

"Tomorrow?" A dance of relief rippled through her. *Tomorrow.* She thought of the way wire transformed into a sculpted creation. Possibilities visualized in a single strand that required time and application to emerge. Relationships were like that, too. She nodded and smiled up at him.

Then he captured her mouth and kissed her, at first long and sweet. Warm. Perfect. In a heartbeat, a light within her ignited and she clutched him tighter, pulling him against her, desperate for something more. He dipped his tongue into her mouth to taste her and she matched his every move. She knew as he drew back that he'd just given her the most delicious kiss of her life. And yet, she sensed he had so much more to offer. As if, he was saving the best for later.

Her head remained tipped back, her eyes closed, for a lingering moment after he moved away. When she opened her eyes again, a roguish smile enhanced his features.

"What time can I pick you up?" he asked. "I want to spend the whole day with you."

"I have to meet with someone at the warehouse in the morning when they uncrate the statue, but I should be free after that."

"Okay, after that, then. How can I reach you?"

Still in a haze from his kiss, they exchanged contact information.

"Call me when you're done," he said. "I'll be waiting."

6

In her room, Emma quickly dressed for bed, feeling a little overwhelmed by the evening. She arranged the usual things on her nightstand: a bottle of water, her touching spoon in case her hands grew hot, and her cell phone. As her eyes roamed over the last, she thought of Venn, and then of Todd, conflicted. Maybe she needed to call Todd tomorrow. Perhaps hearing his voice would relieve the unsettling twitter she was experiencing, snap her out of this longing for another man, for Venn.

Punching her pillow, she settled into the mattress and dragged the covers to her chin. She closed her eyes with a long sigh. She'd sort out her feelings in the morning when she'd be refreshed and have a clearer perspective.

But despite her resolve to put everything out of her mind, her thoughts kept flickering from one problem to another: the Paris fire, Venn, Todd, working with Jacob on the statue project. She hadn't expected this trip to be so complicated.

Finally, after about thirty minutes she gave up on sleep, got out of bed and donned her robe. Perhaps she should get a book and read. As she went for the paperback she'd brought with her, the moon shining through the window caught her attention. Tucking one arm over her rib cage, she drew open the curtain with the other hand and peered out.

The night was shimmering and quiet with an overcast sky, the moon peeking from behind the clouds. Snowflakes danced and waved, reflecting gentle rays of light. When her gaze arrived at the ground, she tensed. A wolf stood a few feet into the yard.

She rubbed her eyes in disbelief.

A wolf. In Tyler, Georgia. No way.

She remembered the vision she'd had in the park, of the wolf howling over a dead woman. She brought her hand to her throat as she looked down at the creature. It seemed to be watching her, too.

No, that was plain silly. She drew a breath, having the strangest urge to call it nearer. No, not *it*. *Him*.

The wolf had the wide muzzle and brow of a male. Her research for her sculptures had taught her a great deal about forms and mannerisms of all kinds of animals, for the right details gave a project life.

Then the wolf tilted his head up to her as she watched him. He *was* watching her back. Did he envy the warmth she possessed inside the house? He traveled a few steps closer, then paced in that spot, seeming undecided about something. Finally, he stopped near a large rock and sat, staring at her window.

Clouds covered the moon, and Emma squinted hard but lost him. She knew he was there, though, could feel his eyes on her. Eventually, the sky cleared again, and he was still there. On a tired, reluctant sigh, she let the curtain fall closed.

With the wolf now occupying her mind, she gave up on the reading idea. As she climbed into bed, she hoped he had the sense to leave before Grams and her shotgun found him. The woman had gunned down raccoons and coyotes poaching her chickens. Emma shivered. He was a beautiful creature, not meant to be killed.

She would speak to Grams about him in the morning, she decided, turning off the light on the nightstand.

Emma closed her eyes on a hushed moan and let go of her worrisome thoughts one by one—the project timetable, the fire, her confusing feelings for Venn—and focused solely on a wolf and how many times a lone wolf had come to her in her dreams and visions.

Hours later, part of her knew she was dreaming as she told herself to wake up. But the sweet essence of the dream was more powerful than her conscious mind.

This was quite the opposite of the intense visions she typically experienced. Although the time period and even her alter ego seemed the same, the feelings the dream evoked were happy. Contentment and joy wrapped her in a pleasant yet misty bubble. She was with a man.

And she'd had this dream before.

Why this person visited her, she'd yet to figure out.

In a huge study, she sat at a gaming table beside a warm fire. She was halfway into a chess game and had just taken a rook. She laughed. "There. See? I have you."

She turned in her seat to view her opponent. He was at the sidebar, refreshing their wine. His back was to her, and his shoulders shook as he chuckled.

"Did you move them around while my back was turned?" he asked.

"I didn't touch the pieces."

"Perhaps not, Amelia. But you used your powers."

"I haven't perfected that yet," she said evasively, and faced the game. It was true—her mastery and control were inconsistent. However, this time she had managed to use her mind to move the shiny brass-and-silver playing pieces where they stood, exchanging a pawn and a knight as they slid of their own accord to a new position on the board. The task transpired even faster than it would have if she'd used her hands.

The echoing footfalls on the wood flooring let her know he was moving closer, and then he paused behind her chair. Her heart stammered as it always did with his nearness.

He leaned over her shoulder, depositing her wineglass on the table. She inhaled his intoxicating scent of spices and musk. With his hand now empty, he rested it on her shoulder and lightly stroked her tired muscles. She closed her eyes at the delicious pressure along the base of her neck.

"I think that knight is still wobbling," he said.

She jerked forward to see. He laughed. It wasn't, of course, but she was caught by her incriminating reaction.

"I'm impressed. Your abilities are improving by the day."

Inside her mind, Emma pleaded with her dream self— her *past* self, really—to turn and meet his eyes, to capture his face so she could at last get a good look at him. The lack of clarity was infuriating, the dream cloaked in mist. One thing she noticed in this instant was she and her past self didn't seem to possess the same abilities. Where she changed metal, Amelia moved things with her mind. Which meant they were not exactly alike. She sighed. The difference pleased her.

The images faded as she awakened to a whooshing noise and coal-black darkness. Blinking, Emma identified the sound of a flushing toilet. Grams must have gotten up.

Rolling onto her side, she tried to call the dream back, but it wouldn't obey. Finally giving up the futile attempts, she sat, patted the nightstand until she found her fidget-spoon, and warmed it between her hands.

Hmm. Some people used stress balls, squishing them to relieve tension. She had a spoon.

In the dark room, the spoon glowed amber. She bent it into a horseshoe shape, then back again, rubbing the pad of her thumb into the spoon's bowl, deepening it. She closed her eyes. Her parents blamed her overactive imagination for making her different, and her father always said it didn't help that she'd chosen art as a profession.

She'd been two and a half years old when she'd had her first past-life experience. She had talked about horses and

people and events that could only have been in the
nineteenth century. At four, she'd learned she could
manipulate metal with her hands—a spoon-bending
technique, nothing more. Although she'd tried to develop
advanced skills, an element seemed to be missing. She
especially felt the disparity whenever she was with Amelia
but couldn't figure out what it was.

At any rate, the dreams had grown fewer and less
intrusive as she'd gotten older. Except when she was here
in Tyler, usually spending summers visiting her
grandmother. And except now that she'd met Venn.

Emma returned the spoon to the nightstand, curled
onto her side, and closed her eyes, begging for some sound
sleep. Her last conscious thought was of Venn's golden
eyes gleaming dark and dangerous, challenging her to join
him. But where?

———————

She awoke in the morning still tired. Snuggling deeper into
the comforter, she glanced at the light slipping past the
curtain thinking, *Not yet.* She wasn't quite ready to face the
day.

On one level, this was like a vacation with life set apart
from her normal daily work schedule. Her friends thought
a self-employed artist had a lot of playtime, but that wasn't
so. If she didn't produce, she didn't earn money. And even
while at her grandmother's, she would need to maintain
her website, update her blog, and keep creating her metal
sculptures.

She yawned. Her hideaway was warm and cozy, the
citrus smell of the sheets soothing. She *really* didn't want to
get up. For some season, she wasn't looking forward to
dealing with Jacob Price, either. He'd been a strange man,
especially disappearing the way he had. But otherwise, the

day promised to be good. And she definitely looked forward to seeing Venn again. More than she should. She imagined the powerfully handsome set of his jaw and how his face changed when he smiled at her, and something melted a little bit inside her.

She took a deep breath and tried to clear her mind of him, recalling the late-evening snow and her nocturnal visitor. Curiosity drew her from her haven, and she rose, donned a robe and slippers, and shuffled to the window. She paused when her fingertips touched the lacey curtain, feeling vulnerable in her anticipation.

She wanted the wolf to be there.

Pushing the thought away, she drew back the curtain and leaned toward the glass. Her breath fogged the window, and she swiped her fingers over the cold glass. He wasn't easy to spot at first. A light dusting of snow covered his coat. But he was there. As if he hadn't budged all night long.

He lifted his head then, and warmth swirled in her chest, spreading into her limbs like the heat she summoned to shape metal. The wolf grew clearer as the sky brightened from lavender to pink. She needed to let her grandmother know about the wolf before she saw him for herself, sitting there in the early light of day. Izzy would be a bite-size meal for a wolf, too.

She headed downstairs. In the kitchen, Grams huddled at the stove fixing her usual grits and eggs.

"Morning, sweetie," Grams greeted. "Did you sleep well?"

Emma made a noncommittal noise and selected her favorite mug, with its etched tree design. She remembered the fair in Tyler where her grandmother had bought it for her when she was a little girl. Rubbing the imprint with her thumb, she filled the mug with coffee from the coffeepot, and then stood at the sink.

The window presented the same view as her bedroom. *Found you.*

She sipped, letting the warm liquid ease down her throat. "Have you had many problems with wolves, Grams?"

"Wolves? Not around here. Don't they live in cold country?" Grams expertly flipped the eggs.

"Yes, usually. But these days, with people keeping wild animals as pets, you never know."

"There's a new fellow around town that has a dog that's part wolf."

"Hmm. Perhaps it's him. You may want to be careful with Izzy, though." As if on cue, the wolf turned its head and looked at her. A tingle of excitement skated along her spine.

"You've seen one. Where?"

"Out there." She indicated the yard with a nudge of her coffee mug.

But the wolf was already loping off, a bare patch of brown grass the only evidence of where he'd been. And only if one knew where to look. "Darn. Did you see him?"

Grams peered past her shoulder and shook her head. "Funny you should mention a wolf. When you were a little girl you used to talk about having a wolf 'friend.'"

Emma's breath caught. "Did I? I'd forgotten."

"I think he was your imaginary friend. And he would visit in your dreams . . . or whatever they were."

The sudden silence made the room claustrophobic, and Emma drifted back into her childhood. Glimpses of a wolf as tall as she was sat beside her. Her arm rested across its shoulders, her fingers laced deep in its impossibly thick fur. She was content, wrapped in tenderness and comfort and love.

A soft, warm feeling spread through her chest. How she missed that feeling. What had caused her to bury it?

"Do you still get them? The dreams?"

"Occasionally," she answered with a half-truth. In the two days since she'd arrived she'd had one vision, a bunch of glimpses, and a dream—a jarring escalation compared with the few episodes she'd had the entire past three years in Paris.

Grams squinted outside, as if she were trying to see something more.

Emma glanced out the window again. Yellow eyes gazed at her from within the forest shadows. Was the animal real or some spirit creature?

At this very moment, it didn't matter.

She pushed aside vague memories from her childhood, along with the thought... *You can't escape who you are.*

True. And she was determined to move forward with the reason she was here.

"I have to meet with Jacob today at the warehouse. Maybe I should rent a car so as to not put you out," she suggested, changing the subject.

"Nonsense. Take my car. I have nothing planned," Grams patted her shoulder, then walked to the table.

Emma's gaze shifted to the edge of the forest again. The wolf stared back.

7

Positioned behind a low-draped oak branch at the forest's edge, Venn paced, debating whether he should return home to bathe or stay put. His stomach growled, an intense reminder that when he changed, he needed to eat more. Food equaled strength, and shape-shifting consumed a ton of energy. It didn't help matters that the smell of eggs and bacon drifted out from the Grants' kitchen.

When the side door creaked open, he snapped his head up and assumed a guarded stance. Emma exited with that little dog on a leash. She was clearly taking no chances. She looked magnificent in her jeans and hip-length sweater, with her hair a disheveled riot of auburn. She threw on a jacket as she walked into the yard, trying to maneuver the leash as she went.

He smiled to himself. No feminine wiles to be found. His voyeuristic behavior produced a tinge of guilt, but he couldn't look away.

The sun inched higher, and he retreated several paces.

At least she was safe. He couldn't sense Io's presence here, either. Yet. Then again, when Emma was near, things within him could get a little messed up. Including his powers.

"Hurry up. Do your business," she grumbled to the dog.

The scrawny thing yipped like a banshee and pitched a fit, and decidedly turned in Venn's direction.

"Yeah. And he'll eat you for breakfast."

No, thanks.

Peewee finally took a shit and tugged on the leash back toward the house.

If Venn had his way, he'd change into his human form as he strolled up to her. Then he'd pull her into a kiss, showing her all the passion and longing he felt for her. And if he knew it wouldn't freak the hell out of her, he'd do just that. But at present, he would have to settle for watching her from distance.

Should he go? Should he stay?

He was normally of an extremely decisive nature, and it irked him that all common sense fled when it came to Emma.

But hell . . . Love. Bonding. Instinct. How did he control that?

Of course, the problem was that he couldn't.

After Emma let the dog inside, she paused and glanced back to where he'd spent the night. Finding the spot empty, she scanned the forest. Did she feel his presence the way he felt hers? She was a heat lamp that warmed his cold soul.

Unable to stop himself, for a heavy chain tether wouldn't have held him, he moved from the shadows.

She glimpsed him then, closed the door, and traveled several cautious steps toward him. To his super acute hearing, her heart rate sounded like a fluttering bird's wings. Yes, she should be nervous.

He eased closer. Not too much. *Mustn't scare her.*

She matched his steps, then upped them by four, the snow crunching beneath each footfall, the color of her slippers darkening as they got wetter and wetter.

The clearing between house and forest became

astoundingly silent, as if every creature held its breath to watch what was transpiring as woman and wolf came together.

Finally, he stopped at her feet and looked up.

"Easy now. You won't hurt me, will you?" She held out her hand, palm down, in the customary nonthreatening way to greet an unfamiliar dog.

He took the opportunity to sniff her skin, nuzzle his nose along fingers, and then pushed the crown of his head into her palm.

"You're friendly. You must belong to the neighbor." She knelt, looked him in the eyes. "Hmm, you're part wolf and part . . . what?"

Interesting question.

He sat still, not moving a muscle for fear she'd bolt. She brushed snow from his coat with light strokes. Then she buried her fingers deep in his thick fur. Sensations bombarded him—tingling, feathering, arousing. Making him wish he were in his human form again, but knowing if he were, she wouldn't be touching him now. He positioned his muzzle along her thigh and pushed the side of his face into her.

Beyond them, he was vaguely aware that the birds took up chirping again, a squirrel rustled in a tree, and the house door clacked.

Her grandmother startled them both. "I think—"

On instinct, Venn launched himself around Emma, assuming a defensive posture between her and her grandmother.

The elder woman backed up. "Oh my."

"Easy now. It's okay," Emma said.

Venn mellowed immediately as he cursed his overreaction.

Hands on her hips, her grandma said, "Protective, aren't you?" Then to Emma, she added, "I think I better give Phil a call and let him know the whereabouts of his animal."

Venn trotted back to Emma and sat, going for the perfect picture of a well-trained canine.

Mrs. Grant narrowed her eyes. "Hmph. You aren't fooling me. Don't turn your back on him, Emma. Better yet, maybe you should come on in."

But he had to hand it to grandma, she didn't harp on the matter and left it up to Emma to make a choice.

"I'll be in shortly."

She would stay. Longer. He moaned, pleased with the way his head fit perfectly under her hand. She stroked the fur between his ears with lingering caresses.

"Did you hear that? Your owner will probably be stopping by later to get you."

Venn knew differently. When Emma walked toward the house, he followed.

At the door, she turned. "Why don't you find a lovely place in the sun to wait?"

When he got home, Venn hopped in the shower and let the vigorous stream of water pound on his exhausted back muscles. He stood beneath the pounding multi-jet spray until the hot water turned cold. Which considering the size of the water heater had to have been a considerable length of time. And the only thing he'd accomplished was pruning the flesh on his toes and fingers.

After Emma had retreated into the house, he'd paced for a half-hour or so until he couldn't stand the thought of being close to her but not actually with her. He needed distance, to be far enough away that he couldn't inhale her scent with every breath. He had pushed himself hard the entire way home, but no amount of running would free him from the ache his body knew. That was up to Emma.

He shoved away from the wall and cranked back the faucet until the water ceased. Cool air whisked over his body, making him shiver. He grabbed a towel, dried, and dressed.

Long before Henry reached the door, the aroma of breakfast drifted into the room. The man was whistling. Venn smiled. He wasn't sure if Henry did that because he liked to or because he was forewarning his arrival. Regardless, Henry always timed his entrance perfectly.

"By the window?" he asked.

"Sure. Thank you, Henry."

The man uncovered a tray with omelet and bacon. "Have you checked your schedule? I see an appointment with your banker."

"Cancel it, please. My plans have changed."

"Of course."

On his way to the seating area, he paused to admire the wolf figure he'd brought back last night. He reached out and turned it slightly, just because he wanted to connect with something that had been part of Emma, touched by her. Out of nowhere, Io's riddle flitted into his thoughts. *From nothing it's formed, light-shadow catching ridges or hollow, surfaces, texture, proportion, depth, shape, mass, space, three-dimensional, all intentional, enduring.*

A sculpture. Yes, that was the answer. And the statue that came to mind was the one Emma had made for the park. There must be an association there somehow.

Venn sat, then remembered he wanted to call his brother in Paris. A quick glance around revealed his cell phone on the nightstand, hooked up to his charger. He drank a long gulp of coffee, then thumbed the latest message on the phone. Nothing important.

Henry gave him an exasperated look. Venn ignored him. He had learned that nothing set the man off more than delaying a meal. If it was hot when he prepared it, he wanted it hot when it was consumed.

"Let me know if you need anything, sir."

"Will do."

As Henry left, Venn dug into the food. When he'd

finished, he poured a second cup of black coffee. The meal was already giving him more energy, and he grabbed his cell phone again. He selected number six on speed dial and hesitated, contemplating how much to reveal about Emma and Io.

Once he called Ian in Paris, he'd be on the Light Realm's radar. No doubt about it. But he needed reliable information about what happened to Emma's Paris apartment in order to get a better handle on what was transpiring here.

Had Io gone that far?

Damn, with no way to travel there himself, his anxiety rose. That was one huge advantage Io had over him, the demon was free to go wherever he pleased...Venn was not. His duty remained to stay within calling distance of his tree.

He leaned back in his chair and hit "Video Chat." The phone rang several times, then quit. No answer.

———

Emma arrived at the city's Parks and Recreation warehouse at nine thirty. She pulled into a parking space near the flagpole as the sun rose above the treetops, snow glistening as it melted. Five cars dotted the lot, and she recognized Jacob's immediately. In the background, a man walked a large dog along a trail. Somehow she couldn't picture the wolf at Grams's on a leash. According to Phil, the wolf dog couldn't have been his. His dog had been lounging on its bed when Grams had called him.

Could that mean she'd been petting a real wolf? She couldn't believe that was possible. Someone else had to have a mixed breed on the loose.

Putting on her businesswoman hat, she turned up the walkway. Inside, Jacob greeted her. He led her to a rear exit, and they traipsed across a patch of gravel to another metal building. They entered a room with large cargo bay doors at the far end for easy delivery of goods.

The screech of nails being ripped from wood greeted them. Two men were hard at work opening the nine-foot crate in the center of the room. Her statue. She couldn't help the flash of pride and excitement that it ignited in her. The moment was like watching someone opening a gift when she knew what was inside. She awaited the men's reactions as they pried the crate top off, then the back and far side, and finally removed the front and nearest panel.

As the statue was revealed, Jacob strolled the crate's perimeter and cocked his head, studying her work from different vantage points.

Was that good or bad?

Emma moved forward, burying the uneasy feeling. "Do you like it?"

"It's perfect," he practically purred, as if enjoying a secret joke. "Yes, perfect."

Ground transport and air shipping had taken three weeks. Weeks that had distanced her from the work. After months of shaping the barbed wire into a 460-pound horse-and-rider figure, she was anxious to see how the statue had fared.

She glanced from him to the statue, seeing her creation with fresh eyes. Heat suffused her cheeks.

Oh. My. God. She inhaled a long, shaky breath as she walked to the left to take it in at a slightly different angle. Her fingertips warmed with each step, her beating heart tripping faster. Now, the vigorous man straddling the horse, magnificent and confident, looked like . . . Venn Hearst.

Her gaze ran over the same firm jaw, broad shoulders, even the tilt of his head, she'd captured perfectly.

Emma stared, eyes wide. Confused. Shocked. Torn. *This* was the reason Venn had seemed familiar to her. But, how . . . How could she have constructed a statue the exact likeness of a stranger? Had she seen a picture of him in a news article or tabloid, and had just forgotten? Had she met him before and forgotten that? She couldn't imagine the latter could ever be true. He was certainly memorable.

She zeroed in on the features of the rider's face and the connection came to her, slammed into her like a Mack Truck. Why had she not noticed it before? Venn was the man in her visions.

But how? Was he a descendant of the guy in her visions? Or was he a reincarnation of the man from her past life? Did he remember her, too? Why had he not said anything?

From the beginning, the statue commission for Tyler had stood apart from other projects. It should have taken her twelve weeks to create, yet she'd accomplished the task in four. Each day she had burned to work on it. Maybe Venn was why.

Heat rushed up her neck and face. Did Jacob see the resemblance? Did he know Venn?

The statue was a gorgeous work of art—the best she'd done. Now its brilliance faded before her eyes as embarrassment filled her. The entire town would recognize its namesake. She had not been commissioned to create a figure of Venn Hearst, current park owner, but one of a fictitious early settler.

Worse, Venn would identify her subject in a heartbeat.

And she would have no explanation.

After his meeting, Io sat in his mansion, lounging in front of the colossal stone fireplace—tall enough for a half-dozen men to stand in—and watched as his current minion arranged his afternoon's quota of Satan's Brew in glasses from the smallest shot glass to the exquisite diamond cut crystal tumbler on a tray. The fire danced and cracked and behaved as if it might jump out of its confines and engulf the house at any moment. Just the way he liked it. He began with Spirytus, Polish vodka, knocking the shot back. Ah, it had been an extremely good morning.

He lifted the fused clump of coins from the end table, and rolled it effortlessly over his knuckles and between his fingers just like a talented magician. He'd made a habit of practicing the trick ever since that fateful day he'd dropped them. Thinking, he set the fused coins aside.

At first glance, the irony of the situation this morning had hit Io like the sun on a cold day. What better means to deliver a fatal blow to Venn and the Divine Tree than through a statue of Venn himself. Io sniggered maliciously.

It didn't take the genius he was to see that she'd been shocked to discover the identity of her subject. She had not realized the similarity until the moment the art was unveiled. The astonishment on her face was priceless. And knowing her background as he did, what she was like as a child, when she'd moved from Tyler and lived with her parents in New York, he was fairly certain that she'd never met Venn prior to her return to Georgia this week.

He paused to swirl his second drink, Everclear, watching it slosh against the glass, and then drank.

Yes, Emma Grant's subconscious had to be working in overdrive. How else would she be capable of achieving an exact likeness of Io's nemesis? If Emma chose Venn as her subject without knowing the man, then the bond between them must be incredibly strong. It was only a matter of time before she discovered the truth about their shared past.

Golden Grain, came next. He delighted in the way his stomach burned as it hit bottom. With a stretch of his neck, he opened and closed his mouth, feeling as if he'd spew fire out like a fucking dragon if he exhaled properly.

Io forced his thoughts back to the issues...he believed in making things happen, not leaving the future to fate.

Relying on fate was akin to being a drug addict. Who knew if the next fix would even be there? He needed to ensure Emma adhered to his plan for the dedication ceremony. He needed her to handle the support stakes prior to setting them in the ground. Only then would they be poisonous to the tree.

The Bruichladdich X4 Quadrupled whiskey, he'd saved the best for last. He admired the crystal tumbler adorned with diamond-shaped spikes cut into the glass. This time he consumed the drink slowly, mmm, tasted like rocket fuel.

If Venn figured out his real purpose was to use Emma to kill the tree, then the Guardian would stop him. Too much sweet talk from Venn might just convince her of the dangers to the tree and therefore to him.

The nagging possibility she would remember her past life was a problem. One he had little power to deal with.

So what if they had another distraction, one that would take their attention away from the real reason she was called to Tyler? Something to do with say...old lady Grant.

Yes . . . yes, that could work . . .

Io stood, giving his minion orders to fix leg of lamb for dinner.

8

A short while later, Io watched over the Grant estate in his owl form, looking for an opportunity to throw Emma off guard. The sun had not quite shown itself in the full light of day, and the morning fog still clung to the trees and blanketed the ground. Possibilities churned through his head. But he kept returning to the grandmother. An accident perhaps . . .

The side door swung open, and Claire Grant exited with her silly dog. She carried two blue rugs and hung them on the line to dry. Man, the old lady was always working on something, but even so, she dressed spiffy, as if she were forty instead of eighty-five.

A good ways from Claire, Fido did his business and sniffed a tree.

The stroke of genius came to him immediately. He would take the dog.

He swooped down, flexing his talons. The little mutt ran but was no match for his speed. He sank his talons into the dog, and the thing yelped and then yipped as he became airborne.

Grandma gasped. "Stop. Let him go," she yelled, staggering forward, shaking her fist.

Io circled as the terrier furiously kicked his legs.

The woman took off for the house, ducked inside, and emerged mere seconds later with shotgun in hand. She fired in his direction, but not at him. How foolish she thought him. No. The gun posed no threat since it also would mean disaster for her pup.

He dipped closer, dangling the bait, then flew away from the house. She focused on him, tripping over roots and logs. Cocking the shotgun, she hitched several steps and fell forward. The gun fired upward, and the leaves of a nearby tree rustled, falling to the ground.

Too bad she hadn't blown a hand off or something. That'd do the trick, wouldn't it?

Io scanned the terrain below. He swooped for uneven, sloped ground, hoping she'd take a serious tumble, maybe even slam into the base of a tree. He envisioned the horrendous car accidents he'd instigated when he was bored, the victims left with broken bones and twisted bodies.

He flew higher, swung around, and dove between trees. Grandma shook her fist, obviously no worse from the fall. Pity.

"Izzy!" She launched into a hobbling run. "Put him down, you damned horned bastard."

He couldn't help but chuckle inside. Deep in the woods, there were a multitude of things that could go wrong, ways that dear old grandma could get injured. He needed only one.

Light flashed, a slice of sunlight peeking from between the clouds, hitting Izzy's dog tag and winking a bright reflection. She shook the gun at him again. The dog went berserk, trying to break free. Could the dog survive a fall from this height?

Mrs. Grant fell again, then got up and kept running. Then a snap, crack, and scream split the quiet forest morning. The old woman had disappeared. One second she was standing on the leaf-strewn ground, the next she'd dropped out of sight.

Io circled back to discover a fissure in the earth half-covered by rotted boards. An old well.

He swooped low and let go of the dog. Then he perched at the well's edge and looked down the dark shaft.

Mrs. Grant lay in a crumpled heap at the bottom, unconscious.

Perfect.

Emma stopped by the drug store on her way back to her grandmother's. She picked up deodorant and mascara that she'd left at home and some shortbread cookies for Grams, her favorite. Still distracted by the events at the warehouse, she walked off without receiving her change until the clerk advised her of the error. "Oops. Sorry, I don't know where my head is at today."

Actually, her thoughts worried over Venn. On top of the attraction she felt for the man, now she had the statue-identity issue to contend with. Plus the concept of reincarnation. What if he didn't believe in it? What should she share with him when they met for lunch?

Frustration set in as she drove with little attention given to her surroundings or the route.

As she approached the house, the side door stood wide-open in silent invitation. Grams did that on occasion to air out the house, but it seemed too cold for that today. A quick trip through the house found it empty, and apprehension niggled her. She went into the backyard.

"Grams?" she called.

Nothing. She shouted several more times. It seemed that no one was home, but the car remained in the driveway. "Strange."

Heading to check the detached garage, a frightened Izzy came barreling out of the woods, barking frantically. Emma knelt, and the dog hustled to her, wedging its tiny body beneath her bent legs, practically clinging to her ankles. The poor thing shook convulsively.

Alarm skipped within her chest. The hair across the dog's shoulders was matted with something. She reached to feel his fur, and when she pulled her hand back, blood covered her fingers. "What happened?"

As soon as she released the dog, he padded in a back-and-forth pattern, yipping.

He wants me to follow him.

With her grandmother nowhere to be found, Emma trailed after the dog. He led her a good ways from the house, and she was about to give up the chase and go back when she saw the broken earth. On closer inspection, she realized it was an old well. Someone had recently broken through the boards, and based on the footprints in the wet red clay, that someone may have fallen in. Panic formed in her chest and spread throughout her body like food coloring hitting water.

She hurried over to the chillingly silent crypt, dropped to her hands and knees, and inched forward to the edge. The wood framing the hole jutted out, jagged and half covered with clay, so it was difficult to tell where it began and how sturdy it was. A thick splintery board wobbled under the weight of her hand. She yelled for her grandmother, and Izzy began barking wildly.

Oh God.

"Grams! Are you okay?"

Nothing. Not a sound.

Why didn't Grams answer? What if she was already dead?

"Can you hear me?" she tried again. Darkness had a new sound, a deep empty echo. "Hang tight! I'll be right back." Distressed at the thought that her grandmother could be at the bottom of the abandoned well and hurt, she stood, moving too quickly, and her foot slipped in the mud. As if she were ice-skating, she tried to recover but to no avail. Her feet couldn't find purchase. She rolled and tried to grab hold of the ground, but still she slid over the edge and down, down into the well. And even though she reached out and strained to cling to something—*anything*—nothing held. Her breath caught in her throat, waiting to hit bottom, and expelled in a whoosh when she landed against her grandmother's legs.

Oh. God. No.

Slowly, the shock of what had just happened sunk in.

She needed a flashlight . . . *and help*. But first she had to see how Grams was.

"Okay," she said with more calm than she felt.

Setting her feet in the deep muck, she positioned herself standing over her grandmother. Grams didn't move, didn't say a word. Emma dug her cell phone from her pocket, thankful it was still there and hadn't fallen out during her tumble.

She thumbed it on. No signal.

Shit. Another of the drawbacks of living in rural Georgia. But she could still use the flashlight function. With a knot in her stomach, she fanned the light around them, taking in the situation. The dim glow revealed Grams's crumpled form half-covered with water. Emma pressed the back of her free hand to her mouth. A wave of fear sliced through her as she realized that even the presence of the light didn't elicit a response. Holding the phone in her teeth, being extra careful not to let it slip and fall into the standing water at the bottom of the well, she leaned down toward her grandmother and touched her cheeks. "Hold on, Grams. I'll get help."

What to do now? She circled the light, taking stock of the interior. The clay walls appeared firm, surprisingly smooth and vertical, and glistened with moisture. But she didn't think she could climb back up them.

With shaking hands, she examined Grams. Luckily, she had landed with her head up and somewhat propped against the inner wall, because with the water and muck, she could have easily drowned otherwise. There was a big gash from her brow to hairline, though, as if she'd struck the planks when she'd fallen. Emma was most concerned by her pale coloring, which, given the poor light source, she suspected wasn't accurate. Could it actually be worse? She checked her pulse. Faint. Very faint.

Emma took a stuttering, nervous breath. Hypothermia was one of the biggest concerns down here. The walls emitted frosty air like a refrigerator. With judicious movements, careful not to allow herself to sink deeper, she peeled off her coat and wrapped it as best she could around Grams's shoulders and torso.

Venn.

Call me when you're done. I'll be waiting. His words had sounded so prophetic at the time.

Even though she didn't have any bars indicating service, she decided to try texting him anyway. Sometimes that got through when a regular call didn't.

Help! Grams and I are in danger. Fell into an old well in woods northeast of her home.

Laying her free hand on her forehead, she thumbed "Send." If anyone could help her, he would. She just knew it.

If he gets the message.

Unfortunately, she didn't know how long she could just wait to be rescued. Her favorite person in the world could be dying. And if nighttime fell and the temperature dropped . . . well, Emma herself may not survive, either.

Refusing to believe they wouldn't be found and rescued, Emma tucked her arms around herself, hugging in every bit of warmth she could. She glanced up to the mouth of the well where light filtered in. The glow barely reached the bottom where they were, and as the sun descended, she knew it would soon be gone entirely.

She glanced at her phone to see if the message had gone through. It hadn't. What's more, she needed to quit checking the status in order to conserve her only light source.

Izzy barked from up top, another reminder of the horrible situation she was in. "We're okay, Izzy. Go get help." The dog had brought her to Grams; maybe he'd find someone else. Maybe Venn.

She waited for what seemed like hours as the darkness within the well increased. She checked her iPhone. Only thirty minutes had passed. And the message still had not sent.

Time to try to climb up. She had to at least try.

She used some of her precious phone light to check on Grams first. Her breathing came in shallow, uneven breaths. Emma held on to the fact that her grandmother was still alive.

She secured her phone tightly in a pocket, then felt the walls. They were made of slick, packed Georgia clay. She tried to brace her feet on one side of the well and her back against the other, thinking she might be able to inch her way to the top. But it was immediately evident that approach wouldn't work. The inside was too large, and she wasn't tall enough to reach both sides at the same time. Her other concern was that if she fell—and she predicted she would in her first attempts—she might land on Grams and injure her further.

Taking deep breaths, she gathered her courage. This time she rotated, placed her hands on one side, her feet on the other, using resistance to hold. Her fingers sunk into the wet clay, but she pushed harder, tightening her muscles. She moved a hand and the corresponding leg ever so slightly. Left hand, left foot, right hand, right foot.

She had accomplished four steps, her breathing growing labored, the muscles in her back complaining. And then the inevitable happened. Her foot lost its grip and slipped, taking her down. Working hard to control how she landed, she hugged one of the well walls with her hands and feet.

As she rested, her breathing came out harsh and labored, so loud in her ears she barely heard the *swish* of her phone delivering a text. Hoping beyond hope that she heard the sound she'd thought, she checked.

Yes! The message had been sent.

Of course, that didn't mean he'd see it. But she noted the time. It was thirty minutes past when they had agreed to meet for lunch. She trusted Venn was interested enough to inquire about her absence. But still, if he didn't see the message, it'd be hours before anyone would realize they were even missing.

9

For the first fifteen minutes, he thought Emma was merely running late. But after that, he grew seriously worried and paced outside the little Italian restaurant where they'd agreed to meet. Located at one end of Main Street, it was a good location to begin taking in the local art festival happening this weekend. His plan to share a meal and then use her interest in art as a means to get to know each other better seemed to be fading with every minute that passed. After twenty minutes, he phoned her, only to get her answering machine. By thirty minutes, he jumped in his SUV, heading to her grandmother's place. Something wasn't right. He could feel it. He stepped on the gas.

A text pulsed on his cell phone. He tapped it and read, glancing between his phone and the road.

The muscles in his neck and chest constricted with fear. How on earth did they end up in an abandoned well? And worse, the Grant property was huge. The well could be anywhere. No, the text had given him a clue. Northeast. At least that narrowed it to a hundred acres or so.

He cursed. Honestly, he may have been able to shift and run or fly there faster, so when he arrived at the Grants' place, he launched out of the vehicle and stopped dead in the yard. He called to his wolf, and the change was almost instant.

He lifted his nose with a long sniff. He sorted through the scents of pine and earth until he found hers. Emma smelled fearful and confused. He took off running, pausing to take a whiff every hundred yards or so. Her scent lingered on the trees she'd passed along the way. It was getting stronger, too, so he must be getting closer.

The abandoned well was in the middle of a clearing. Izzy was stretched out alongside it, his chin resting on his front legs, standing guard. Running in long strides, Venn changed into his human form.

"Emma!" he called out.

"Venn?" Her shaky voice seemed far off. "Venn! We're down here."

He hastened toward the opening of the well, toward the sound of her voice. When he peered down, she lit her phone. At the sight of her deep within the hole, his stomach clenched. She stood plastered against the wall, her hair wet and dripping, and Mrs. Grant lay on the bottom, propped up but surrounded by more water than he expected in an old abandoned well.

"Are you all right?" he asked.

"Grams is hurt badly. She's still unconscious, but she's breathing."

Venn could tell her grandmother was in poor shape even without the update. In the same way animals sensed when other animals were in distress and made easy prey. With his extremely acute hearing, he picked up her very faint, very slow heartbeat.

"Thank God you saw my message," she said. "We could have been out here for days otherwise."

Yes, thank God. Because had he not . . . He hated to think of the outcome. "What are the well walls like?"

"Clay, slippery but firm. I tried climbing them, but I could only make it a few feet."

He took in the information, calculated the size and the

depth of the well. Maybe he should go for help, contact the fire department. His gaze snagged on a bloody piece of wood. One of them had collided with it. The thought of Emma down there for a second longer than necessary tore at him.

Her grandmother's breathing hitched. "Something's happening with Grams," Emma said. "I...I don't know, her breathing is becoming erratic."

He watched Emma's slumped shoulders move as she swiped the heel of her hand over her eyes.

No. He could get them out, by sheer determination and grit if need be. But he would have to change forms to do it. He needed his hawk to lift them out, but his wingspan would be too wide. It would have to be his wolf. He should be able to maneuver the clay walls in that form. He closed his eyes and palmed his hand across the back of his neck. This was not what he wanted to do on their third meeting. She might be frightened away before she ever got to know him. Damn.

But there was no time for second-guessing.

"Listen to me. I'm coming down to get you both out." He shrugged out of his coat, collected it into a ball. "I'm dropping my coat down." He let it go, and Emma caught it.

"See if you can tie the sleeves around your grandmother's torso."

Next went the boots. Normally, he didn't have to bother with clothes when he transformed, but he intended to go down in human form and use the wolf to drag them up. No need to inadvertently clip the old woman, and his toes might better grip the sides.

Venn inhaled deeply, exhaled slowly. "Okay, here I come. Close your eyes and protect yourself in case any dirt falls." As he lowered his body into the well, a board snapped, raining a shower of debris. He caught the largest chunk before it dropped and threw it up onto the ground. With solid, economical movements, he worked his way down, moving feet and hands inch by inch.

His biceps bulged, but he wasn't fatigued. He glanced below, then rotated to the right in order to take position for the remainder of the decline. It wouldn't do to land on the women and crush them. With legs extended to equal the width of the well, he tested the next section of wall with his toes. Promptly, his feet slid and fell away. Shit, the stuff was like grease.

He heaved a breath of stale, musty air mixed with determination. Willpower.

He jabbed footholds into each sidewall and then followed with his hands. He pushed with everything he had. The muscles in his neck and shoulders, thighs, calves, and abs strained.

"This is no picnic," he growled at the slick walls. Then he methodically inched downward one piercing toehold after another. Slipping. Gouging. Fighting.

He forced control to the very last moment. When his feet sank at the bottom, a groan formed in his chest. He had to steel himself from wrapping Emma in his arms as enthusiastically as he desired. With control, he hugged Emma and kissed her face and lips. She was okay. He breathed deeply. The muck oozed around his feet like quicksand. Every movement sucked him down.

She moaned, and they pulled apart. "You are terrific," she whispered.

He crouched to check the coat Emma had fixed around her grandmother, tugging at the sleeves to make sure they were tight enough and using the belt to create a kind of sling. "Your grandmother probably benefited from being unconscious."

"Take her up first," Emma implored.

"Yes, I agree, that's the best way to do this. Then I'll come back down for you."

In the narrow space, he and Emma brushed arms, their bodies touched hip to hip, chest to breast. But he didn't have the luxury of actually enjoying the closeness. He lifted the old woman's limp body and tested the sling's hold.

Good. Secure.

Satisfied, he positioned it over his shoulder so she hugged his back. Emma helped get her settled. She didn't weigh much, but that wasn't the point. Getting just himself out of this place would be a near impossible feat, and rescuing someone . . . There was only one possible way.

He placed a palm on her upper arm. "Emma, you know how you do special things with your hands? Well, I have a few tricks of my own. In order to get you out I'm going to have to use those powers." He paused. "I'm going to have to shape-shift . . . into a wolf. Don't be alarmed. You can even close your eyes if you want."

She nodded, despite the surprise on her face. "It doesn't matter what you have to do. Just get us out."

He lifted her chin with his knuckle, proud of her bravery, and brushed his lips across hers. "I'll be back," he promised.

On three long breaths, he hyper-extended his lungs and summoned the change.

The atoms in his body dilated, hyperactive, and converted to energy, then reshaped. He sensed her plastering herself back against the wall.

His long, sharp lupine claws released, and he dug them deep into the clay walls. With grappling hook strength he climbed, dragging them up with his front paws, supporting with his back, concentrating, ascending one painful half-foot at a time.

His belly pressed to the wall. There was barely enough room for the both of them, but that worked to his advantage. Yet he didn't dare use his weight against the elderly woman to wedge them in, for fear of crushing her delicate bones.

It seemed an eternity before his front paws hit topsoil.

Four more brutal steps and they were free. A deep growl built in his chest, burned his throat, and whooshed over bared teeth.

He gently rolled Mrs. Grant from his back onto the

damp earth.

Panting as if he'd run a marathon, he watched the unconscious woman, unable to hear her vital signs over his own labored breathing.

After a second, he changed back into a man to repeat the process with Emma. With the narrow walls, it was the easier way.

Emma held her breath a lot while Venn, as a *wolf*, hauled her grandmother out of the well. Her heart hammered against her ribs so hard, for so long, she thought her chest might bruise.

"Move back against the wall," he instructed when he reached the top. Even though she couldn't see him, she knew by his words he must've changed forms again. "I'll be coming down faster this time."

She did as he said, and the second descent turned more into a jump than a climb. He barely touched the walls, using them only to control his position so that he wouldn't land on her. He dropped in front of her with a splash, but also with amazing control.

"Is she okay?"

"She's alive. We'll need to get her to the hospital."

"Thank you." She held his face between her hands and ran her thumb over his cheek bone, trying to take in what had just happened. "You were magnificent."

"Do you think you can hold on to my back as I climb up?"

Even with the dim light in the well, she could make out his golden eyes searching hers. "Yes," she said.

"Good." He turned. "Lace your hands around my neck and interlock them."

She did, feeling her breasts against his back.

"Now lift your legs and wrap them around me."

If they weren't in this horrible predicament, this would've been fun. He helped her into position by reaching around with his hand and scooting her ass higher.

"Okay, when I turn into a wolf, don't be shocked by how it feels. Unlike your grandmother, you're going to know exactly what's going on." He paused, as if preparing himself. "Ready?"

"Yes," she said, her voice sounding peculiar in her ears. Maybe it was that the well absorbed the sound. Or maybe it was a tinge of fear. She didn't have but a heartbeat to wonder about it before Venn's body began to shift. One minute she held on to a man, the next a wolf. Massive, firm muscles moved against her arms and chest and belly as he leaped up, climbing, climbing, climbing.

A whimper had built in her throat, but she forced it down, and air filled her lungs like a billow when she buried her face in his pelt of thick gray fur and held on tight. So tight. The wolf's feet slid down the walls a few feet. She stifled a gasp and slammed her eyes shut.

A blast of cool air hit her and she knew they must be at the top. She looked up when she felt him stop, and it took her a minute to realize she could dismount from his back. She slid to the ground and her legs gave way, landing her on her bottom.

Grams? She looked sideways and found her grandmother still wrapped in Venn's coat. She sighed in relief.

Her eyes blurred. No. It wasn't her vision; it was the wolf. His fur shimmered and sparkled, a million diamond particles. Like a "Star Trek" transporter scene, except . . . except instead of completely disappearing the wolf changed into a man.

Venn.

"Holy shit." She blinked, hard. The extent of its impossibility hadn't hit her fully until that moment as her adrenaline began to lower and she got a good look at him. One minute Venn was a wolf, the next human? How was that possible?

It wasn't.

Hysteria warred with common sense.

His golden eyes fixed on her. "Emma . . ." His voice sounded strained, hoarse.

"That's not . . . People can't do that."

"Don't panic. I'll explain later." Thankfully, he didn't advance. "Right now, we need to get your grandmother to the hospital. That's our first priority."

It took several long moments before his words penetrated her thick skull and stupor. Heart thumping against her sternum, her gaze shifted to the woman on the ground.

"We need to get some dry blankets," he said.

Her feet wouldn't move, though, not until he said her name again. Numbly, she padded forward to help him with her grandmother. Together, they repositioned Venn's coat and wrapped the frail woman who was so dear to her heart.

Minutes earlier, he'd been a wolf. Unbelievable. Just like in her visions and dreams.

Finished, he bent and gently lifted and cradled Grams.

"Are you okay? Can you make it on your own?" he asked.

"Yes. I'm just so worried about Grams."

She followed him to the house, staring at his broad-shouldered back, recalling what he'd felt like as a wolf. "I don't know what I would have done if you hadn't come," she said. "Who knows how long a rescue would have taken. It's a good thing you could get her out. I was going to ask you to call a friend."

She was babbling.

He looked at her and gave a small smile of understanding, and she quieted. "Let's take my car," he said. "The keys are still in it."

She nodded and opened the back door for him to put Grams in.

"Do you want to run and grab a couple changes of clothes for you both to change into at the hospital?" he asked.

She took in her muddy, clay-covered clothes. "Excellent idea."

Inside the house, she grabbed a few things straight from the laundry pile. At least they were dry. Then she searched for Grams's warming pads—flannel bags filled with rice that would warm her on the drive. Emma dug a couple out of the cabinet and popped them in the microwave. While they heated, she ran upstairs to grab her and her grandmother's purses, plus a blanket.

When she got to the Explorer, Venn sat behind the wheel, waiting. She slid in, giving him a faint smile and glancing back to see how Grams was faring. As he primed the ignition, she raised to her knees, leaned over the seat, and positioned the warmers in the folds of the blanket. It wasn't near enough to do much good, but it was something.

She sat back in her seat and fell into the silence of the drive. She desperately needed things to occupy her, because she kept seeing Venn's conversion over and over again in her imagination. She couldn't believe she was sitting there as if she hadn't seen such a bizarre transformation.

She stared out the window at the varying landscape, her palms sweating. She wiped them on her jeans, brushing wet globs of dirt to the floor. She tugged at her hair next, not actually caring about the mess she presented but because she couldn't sit still.

She bit her tongue, assuring herself it was more important to concentrate on her grandmother's welfare, than to flee this man's—er, creature's?—presence. But then her mind settled. He had saved them. No matter what he was, he had been there for her. And her heart warmed with thankful appreciation. The rest of it didn't matter, did it?

They pulled into the hospital parking lot sooner than she expected. The emergency sign winked before her eyes, then the SUV lurched to a stop. Venn climbed out of the Explorer before she flipped the door handle. He gently pulled her grandmother from the vehicle, and a minute later he was tromping through the sliding doors. All big, demanding, and in charge.

Emma was extremely grateful. She wouldn't have been able to handle this alone.

From the moment he stepped through the door, he snapped orders at nurses like an emergency room pro on an ER TV show. But this was backwoods Georgia, not big-time New York. Still, the personnel listened and reacted as he spit out Grams's pulse, blood pressure, and temperature. The numbers couldn't possibly be accurate; he hadn't used a blood pressure cuff or thermometer. She couldn't see the harm in misleading them, though, if it jump-started them into action.

Moments later, Emma and Venn stood in the corner of a small room with the curtains drawn as hospital staff hooked her grandmother to machines. The slow *beep beep* of the monitor bled over the sound of shuffling feet, clang of metal as something hit the bed, and rumble of voices as the nurses called out stats.

Emma stared at the action in dismay and disbelief, fighting mind-numbing bewilderment. Every one of the figures Venn had quoted was too close for comfort. But how could he have known?

And could someone live with a BP of seventy over thirty-two?

Vaguely aware that Venn had slipped a strong arm about her shoulders, she leaned into him. "Hey," he said. "You okay?"

"Yeah. Sure." Her voice sounded distant even to her.

"Can you give this nice lady some information?" he prodded gently. "How old is your grandmother?"

Emma turned her head. A woman with brown hair

twisted in a bun and Admissions written on her name tag waited with a pen poised above a clipboard, all sympathetic eyes.

"Eighty-five." Taking a deep breath, Emma pulled herself together and answered the woman's questions. Venn's hand traveled up and down her arm as she did so, a subtle reminder of his presence and strength that surprisingly comforted her.

"Good, that's it for now," the woman said. "All I need is a signature."

Venn let go of her, and the sterile smell of the hospital hit her as she signed the paper.

As the woman left, a doctor entered. He studied Grams's chart, examined her head, and flashed a light in her nonresponsive eyes before stepping away from the bed. "So, what's the story?" He clasped his hands behind his back.

Emma bristled. What an odd way to phrase it.

She cleared her throat. "I don't know how she got there, but I found her at the bottom of an old well," she explained. "She's been unconscious for at least two hours now." She glanced at Venn. A muscle throbbed in his sternly set jaw. She lost her concentration, paused.

Was he annoyed or worried? Did he think she would tell the good doctor *exactly* how her grandmother had gotten out of that well?

She blinked rapidly, then focused on the doctor and resumed the telling.

10

That she might spill his split identity didn't concern Venn. The tale would be deemed preposterous. But listening to Emma explain what happened made it clear to him that Io had his hand in this. Or claws, as the case may be.

The idea chilled him. And worse, Emma remained clueless of the danger, which made him more determined than ever to stay with her and make sure she remained safe.

"Will she be all right?" Emma asked the doctor, her shaky voice tugging his heart.

"I can't say until we've done more tests."

Using his keen senses, Venn read the vital signs of Claire Grant better than the machines connected to her. Her condition was grave, and she hung on by a thread. But was it one made of cotton twine or fifty-pound monofilament?

He met the doctor's gaze, which revealed concern beneath his practiced physician's smile.

"Obviously, we'll admit her," he went on. "Why don't you get comfortable in the waiting room?" The doctor turned his attention to the nurse and began to give instructions.

Emma seemed frozen in place, staring at the bed. With

his hand at the small of her back, Venn guided her out of the room. "I could use some strong coffee. How 'bout you?"

He sought out a private corner in the waiting room. She sat and shivered.

"I'll be right back," he told her.

He got two cups of coffee with fixings and stopped at the reception desk to check in, leaving their names and patient info. "Do you have a spare blanket?" he asked as the volunteer smiled pleasantly.

"I'll check." She dipped into a room and returned with a thin white flannel draped over an arm.

"Perfect. Thank you."

"No problem." A pink blush eclipsed her unease as her eyes met his, then quickly looked away. The poor woman didn't know what to make of him. Most women didn't.

Walking back to Emma, the tan walls pushed in on him. What if Claire Grant died? He'd always liked the gutsy lady. She spoke her mind and didn't back down in a fight. Emma would be devastated if the worst happened.

He set the coffee on the table next to her. "I wasn't sure how you take your coffee, so I brought a bit of everything—sugar, Splenda, creamer." He shook the blanket. "And this."

He wrapped it around her shoulders and grinned inwardly at the soft purr that escaped her lips. "Mmm. It's warm. Thanks."

"My pleasure." And it was. He liked taking care of her, watching over her. "Sugar?"

"Yes. And creamer."

After fixing her coffee, he sat. His bones chafed as he stretched his legs out. A lingering effect from his changing, a shape-shifter's arthritis. Like other miracles of life, transubstantiation had its side effects. Kind of like the pain of childbirth: You didn't get the miracle without the pain. And while the shift itself didn't hurt, there were other issues he certainly had to contend with.

Emma drew the blanket tighter around her. Venn's kindness added an oppressive weight to the one already settled in her chest. Pressure built behind her eyes and she fought the spill of tears.

Anger would have pushed them back. Fear would have dammed the ducts. But at his thoughtfulness, her mouth quivered. She sunk her teeth into her bottom lip, closed her eyes, and conjured the memory of him turning from wolf to man, drawing on the absurd to stifle the downpour that was imminent.

She slowly drew air into her lungs and held it, unwilling to let go. Predominantly because once the floodgates opened, they'd be impossible to control. And she'd learned long ago, to her embarrassment, she didn't cry sweetly or quietly.

The strategy worked, though her eyes burned with unshed tears. She swallowed. In her mind's eye, the wolf formed, dragging her grandmother from the hole. The animal turned his head, his eyes a living kaleidoscope of gold and burnished mahogany.

Why she went back to that moment, she couldn't say. What made the mind choose one thought over another wasn't something she was privy to.

The scene in her mind enveloped her and altered, skipping to another similar event. Although the emotion gleaned from this new one was different, calming. She latched on to it, tipping her head back until it rested against something hard.

The odor of wet animal fur mingled with earthy, musky smells in the air. She wrinkled her nose, vaguely aware of the shade line of the tree under which she sat and the rough bark grazing her back. As she wove fingers deep into the wolf's thick fur, his ribs expanded and contracted on a sigh.

She argued with her senses about what she felt. It wasn't real. But she had done all this before in a past life. Did her senses lie?

God, the horrific day was taking an exhausting toll.

"Your coffee's getting cold."

Venn's voice caught her attention like a door slamming. She whipped her head around to gaze at him. He held the coffee for her to take, his arm outstretched. A small lapse of time passed as she stared numbly at the white Styrofoam cup in his large tanned hand. Finally, she took the cup and brought it to her lips. He was right—only lukewarm now. But the liquid helped wash down the last of the tears.

"Is there someone you should call? Your mom or dad?"

Her mind rebelled. Did she have to contact her father? "Not yet," she decided aloud. "I'd like to see how things go first." She drained the cup and placed it on the table.

He leaned toward her, resting his elbow on the chair arm, his massive shoulders blocking the view of the entrance. The movement brought them eye to eye.

His golden gaze held hers, intelligent and striking. He oozed sincerity and empathy. "Emma, I'm not certain how to phrase this." He paused. "But I think you should be prepared. Your grandmother is in very serious condition. Perhaps—"

"You can't know that," she snapped.

"I do."

She shook her head. He sounded so positive, but it couldn't be true.

"The next few hours will tell," he said.

"Dr. Myer will treat her. She's a fighter." Emma rose, taking the blanket with her, and began pacing.

"True. But at her age, it may not be enough," he said softly. "You have to be—"

"No. You're wrong. She's healthy. You're not qualified

to make those calls. You're a—" She glanced around then leaned closer to him, whispering, "You changed into *a wolf.*"

His eyes narrowed at her. "Which is precisely why I know about her health."

Confused, she leaped back as if struck. What was he saying? He confirmed he'd changed into a wolf. Her heartbeat escalated. She ran a hand over her face. No, she hadn't seen what she thought she had. She'd just been upset over her grandmother's ordeal. Or her visions had somehow warped reality. Venn Hearst had not changed into a wolf to save Grams.

Shape-shifters were creatures of novels. They did not exist.

She paced in a circle, ending back at her seat, where she collapsed onto the cushion. She wrapped herself cocoon-style. "Go away."

But her words had no heart to them. She knew Venn and the wolf were genuine.

"Some animals have a sixth sense. They can tell when another is injured, dying. I think you should call—"

Enough. She stood, threw off the warm length of flannel and picked up the extra clothes she'd brought with her. "Where's the restroom?"

He pointed in its direction, giving her space.

It was all she could do not to run, and dammit, he knew it. She felt his intuitive eyes follow her as she bolted for the hall.

As she turned left, the passageway narrowed. Inside the bathroom, a weak light shimmered above a mirror, and she rested her hands on the porcelain sink as her eyes adjusted.

Venn was wrong. No way was she calling her father. He probably wouldn't set foot in Georgia, anyhow.

She didn't need anything else to complicate her life. Venn may be a man from her past, who can also turn into a wolf, and her grandmother might be dying. That was plenty for any one person to handle.

With the world closing in on her, Emma considered her pale reflection in the ladies' room mirror. She splashed cool water on her face. Two weeks ago she'd been sitting on her balcony overlooking the Seine, where the most important decision she had to make was what wine to have with dinner.

She dried her face with a paper towel. What if Grams needed surgery? What if she was incapacitated for any length of time? What if she died?

When Venn had alluded to as much, denial had hit her like a blast of a blowtorch, hot and furious. What she needed was someone to show her the positive side of the situation, not pummel her with negativity.

Numbly, she changed into her dry garments. She took a deep breath. She had to go back out there.

She pushed open the door and stepped into the hall, nearly running into a strange-looking man who was a little rough around the edges. His long dark hair was pulled back in a ponytail, and he had a volunteer badge pinned on his jacket.

"You're Claire's granddaughter, aren't you?" he asked.

"Yes," she said warily.

"I'm so sorry about your grandmother, dear. I'm Venn's friend, Seth. If there's anything I can do, just let me know."

Turning back the clock would be nice. Emma narrowed her eyes, glancing around, looking for answers. *Who is this guy?*

"That's very thoughtful, thank you." She started to walk on. "Where's Venn.?"

The man hitched his thumb in the direction of the corner and gave her a tight smile. He moved past her down the hall.

Venn was getting more coffee when she returned to the waiting room, and they had both just sat down when the doctor arrived again. She checked her watch. Had it actually been an hour and fifteen minutes?

Her stomach did trampoline-style flip-flops as Dr. Myer crossed the space. He swung a chair around and sat, looking dog tired.

She raked her gaze over Venn, noting that despite the rescue and carrying her grandmother to the car, he didn't appear fatigued. The implications both fascinated and worried her.

"All right," the doctor began. "This is where we stand. The blow to her head caused some damage. How much, only time will tell. Right now she's in a coma. Her oxygen levels are also too low, so she's on a ventilator."

Emma swallowed. "Can I see her?"

"Certainly. However, she won't know you're there. You may want to go home and get some sleep, though. You're going to need your rest."

She lifted her chin. "As soon as I see her with my own eyes, I'll head home for a while."

"I'll see she sticks to that plan," Venn said, his voice softening and his concerned gaze landed on her.

Emma turned to glare at him but held her tongue. Were Venn and Dr. Myer sharing some kind of men's-club nod? She thought so. But from what Grams had indicated, he was a recluse, so his manner came across as confusing.

The doctor rose, and they did the same. He paused and looked at Emma meaningfully. "By the way, according to our records, your grandmother has a living will."

Emma met his compassionate gaze. All traces of humor had vanished from his crinkled eyes. "I'm certain that she does."

11

The following evening, Venn guided the Explorer through the KFC drive-through line. It was far from the kind of food he liked, but it was on their way back to the Grants', and his exhausted Emma needed food and rest. He meant to see that she got both.

"I can fix something. It's no big deal," she protested.

"Look, believe me, as soon as you let go and relax, you're going to crash."

She grumbled something under her breath. Which sounded to his excellent hearing suspiciously like, *Know-it-all.*

He grinned to himself.

The second day of Claire Grant's hospitalization had proved long and grueling with no progress for the old lady. The woman still breathed, albeit with mechanical assistance.

"You didn't have to come to the hospital with me again, you know," Emma told him. "Even though you saved us, we're not your responsibility."

"I realize that. But I wanted to, and you don't have anyone else in town, right?"

Her face tightened, and she glanced away. "I'll be fine. Grams will get better. We'll do the dedication. And I'll go home to Paris and put my life back together."

But nowhere in that scenario had she mentioned him. He planned to change that.

Today, Emma had brought a sketchbook filled with drawings with her to the hospital. She seemed to retreat into another world when she drew. Once, he'd glanced over her shoulder as she worked on a picture of her grandmother lying at the bottom of the well.

Therapy for her, perhaps, but it struck him as creepy.

He paid for the order and drove on.

The aroma of fried chicken filled the car as he passed the bag over for her to hold. They inhaled in unison, and he heard her stomach protest.

"Okay, so it smells good," she admitted.

Before they knew it, he was parked in the Grants' drive. He met her in front of the car, and she paused. Obviously, she was just figuring out that he intended to eat dinner with her.

He shrugged one shoulder. "We have things we should discuss."

With a sigh of resignation, she marched past him. He followed. Halfway up the porch steps, her cell phone rang. She swung around and shoved the KFC bag into his gut. The plastic crinkled as he grabbed hold.

Her face turned ashen beneath the deck lights, and she squinted at caller ID.

Was it the hospital? From her expression, he guessed she was wondering the same thing.

"Hello?" Her shoulders rolled forward, relaxing, and she dug in her purse for the house keys. "Hold on a second."

Venn dangled her key chain in the air, revealing he'd picked them up from the console where she'd left them. She nodded and he led the way, unlocking the door and heading straight for the kitchen. Each room had a night-light to show the way. He flipped on the overhead light.

"Mr. Price, I'm sorry," Emma said into the phone

behind him, "but I'm not of the mind to discuss this right now. My grandmother is in the hospital. I'll call you tomorrow."

Venn plunked their dinner on the table. He heard the imperceptible sneer in Io's voice as he offered his condolences. He wanted to snatch the phone from Emma and slam it into the nearest wall. Instead, he fisted his hands.

The son of a bitch was playing them, and there wasn't a damn thing he could do about it. Yet.

But the deadly menace would pay. Soon.

Emma would be crushed when she learned Io had caused her grandmother's accident as some scheme to get to Venn. Emma and Mrs. Grant were only tools to hurt him and the Divine Tree, and if the blame landed anywhere, it was with him.

But Io continued to badger Emma with the importance of her responsibility to the project. Venn had heard enough. He pulled out a chair and eased Emma into it. It didn't take much to pry the phone from her fingers.

"She told you she'd call tomorrow." An unnatural explosion sounded on the other end, and then the line went dead.

Venn savored the wicked satisfaction of knowing that Io was royally pissed. He set the phone on the table and unpacked dinner. Emma slumped in the chair, on the verge of collapse.

"Thanks," she said tiredly.

"Glad to help. Now eat." He made sure she had utensils, salt, and pepper. "Something to drink?"

"White Merlot. In the fridge."

He found the glasses in the cupboard. After he poured them both glasses, he lit a fire in the country hearth and then sat beside her. He unloaded the bag and prepared her a plate of chicken, mashed potatoes, corn on the cob, and baked beans, with a biscuit on the side.

"I'll never eat that much," she complained.

"It doesn't matter."

As they dug in, he noticed that she ate one item at a time without mixing foods. She'd devoured the chicken first, corn last. He enjoyed watching her bite into the kernels and then flinch when a spurt of juice shot out. A smear of butter trickled down her chin. Squelching the desire to lick it away, he handed her a napkin.

She dabbed her face. "Mmm. I have to admit, this was a good idea."

Yeah. And being with her made any ordinary meal gourmet.

His eyes feasted on her sensuous mouth. He could see her color returning—the warm glow to her skin seemed close to normal. And as her strength returned, his concern for her segued to burning need. He longed to possess her. Cover her with his body. Taste her with his tongue. Love her with his hands.

On the table, their wine began to boil, the gravy bubbling. Another sign of how he couldn't control how she affected him.

She slid her gaze to capture his, lifting a quizzical brow. "That was you at Aunt Fay's? You made the coffee boil over?" she questioned.

He summoned an arctic blast to cool his surging desire. Well, at least it gave him a minuscule measure of control. With a wicked smirk, he said, "Yes. But it's not like your hot hands. Somehow there's an energy I can't control inside of me and it causes liquid in my vicinity to heat up." His voice grew deeper as he added, "It's only ever happened when I'm with you."

"Only with me? Why's that?"

"Because I'm attracted to you," he admitted, his body reacting to his words, his heart hammering.

Her face flushed a pretty pink. "I guess that makes sense since you asked me out."

He straightened. "Are you ready for me to explain some things?" he asked as he moved across the room to get her a fresh glass of wine. The steps back and forth to refill her glass allowed him to control the driving desire coursing through him. At least a little. Back at the table, he handed her the goblet.

She downed her Merlot in one long gulp, then stared at him with trusting eyes that communicated her conflicted feelings, *yes* and *no* at the same time. A long moment hung between them, as if she had a choice. "Yes. Tell me."

————————————

Venn wasn't the only one who had things to share. She didn't know how he'd infiltrated her subconscious, but the proof was in the statue. How was she going to explain that, to tell him that they were somehow connected in past lives? Or so she thought.

"Let's sit over there," he motioned to the hearth end of the farm table.

"My favorite spot."

She moved to stand by the fire, seeking its heat, wrapping her arms across her middle. As she watched the flames dance, she was aware of him placing their glasses on the table. The light clink of glass on wood. The creak of oak flooring beneath his weight. Tucked in the corner by the hearth, she craved the warmth and security of his powerful body more than that of the blaze.

He came into her peripheral vision, and she swung around, stepped forward, toe to toe, willing him to hold her. She looked up into his golden eyes, and the feeling of his arms circling her felt so right—part of him touching something deep inside of her. Better than any hug she'd experienced in her life.

She leaned into him, turning her head to rest her cheek on his solid chest. The embrace felt right, not awkward or embarrassing, but familiar.

Her suspicion that he was connected to her past felt all the more right, now.

As the fire flickered hotly, both in the hearth and in her abdomen, she needed, wanted, him to kiss her. What's more, she didn't want to have to ask.

She ran her palms up his muscular back, and he reciprocated, dragging her tighter to him, his biceps pressed against her upper arms. A yearning bloomed in her chest, her nipples itching for attention. She tilted back her head.

Slowly, intimately, he touched his mouth to her forehead. Brushed soft kisses along her brow and down her cheek. By the time he captured her mouth, her lips were quivering with anticipation. He dipped his tongue inside, grazing her teeth. When he deepened the kiss, a little moan escaped her throat.

More. God help her, she wanted more.

She sensed his reluctance as he released her mouth and held her, threading his fingers through her hair, cradling her head into the hollow of his shoulder.

"Is that what you wanted?" he murmured.

"No . . . yes," she whispered huskily, willing to own up to that much. "I . . . I don't know why I'm not afraid of you, why I haven't spun on my heels and run, or at least kicked you out the door. You turn into a wolf, for heaven's sake."

He pulled back and peered at her as a crooked smile curled his lips.

He'd been kind to her. When she needed him, he'd been there. And he hadn't dictated what she *should* do. There were strange things in this world. She knew because she was one of them. And dealing with her own crazy peculiarities—her visions and dreams and reincarnation and hot hands—made her curious, as well as tolerant of others with special talents.

"I can't say that I trust you completely," she admitted, "but you don't frighten me."

"I know what's happening," he said with a small smile. "Sit down, and I'll explain."

He eased her back until her legs hit the chair, and she plopped down, dissolving into a pile of mush. The weight of her problems felt overwhelming. But at this moment she allowed herself a respite and gave herself permission to discover how Venn could possibly be a wolf. As farfetched as it seemed.

As he settled into the chair beside her, his knee brushed hers, and his fine masculine scent drifted over her like a mist. She swayed, dizzy. The wine? She looked at her almost-empty glass.

"There are things in the universe that can't be explained within the confines of human experience," he began.

"You're a werewolf?"

"No."

"But you changed—"

"I'm predominantly human . . . with some gifts, abilities."

"One being that you can shape-shift."

"Yes. I can change into a wolf and hawk. Technically, it's a sort of facilitated diffusion, where molecules change and equalize."

She knew something about that sort of thing. After all, she could essentially change metal molecules with her bare hands.

"I'm an immortal. Something called a Guardian."

"Immortal?" She scrunched up her face in disbelief as she drew her feet beneath her bottom and angled legs and knees away from him. "What do you mean? Like a spirit?"

"No, not a spirit. I'm flesh and blood."

There were exceptions to the laws of physics, weren't there?

"And you've lived a long time?" she added.

"A very long time. We are the Guardians of—"

Her jaw dropped. "We? There are more of you?"

He nodded. "Yes. We make up a sect charged with protecting the Divine Trees."

She knew immediately which tree he protected. The aura of the oak in the park was unmistakable. "So the town square houses a Divine Tree."

His eyes widened. "You're aware of it? Humans can't usually sense its uniqueness," he said, his gaze narrowing. "Then you're already closer than I thought . . ."

"Closer to what?"

"To figuring out your destiny."

She blinked and folded her arms over her chest. What an evasive answer.

He smiled, seeming to read her thoughts. "My brothers are scattered throughout the world."

"How many brothers? And what is it exactly about the tree that you protect?"

"I have eleven brothers. The rest you'll learn later."

"Because I'm an outsider?"

He raised a brow.

Bingo.

"Let's just say I'm bound by rules," he said, then stood to tend the fire.

"Who makes up the rules?" she asked.

When he returned, she watched him move closer and closer until he stood over her. He took her hand and drew her to her feet. She tilted her chin up and he caressed her cheek. "You're tired. Another time."

He was right. She was exhausted. Gripped by fatigue, she let the subject drop for a while as her mind absorbed what he'd told her so far. If there was one thing she understood, it was being different. She'd had "impressions," as her parents had labeled the episodes, her entire life. They were as much a part of her as her eyeteeth. And how many times had a wolf been part of her visions?

A niggling suspicion bloomed within her as she met his gaze. In her mind's eye a triangle formed between her past life as Amelia, Venn, and the person she was today. She flattened her palm on his muscular chest, where she found his heart beating just a rapidly as her own. His earthy and spicy scent teased her nostrils. She inhaled a deep breath and closed her eyes. The strange connection she felt with him wasn't at all clear, but one thing she knew...she desired Venn Hearst like no other man.

She pushed herself away and picked up her glass. "Just one more," she muttered. A minute later, as he handed her the glass again, she said, "You didn't answer my question. Who makes up the rules?"

12

"Not me, I assure you." He paced a few steps. What more could he tell her?

Not much. At least not about the tree. Guardian rules didn't allow it. As for Io? Well, he definitely needed to warn her about that demon. But with everything that had happened today, he'd save that part of the story for later.

Venn hated dancing around the situation. Let him wield a weapon, change form, fight. Act. Anything but evade. Io was the devious breed, not him. Tomorrow, when things settle with her grandmother, then he'd talk to Emma and discuss their past. Yes, better to introduce these strange ideas over time and allow her to come to terms with them.

"There is a Light Realm and a Dark Realm, a heaven and hell if you will. The rules are ultimately dictated by the Creator. But things get dicey when the Free Will component is mixed in."

Venn cringed at the thought of the consequences to wrong choices. The thing was, Emma had to choose him of her own free will. For her, their bond may not be a solid contract. She had mentioned someone else in New York, after all. He held back a shudder. The thought of her with another man caused anger to build in his gut.

No. She was *his*.

At the same time, his first duty was to protect the Divine Tree.

It occurred to him, then, that he'd been gifted with the very thing that could make him weak. His love for Emma. How had Io figured this out before he did? The demon knew Venn could never choose Emma over the tree. And he would use that knowledge to twist the knife in Venn.

He could confide in her very little, actually, but he had to give her enough to explain their relationship and his unique abilities. How could he convince her of Io's danger without scaring her away?

He'd had two hundred years to think about what he'd tell her *if* he saw her again. He'd known it could happen but had given up hope after a century. Now he couldn't recall a single word of what he'd planned to say.

Restacking the logs allowed him to stall. By the time he sat, she'd changed positions again. Her jaw worked, suppressing a yawn. He sensed her fatigue, but also something else. A yearning, perhaps. He longed to kiss her again, hold her, lie with her. He settled on lifting her legs, positioning her feet on his thighs. She wouldn't run away if he had her by the ankles.

To his astonishment, she allowed him to remove her shoes, and he wanted to believe it was because she felt the same connection that he did. "How do you feel about reincarnation?" he asked.

Her eyes, open and accepting, met his. "Actually, I've researched the subject a great deal. My life has been somewhat . . . odd, in that regard." She paused. "It is something I believe in."

"Good. That's why you're not afraid of me. It's a karmic bond. We have deep past connections that have carried forward," he explained.

Her expression didn't change with his words, though; she seemed oddly calm about it all. Which surprised him. Perhaps she'd already figured out a great deal on her own.

That would explain her composure. But it made him wonder if that was the case.

He sat quietly and let her absorb what he'd said as he took one graceful foot in his hand. Pressure points were linked to other parts of the body—he was familiar with every correlation—and he began with a slow massage of the entire foot, then zoned in on one specific spot at the very back of the heel, a place few realized the importance of or how it affected one's memory. He pressed down with his thumb and rolled gently inward.

Her eyes flared. "Oh my."

"What?" he prompted.

"Nothing."

"Tell me."

"You've done this before. T-to me."

He smiled, and the warmth in his chest deepened. "Yes." He moved to the other foot. "Now you see why I can't leave you alone."

"We were lovers?"

"Oh, yes."

He felt her shiver, and an answering vibration ran through him, straight to his burgeoning erection.

She must have sensed the tension in him. "What's wrong?"

"Uh, let's just say I like your reaction," he said.

A reaction she immediately attempted to hide by talking quickly. "So let me get this straight." She wiggled her toes. "You're a Guardian who can change into a wolf and hawk," she said as if testing the idea, as if her mind tried to put the pieces of their complex relationship together. She gasped and tried to sit forward. "That was you the other day."

He shrugged.

"So wolf *and* hawk," she listed. "Anything else?"

"No."

The fire cracked and sizzled. He figured she could only digest so much, and sticking to the details surrounding

their relationship so far seemed the best way to introduce
things. When she trusted him, he'd tell her more.

Soon, he'd be able to speak of Io, and she'd
understand.

But for now, Emma had been through a helluva lot the
past few days, and he'd already given her a ton to take in.
How much could he ask her to accept at one time? He
couldn't add pressuring her to save the tree, or telling her
about his enemy, or for that matter, risk letting her know
that Io was the evil demon behind her grandmother's
"accident."

No, all in good time.

Emma rested back into the chair. He adjusted her feet
and brought them further onto his thighs. He wished she
weren't wearing jeans so he could slide his hands up and
down her long, slender legs and caress the soft hollow
behind her knees. Fingering her ankle, he came to the
indentation between her Achilles tendon and outside ankle
bone. He applied a bit of pressure. The spot could warm a
woman from the inside out . . .

A glow simmered low in her abdomen. On a soft purr,
Emma pressed the small of her back into the chair and
curled her hips up off the seat.

Oh, that felt incredible.

She held his gaze as she inhaled. "I've seen us together
before." Her breath leaked out on a sigh.

He lifted one brow. "I savor those memories. And
lived for the time you'd return to me."

With what seemed like expert precision, he pressed the
same spot on her foot again. At the same time, flames
licked her insides and sweet sensations flickered over her
crotch. If it felt this magnificent sitting here in front of the
fireplace, she could only imagine what sex with him would

be like.

"Peeerfect. Umm, I mean, maybe you've had too much practice," she said, wondering how many women he'd stroked and lavished care on in the past two hundred years, unable to control a tinge of jealousy.

"I haven't used the technique since you."

"Really?"

Was he saying he hadn't had sex since . . . ? No. She couldn't even fathom it.

Life's short. Grab it with both hands. Grams's voice drifted around her, repeating the lesson.

Her grandmother had never declared it, but Emma wondered if Grams had visions of her own. Geez, she hoped and prayed that tomorrow her grandmother would be well enough to nail Venn with another saucy wink. *Life's short. Life's short.*

She closed her eyes and, for the first time *ever*, intentionally summoned a vision. She wanted to see if she could recall Venn and their past, their lovemaking, and figured with the feelings she was experiencing at this very moment, the connection might be strong enough.

Amazingly, the first thing she saw was the wolf, not the man. Since she knew he was one and the same, she gave herself over to the image.

He prowled along a balcony, pacing back and forth in front of a balustrade. The creature paused, then changed form, a shimmering glow of energy. When the transformation was finished, Venn stood in profile, fully clothed. Frustration pushed her mouth into a pout. Why couldn't he materialize nude?

As the idea flitted though her mind, she realized she'd seen his silhouette many times before. Just never his face.

In exquisitely slow motion, he turned, strode toward her, and shed his clothes one piece at a time.

Now that was more like it. He paused at the end of the bed, magnificently naked.

She raked her gaze from his shadowed jaw, down his

chest and ribbed stomach, to the dark thatch of hair and jutting erection. And as he lowered down into her, her vision glimpsed a three-ringed raised scar on his left hip.

Then there was weight and pleasure and—

She climaxed. Not a fireworks finale but yummy pulsating ripples of warmth that laced through her abdomen, spreading out and up and over her heart.

Flipping her eyelids open, she yanked her feet away from him so unexpectedly that he had no choice but to let her go.

She stood shakily.

"That good, huh?"

"What?"

He took a long, slow whiff of air. And she thought of a wolf tracking a scent.

By the grin on his face, she was pretty certain he knew that she'd just come without him even really touching her. There was no way she'd admit it, though. "I should go to bed."

"Yes, you should." He brushed his thumb over her bottom lip. Unmistakable desire showed in his eyes, lingered in his touch.

A delicious shiver danced down her neck, over her shoulders and breasts, and into her tummy. God help her, her body craved him. *Oh, no, not a good idea.* Even though she had accepted reincarnation, when it came to a relationship, she drew a distinction between her past self and her present self. She didn't want to be just a substitute for Amelia. She wanted him to love her for herself.

She released a slow breath she hadn't realized she'd been holding.

"What time do you want me to pick you up tomorrow?" he asked.

"You don't have to drive me," she insisted, "I'm going to go in early in order to be there during the doctor's rounds."

"I don't mind taking you."

"No, I have Gram's car. I'll manage just fine."

He gave a reluctant nod. His dark lashes lowered, he turned and went out the door.

His name was on her lips to call him back. Instead, she peered out the window. He tromped down the steps where he seamlessly transformed into wolf in mid-stride, then looked back with those golden animal eyes.

She suppressed a gasp. It seemed so surreal. Even after his explanations, she struggled with the concept of him being an Immortal Guardian, a wolf, a hawk, *and* a man.

He broke into an all-out run down the drive.

And the animal in him, all the wild, pent up energy she sensed lurked just below the surface—Well, that really turned her on.

13

After Venn was gone, she realized he'd left his vehicle in the driveway. How strange. With a yawn, Emma phoned the hospital. She spoke with the on-duty night nurse. No, her grandmother hadn't awoken, and there was no change.

Guilt started eating at her stomach. She flipped over the numbers in her cell directory, landing on her father's. Her thumb lingered, vacillating. Would he want to know? It was too late to call tonight, anyway, but she could text him.

No, no. She'd cross that proverbial bridge only if things took a turn for the worse. And she refused to think about that.

With a heavy heart, she trotted upstairs, showered, dressed for bed, and climbed beneath the covers, utterly exhausted. She glanced at the clock on the nightstand. Only ten-thirty, rather than the two a.m. it had seemed.

The things Venn had told her flicked in her head like windblown fire. Reincarnation. She didn't doubt she'd lived before. But there was more in what he hadn't said. Much more.

She clutched the covers to her chin, savoring the soft brush of fleece against her face. Her eyes grew heavy as sleep pulled her under, and she dreamed of Venn.

She wore a dress the color of dark-pink roses. A shade she'd never wear today because it clashed with her hair. Perhaps she should rethink that. The hue was stunning and bold.

For the first time ever, she saw her dream man's face. Excitement built in her breast.

Venn.

He clasped her hand and led her past a crowd of people at an old-fashioned fair. Dry red dust covered the tops of her ankle boots and clung to the hem of her skirt as they wove between people at game booths. Ring toss, beanbag throw, button in a jar, bobbing for apples.

Venn stopped at a shooting venue. He plunked down a handful of coins, and a man with slicked-back dark hair and a gray-dappled goatee set up a line of milk bottles some thirty yards away.

Venn grinned. "Which animal would you like?"

She perused a lopsided wood shelf overflowing with carved animals. With a teasing smile, she said, "The wolf."

He nodded. After inspecting the pistol the man offered, he took aim and picked the entire row of bottles off the fence. They popped and dropped in quick succession.

"You're fast," she said.

"Fast doesn't count without accuracy."

The carnival vendor passed him the animal he indicated, and Venn gave it to her. She stroked its neck, disappointed that the toy wolf lacked his soft fur and musky scent. She curled her fingers around the wood form. "Thank you."

Wrapping his big arm about her shoulders, he drew her to him and kissed her head. "Come on."

They left the fair then, but on the way out, he bought an apple pie at a table of baked goods. He helped her into a buggy and drove to the tree, where they laid out a picnic in the shade of the oak.

It was like a scene from a romance movie complete

with a red-checkered tablecloth and picnic basket filled with every delicious gourmet snack she could want. They munched on cheese and bread, peaches and grapes. The lemonade was cool and refreshing. When Venn couldn't find a utensil to slice the pie, he whipped a pocketknife from his hip pocket and cut a small wedge, carefully lifting it out the dish with his fingers.

They ate the cinnamon-laced dessert from his hand, him giving her a bite, then taking one himself, until she licked his fingers for the last taste.

They laughed, and she felt a joy in her heart that she'd never known in this life. Clearly, she'd loved him, and he'd returned her affection. She wondered if they'd been engaged at the time.

The poignancy of the moment didn't escape Emma. She knew the happiness they shared wouldn't last. She was at the very spot she would die, if her vision a few days ago were to come true.

The image abruptly changed to that of an arrow flying through the air in slow motion, the red-and-yellow fletching whirling in a spiral spin as light winked off the shaft.

She awoke with a start.

Fighting what would come next, not wanting to experience Amelia's death again, she opened her eyes and peered into the darkness. Were her visions now intermingling with her dreams? She sighed. Venn had truly been her romantic interest in the past. The dream seemed to confirmed it.

She stretched in an effort to clear her head.

She tossed three times, four, and pulled the covers over her and tried to go back to sleep. After minutes of listening to her heartbeat in her ears, she got up, slipped on her robe, and padded downstairs.

The clock glowed 5:23 in blue letters. She fixed a pot of coffee and stared out the window, taking comfort in the sound of the coffee brewing.

The sky grew a lighter shade of indigo black as she thought about Venn. She had loved him before. Was it possible to love someone through time? Was that the reason she hadn't felt this all-consuming feeling for someone else? The rationale as to why she'd settled for a long distance relationship?

Funny, she looked forward to calling Todd and officially ending it. Better yet, given the hour and everything she had going on with her grandmother, she decided to email him this minute. She sent the missive from her phone, sharing with him about Grams's illness, too, and explaining that she'd call him later.

Now at least she wouldn't feel guilty, and she'd be free to pursue whatever Venn had in mind.

The idea made her giddy, warmth building in her chest and spreading to her limbs and head. And not just because he was sexy as sin and irresistible but because little things like a well-planned picnic could make a girl feel special.

And loved.

Within the Divine Tree, Venn sat in his recliner with his laptop across his thighs, engaged in an online search. As the low battery warning flashed on the screen, he reached for the plug. Although the oak was not wired for electricity per say, the living area was powered by a large battery bank housed in a garage across from the park. Another benefit of modern times. It worked just fine, and a hot spot connected to his phone gave him the Internet connection. He needed to know where Io lived, and County Records was a good place to start.

His mind racing, he'd given up trying to zone-out and escape his pent-up lust and desire. After he'd left Emma last evening, he had launched into another punishing run and kept it up for hours, staying to the woods, leaping over fallen logs and debris, diving recklessly through briars that ripped and cut through his fur.

When that wasn't enough, he'd transformed to hawk and flew to Atlanta and back again.

But nothing alleviated the sense of urgency to be with Emma. Lie with her. Hold her. Love her.

Eventually he came to the realization that he'd have to live with his intense longing and frustration for now. One day soon, she'd be his completely. Stay in his home, share his bed, and he would protect her forever.

Despite the fact that he was unworthy. He had failed to keep her safe before.

Guardian.

Protector.

Fraud.

He shoved the inner demons aside. *Not. This. Time.*

But hidden in his thoughts, the bothersome voice whispered that he was immortal. She wasn't. An issue they had not had the opportunity to deal with before. Which brought to mind how fragile their relationship was.

On the next mouse click, a sprawling country mansion home filled the screen. No bank loan, it had been a cash purchase seven years ago, and it was practically located in the next county. Venn positioned the address at the top of his mental list. Io would have used a fictitious name, perhaps the Jacob Price identity he was using now. That was inconsequential. Venn needed only to sniff around a bit for the right stench to know if the beast lived there or not.

It seemed he should have paid more attention to the local politics, given Io was on the City Council's development committee and Venn hadn't even realized it. Then again, the demon worked that way, damned underhanded.

He checked his watch. Time to head to the hospital.

. 14 .

Emma strolled into the hospital at six thirty in the morning. The doctor made his rounds at seven, and she was going to be there when he showed up in Grams's room.

Venn greeted her in the lobby with a cup of coffee, looking incredibly handsome with his hair combed back, in a finger-combed sort of way. He must have seen her arrive. How else could his timing be so impeccable?

She didn't have the heart to tell him that she was already floating from too much brew, so she accepted the paper cup. "Thanks."

She inhaled deeply. Day three. Grams would be better today. She had to be.

"They moved her to the third floor," Venn told her. "Room 304."

"Is that good or bad?"

He shrugged. "Good, I think. It's not an ICU floor, at least. The receptionist downstairs didn't know anything."

They walked to the elevator side by side, and he hit the "up" button. "Did you get a good night's rest?" he asked.

"Not really." Because of an incredibly sexy shape-shifter that she wanted to make hers, all hers. She didn't even want to share him with Amelia. "I woke early and couldn't go back to sleep."

The elevator doors opened, and he waited for her to enter first, then they were shut in.

"How about you?"

"The usual."

She refrained from asking what that was. Did immortals sleep?

Repositioning her purse strap on her shoulder, she glanced up at the yellowed light fixture on the ceiling. The drag of gravity as they moved up made her swallow nervously. She wasn't a fan of elevators. It wasn't so much claustrophobia, but trap-o-phobia. She didn't fear small spaces, necessarily; as long as she knew she could get out, she was okay. But being trapped somewhere, that was a different matter altogether. She was certain the fear had a professional name, something with *phobia* attached to it.

The elevator dinged, signaling their arrival at the third floor. The doors opened, and she gave a silent sigh. Again, Venn motioned for her to precede him.

She led the way into her grandmother's room, her heart racing in anticipation of the *whoosh whoosh* of the ventilator. The sound got to her every time. Without it, would Grams be here?

Inside, everything seemed still, and too quiet. Panic gripped her as she looked around and realized Grams was free of the breathing machine.

Emma ran her fingers along the top of the blanket, smoothing the covers. The beep of the monitors set an uneasy yet at the same time reassuring tone.

A sense of helplessness gnawed at her. She went to the curtains and tugged them open. Like her, Grams appreciated the sunrise. Maybe that's who she got it from, even.

She heard the lazy scrape of feet on the linoleum and turned as Dr. Myer entered.

"Good morning." He sounded almost cheerful.

Emma and Venn reciprocated with less enthusiasm.

"Well, I have some good news. Claire woke up earlier this morning. She's not out of the woods, yet, mind you. But we weaned her off the ventilator. I've prescribed enough medication to keep her comfortable."

A raspy, mumbled whisper came from the bed.

Emma took her grandmother's hand in hers. "Hey there."

"Quit talking about me . . . as if . . . I'm not here." After having the trach, Grams sounded very hoarse. She spoke with hesitations to breathe in between phrases.

"I'm glad to see you're awake," Dr. Myer said.

"My teeth," Grams demanded as best she could.

Dr. Myer nodded and marked something on his chart. "I'll let your nurse know."

"I'll see to that," Venn added and stepped halfway out the door.

Grams gave a painfully weak chuckle, which turned into a cough. She glanced at Emma. "Noble aura."

Dr. Myer ignored the comment. "If things go well, we'll begin weaning you from the pain meds tomorrow." He gave Emma and her grandmother a genuine smile. "I'll check back this evening."

A spark of promise and hope ignited in Emma's chest. "Thank you."

As Dr. Myer went out, Venn ushered in the nurse. With the same unexpected tenderness he'd shown last night, he came over and draped his arm around her shoulders. She easily relaxed into him.

He tugged her closer. "See, I told you she'd pull through," she said.

"Uh-huh."

Grams opened her mouth like a baby bird, allowing the nurse to slip her teeth into place. A second later, she moaned and rolled her eyes in an oh-no expression. Something was wrong.

Emma leaned in and bent over the bed for a closer

look. "I think you're holding the teeth upside down. That looks like the lowers to me."

Grams half smiled with a confirming nod. The nurse rotated the dentures and they slipped easily in place.

Emma and Venn chuckled, making light of the silly error. A flicker of happiness and extreme gratitude melted away her doubt. There was something to smile about, after all. Things could have been much worse.

"Izzy?" Grams mouthed.

"Is fine," Emma told her, and because it felt good to talk to her, she offered an update about the statue. "We unboxed the statue the day before yesterday. Mr. Price says everything is perfect."

Emma took her grandmother's head movement to be another nod, and then she seemed to drift in the hands of sedation.

Venn seated himself in one of two wooden chairs with a padded seat and back. "What are your plans? Will you hang out here throughout the day?"

"Until lunch. Then I'll need to let the dog out and check on the project."

"I don't like you being alone with that man."

"He's okay. Just a bit odd at times," she confessed.

"No. He's more than odd. I want to accompany you." His eyes flashed a golden warning.

She drew back. The flex of his jaw was a clear indication he'd boxed up his emotions. She could definitely sense anger.

Her back straightened as memories of her controlling father surfaced, a warning signal blaring in her skull. Venn's insistent tone grated on her already-frayed nerves. She turned her back to him and focused her attention to her grandmother, on anything other than Venn.

Over her shoulder, she said, "I don't need a chaperone."

Venn watched Emma fuss over a brush and comb on the nightstand, lining them up perfectly side by side. Pushing the subject might distance her, and he knew he should let the topic drop, but he couldn't.

"Jacob is bad news."

"Who's Jacob?" a baritone voice rumbled from the door.

"Dad!" Emma crossed her arms like a shield. "What are you doing here?"

Venn could nearly hear the hairs on her body raise as she tensed. Like any animal on full alert. Animosity rained from her pores. The absence of affection conveyed the nature of the relationship, and she seemed frozen in place. There was no hug or embrace. Only cold space.

Her father moved into the room. "Were you going to call me?"

"Only if I needed to."

"In which case, I'm glad the chief of police phoned me," her father returned, his tone emotionless. "Or else I wouldn't have known."

Venn stepped forward. The place had just turned into a furnace. He extended his hand. "I'm Venn Hearst."

"Carl Grant." He offered a firm, quick handshake.

"We have Venn to thank for saving Grams. He pulled her out of the well."

"Indeed. Thank you." Mr. Grant gave him a curt nod, which Venn responded to with a tight smile.

"Glad to help."

"Dad owns a law practice in New York. I didn't want to bother him just yet, as I know he's very busy," she explained, her voice thread-like and anxious. Her hands and fingers flexed and wriggled at her sides.

Anything that made her this uncomfortable didn't sit well with him, even if the guy was her father.

Emma scowled as Venn assumed a possessive stance beside her, arms folded and feet set wide. He wanted to mark and guard his territory. He could practically see those lawyerly wheels turning in the man's head, summing things up. Mr. Grant didn't seem to miss much, his eyes shifting several times between Venn and Emma.

"Has the doctor been in yet?" he asked.

"Yes. A few minutes ago," Emma said. Her voice lightened as she relayed the latest information on her grandmother's progress.

Mr. Grant traveled to the chair Venn had vacated moments earlier, sat, and crossed one leg over the other. "Well, good. It sounds like she'll be okay. Perhaps I made an unnecessary trip."

Emma paced, but with the smallness of the room, there wasn't anywhere she could go. "I'm surprised you could get away."

"So, who is Jacob?" her father asked bluntly. "From Venn's tone, the man seems like one of the maniacs I'm up against in court."

She stopped pacing, her shoes squeaking on the linoleum floor. "Wait a minute. You lost the right to interfere in my life years ago."

"Touché." Her father tossed up a hand, his gaze slanted sideways and his mouth pinched, clearly displeased.

Venn suspected the man didn't appreciate airing the family's dirty laundry in front of strangers, but he didn't press the issue.

Tension swirled in the room as the silence stretched. Venn could almost taste the bitterness between the two of them. The urge to gather Emma in his arms and protect her surged through him. It didn't matter if it was family or not, no one was going to hurt his Emma, physically or otherwise. She clearly had problems with the man. And he trusted her judgment.

The glares firing between father and daughter felt like lightning ricocheting inside the four walls.

As if it just occurred to her, she asked, "Where are you staying?"

He raised his brows. "In my old room."

She nodded. "Fine. Let's just stay out of each other's way, okay?" Emma grabbed her purse and headed out the door without waiting for a reply.

Venn hustled to match her quick steps. "Wow, you two must have some serious baggage."

"When you have a couple of free days, I'll fill you in."

"Promise?"

She marched past the elevator in favor of the stairs. When he lifted his eyebrow, she said, "It's only three floors."

"Right."

Their footfalls echoed the staccato rhythm of flight— her fast clip-claps, his heavier tromps. He didn't speak, giving her space, until they were at her car and she clicked the remote to pop the lock.

He opened the door. "Stop. You need to calm down before you get behind that wheel. Take a couple of deep breaths."

When she looked up at him, her dark eyelashes were wet. *Damn.* His chest tightened.

Her slender neck contracted as she swallowed. Whatever her SOB father had done was obviously still painful, and she had yet to get over it. She was working so hard to hold it together. Venn's hands curled into fists.

For once she didn't argue and inhaled deeply through her nose. Again. And again.

He cupped her face in his large hands and smoothed back some loose strands of her hair. "Excellent. Okay. The plan hasn't changed, right? You're going home and then to the park?"

"Yes."

The keys jangled in her hand. She was still worked up but at least not ready to blow apart.

"When you're at the park, I'm going to be there shadowing you."

"That's—"

"Yes. It *is* necessary," he said, anticipating her

objection. He dropped his hands to her shoulders. "The hawk or wolf will be just out of sight. Trust me, Emma. Jacob isn't what he seems."

15

When Emma arrived at the park a few hours later, she sat in the car, gripping the steering wheel long after the purr of the engine ceased. Her stomach rolled through spasm after spasm. Jalapeño peppers? Hadn't eaten any. More like her father's unexpected arrival.

This visit with her grandmother sure wasn't what she'd imagined it would be. She centered the heel of her hand against her chest and rubbed. Then she disengaged the keys from the ignition and made a mental note to stop at the drugstore on the way home to pick up some antacid medication. If only everything were that easy.

At least Grams was showing so many signs of improvement. Emma tenderly ran her thumb over the warped-butterfly key fob while clutching that encouraging thought to her breast. On a heavy sigh, she stepped out of the car.

With her attention finally focused on the park, she was shocked to discover the amount of work that had been done in a few short days. Pretty soon it would challenge the gardens in Paris. The place had been transformed, the earth smoothed and covered with new grass. Fresh off-white sidewalks led the way to granite benches, and a restroom facility had been partially erected. Someone obviously had major connections.

Jacob? He seemed to be in charge, but could he have pulled this off? Did he have that kind of clout? She inhaled deeply, exhaled slowly. If the guy was as bad as Venn alleged, then what had her grandmother bought into? Was there something going on behind the scene? As far as she knew, he was just on the city planning committee.

Emma thought of Venn's warning. Unease grew as she neared the statue platform in the shadow of the oak. Venn's "Divine Tree," as he called it.

Within her peripheral vision, Jacob slithered from behind another tree. Emma gasped. "What's with the sneaking around?"

He chuckled. "My goodness, you have an active imagination."

"No. You're just behaving oddly." Emma couldn't help the rude remark. Now, more than before, he was putting off a creepy vibe.

"We were scheduled to meet here, right?"

Emma swallowed her angst. It was simply Venn's attitude transferring to her. Jacob had never done anything to her. Then again, Venn wasn't what he'd seemed at first, either.

She controlled her breathing. "Yes. I'm sorry. I guess I'm just stressed over things."

"How is your grandmother?"

Emma lifted her head as the muscles along her spine bunched. "Doing much better, thank you."

"That's cool." But his voice sounded hollow and stilted, like he didn't use those words often.

A slip of irritation kicked along her nerves. She couldn't stand talking about Grams with the guy. He didn't seem to genuinely care, and it was none of his business.

"So, what do we need to cover?" she asked, directing the conversation to their business.

He smirked a little. "The dedication on Saturday is all set. The mayor and even a state senator will speak. Three days and you can head back to Paris."

"Okay," she replied, wishing the ceremony could be postponed. There was no way Grams would be well enough to attend by then. But maybe it was best to keep the two things separate. She'd snap lots of pictures so her grandmother wouldn't miss out entirely, and perhaps the local news would cover the event.

Grams needed to heal, first and foremost. Emma sighed. She really should delay her return flight in order to lend a hand for a while.

Unable to shake melancholy feelings, she settled her gaze on the tree. A welcoming spark ignited inside her, followed by a warmth that proclaimed everything was going to be all right. A longing for more reassurance called her forward, and she went to a polished granite bench protected by the arched oak branches, and sat.

She glanced about to see if Venn was around as he'd promised, but she couldn't find him. Disappointed—and anxious on so many levels—she turned to Jacob.

"What is my part in this? You already have the artwork." She figured that once he gave her instructions, he could leave, and the sooner the better.

His brow pinched into an ugly frown, then held. He trotted over and hopped up onto an empty granite slab that coordinated nicely with the benches. "The statue will be placed here. These holes accept the support anchors. Eight long spikes. You will set them in place and ceremonially drive them home. Not all the way, of course; the work crew can finish the job."

"And the crowd will cheer or something?"

"Louder than you realize." His tone suggested an inside joke.

She narrowed her eyes, confused.

Come to think of it, she really didn't much like Jacob. The only positive aspect in recent events was Venn, except *he* was an Immortal Guardian. She stared at the tree and calmed her escalating pulse with a deep breath.

This was their picnic spot.

An invisible current whirled around her. The electric vibes sizzled and crackled, her internal chemistry changing. It reminded her of when she knew she was coming down with the flu. That expectant moment when she didn't know what awaited her. She reflected on the origin of the exposure.

From behind another ancient oak halfway across the park, a wolf edged toward them in menacing steps.

Venn.

With a revolted wince, Jacob straightened. Emma heard a throaty growl but wasn't certain from where it came. But she was certain the air crackled with hostility.

She was a spectator on a battlefield. She ping-ponged her gaze between the two beings. Apprehension sent a tingling warning over her neck and along her spine. And a flash of her horrific vision came to mind.

That arrow striking her chest and ruining what she and Venn had. This time she saw everything as if an omniscient story, allowing her to discover some missing details, like Venn changing into a wolf in his grief.

That same wolf kept advancing now, like a proud warrior, and Jacob fisted his hands, his face reddening. In that moment, Emma witnessed the danger Venn had warned her about.

She caught the strong, woodsy odor of the tree, and her body went limp as everything turned black.

The desire to kill Venn clawed at Io. He was a breath away from changing into his barghest and ripping the Guardian to shreds. But that would just be like playing video games, nothing permanent. Venn was the link to the Divine Tree's destruction. And vice versa.

Control. The surest way to destroy Venn was by killing the Divine Tree. Not only would the protector be dead but he would have failed. And Venn's failure would be the greatest satisfaction of all.

But his archenemy abandoned all discipline, launching an attack as huge paws rammed into Io's chest, sending him to his back with a snap and thud. His vision filled with vicious fangs.

A wicked laugh bubbled up from deep in Io's belly. "She's your Achilles' heel."

"She's mine. A love and passion you'll never have."

Hot rage filled Io. But before he could act, movement by the Divine Tree caught his attention. Seth stepped out from behind it. Damn his brother's interference. Io's anger rose to volcanic proportions as he burst into flames and disappeared, leaving behind a whirl of smoke.

"Coward," Venn snarled as Io's invisible form vanished beyond reach.

Live to fight another day. Io muttered his mantra. He had learned the finest means to make a person suffer was to go after someone they loved.

Two would experience the agony of loss this time.

Venn rushed to Emma, slipping into his human form mid-stride. He knelt alongside the bench and swept her fiery hair back from where it had veiled her face. Her cheeks were rosy, a good sign. "Emma?"

She was out cold. What had Io done?

Impulsively, his hand went to his hip and the carved hilt of a knife.

She is fine. The voice of the Divine Tree curled around them.

Venn snapped his head up, confused at first until his anger settled enough for reasonable thought. No, this wasn't Io's style. Too peaceful, for one thing. He frowned. "Who?"

"Not me. Not this time." Seth's golden rasp dripped with humor as he appeared beside the tree.

It infuriated the hell out of Venn that anyone would send Emma to la-la land. He overlooked the fact that he had used the technique a few days earlier, but really, it wasn't the same at all when he was the one in control. He was not using it to harm her.

Venn frowned. *Then who?*

Seth stretched his massive wings, then folded them behind him like a packed accordion and hitched his thumb toward the Divine Tree.

The tree? Custos put her to sleep? Venn was not in the mood for games. "Go home. I don't need complications."

"Is that any way to treat a friend?"

Friend. Ha. There was something else going on with Seth these days. But he didn't have time to figure out what.

Ignoring Seth, he gently scooped Emma into his arms. He'd take her to his place. It was a fortress, after all.

Her throaty moan made his heart squeeze. His sleeping beauty rested her head against his chest. With a quick flip of his wrist for the anointing ritual, the tree allowed them entrance. Her breathing whispered the sweet rhythm of slumber, and her dark lashes fanned across petal-soft cheeks. She looked so vulnerable.

And she was his to protect.

He pressed her firmly against his body. The urge to keep her there outweighed logic and responsibility and loyalty. Which meant he didn't care why a certain angel had showed up. Or why Custos had interfered and put Emma to sleep. At the moment he was angry with everyone, including himself for putting Emma in any kind of danger whatsoever.

He carried her through the main room and headed for the tunnel, since it was the quickest route to his home. Still, the trek seemed to take forever as his anxiety climbed with every step he descended. Not to mention that Seth silently padded along at his back. The angel could have transported himself in ahead of them if he'd wanted to, but no, he had some inclination to live on the wild side.

Venn was ready to deck the angel.

"Hey, where's the attitude of gratitude, man. You've got your mate, right?"

For that, he *was* grateful. "Get over it. You're too cocky as it is."

He'd thank Seth one of these days, he knew, but at the moment, his world centered on Emma. He'd figure out the rest later. When they got to his house, Venn kicked the door closed behind him with his heel. "I liked it better when you *thee*-ed and *thou*-ed everything."

Seth shrugged. "Times change."

No shit.

Venn marched upstairs to his chambers. Carefully easing Emma onto the sofa, he slipped a throw over her shapely legs, wondering how long it would be before she came to.

"Your room? Really," Seth said.

"It's the best place for me to keep my eye on her. Besides, we were already lovers. If you recall."

"Ah, yes."

As Venn took his usual place at the window, Henry miraculously appeared with what smelled to be a stiff drink. Not long after they'd entered the house, Henry had joined the procession, but for once, he'd wisely remained silent. Venn accepted the glass, then clapped a palm on the assistant's shoulder. "Well done. I believe we'll need a tray of food."

"Of course."

As Henry left, Venn drank and paced toward Seth who had fired up the TV and stretched out in the recliner. Hell. Booze was one thing that hadn't changed much since that tree-splitting day eons past. Venn frowned and looked at Seth. "So why are you here?"

"Awesome. The Falcons against the Chargers."

"Like you don't know who'll win." Venn dropped into a matching recliner.

"Can't foretell the future, man."

Venn still didn't believe that, but no harm in testing. "Fine, back to our problem at hand."

"You asked me to hang around, right? I'm just checking on you. I mean, Io has been known to play dirty. There are some things that even I am not privy to."

"What are you not saying?"

The angel's gaze settled on Emma, and Venn's chest constricted with uncertainty. Why Seth's sudden interest in his mate? In their past life, the archangel had given them little notice.

"Two concerns. One, she is connected in some way to the tree, now. I sensed it when the tree initiated the spell to protect her by rendering her unconscious. I don't know how Custos did it, but the Divine Tree knows more than it's telling us."

Venn scoffed. "Imagine that, the keeper of the universe has secrets."

"Don't be snide. I'm just laying out the facts. Plus, Io is getting stronger."

"Which means I shouldn't let her out of my sight," Venn said.

"She was destined for you before; that may not be the case today."

Venn leaped to his feet. "Fuck off. I won't let her go. Or let Io kill her."

"I didn't say that."

"Go. I can fix this."

"Not quite." Seth turned to Venn and raised both arms in the universal touchdown gesture. "Yes." He sighed dramatically, recovering his composure. "Io has an agenda. We need to figure out specifically what it is."

"I will die before I let him harm her." He drained the last of his drink with a virulent survey of the sofa. He'd make her stay if he had to.

Emma moaned.

"That's my cue." Seth's form faded to nothing.

Glass clinked against wood as Venn set his empty tumbler on the side table. It would have felt so damn good to pitch the thing in the fireplace. God knew he longed to hit something.

16

Emma came awake in an oddly familiar, enormous living area. A shiver of déjà vu caused her breath to hitch as she gazed at the magnificent wall of windows and the moon cresting the treetops. She slowly grew aware of several things. Fine, cool leather cradled her exhausted body. A soft fleece throw covered her bare feet. Two male voices rumbled in conversation beyond her visual field. The temptation to retreat again into the cocoon of darkness beckoned.

What had happened? Her lids dragged downward.

Amid her muddled thoughts, she noted an abrupt silence.

The park . . . That was the last thing she recalled. Venn, Jacob, the power of the oak. She pushed up on one elbow.

Ten-pound sandbags had to be attached to her eyelids. She forced them open several times before they held.

Venn walked over, his footsteps resounding on the wood floor. "Welcome back."

"Where am I?"

"My home. I live near the park."

"The park!" She bolted upright until his touch on her shoulder stopped her. It sent a delicious sizzling jolt along her nerve endings, despite the dizziness that overcame her.

"Take it easy." His weight settled on the edge of the sofa where her feet tucked back. She drew her legs up to allow him more room, taking comfort in his concern for her well-being. His knees brushed against her. No, not comfort. *Warmth.*

"What happened?" she asked.

He cleared his throat softly. "Jacob and I had a meeting of the minds, shall we say. Evidently, this time our little clash produced an energy wave that caused you to pass out." His gaze broke from hers the way the guilty avoided authority.

"This time?"

After a moment of silence, he raised his proud chin, rubbed his neck. "At your grandmother's, when you first met with Jacob, I put you to sleep. It seemed—"

"You what?" She struggled to rise, her hands slipping on the leather.

"I'm sorry." He pressed his strong hand on her leg, effectively signaling her again to stay put.

She batted him away. "Let go of me."

"Wait. Listen. It was the best solution at the time. I had to make Jacob leave. You were in danger! Plus, you didn't know what was going on yet."

"I still don't!" She scooted as far from him as she could, crossing her legs beneath the blanket. "Tell me *everything*. What's the deal with Jacob?"

With his jaw set firm, he rose and hauled a footstool in front of her. Then he sat, elbows propped on his knees, his strong hands casually clasped, and he leaned toward her.

She craned her neck, searching behind her. She'd heard someone else nearby.

"My personal assistant just left."

"Henry?"

"Yes. He brought food." Venn moved the tray within easy reach, but she shook her head. He snatched a slice of cheese and ate it.

"Back to Jacob." She stared up into his darkening eyes.

As before, something deep within her crackled to life. The feeling terrified her. What it could mean terrified her. She was used to going it alone, being independent. But to put her trust in this man, well—

Impressions flashed into her mind's eye. Expertly stacked boulders created a solid barrier, a moat protecting its castle, a wolf guarding its lair. All impressions related to Venn. She dragged in a fortifying breath as his lips parted.

"First off, his name isn't Jacob, it's Io."

"Io Price?"

"Yes. You, Io, and I have past history. Do you remember?"

"No. I . . . How would I recall it?"

"I need *you* to tell *me* that."

She hesitated. "Since I was a child, I've had visions and dreams. The dreams appear to be delightful, the visions horrific." She paused, thinking his eyes seemed to whisper, *I understand.* "But lately they seem to be all mixed up. And I recently discovered that you are in many of them. Although until yesterday, I never saw your face. You were always just a profile or cast in shadows."

His irises changed, mesmerizing her, as flecks and ripples of gold and garnet swirled. Extraordinarily intriguing. He seemed so powerful, strong, and intense. She wet her lips. All of a sudden, there wasn't enough air in the room, and when she finally gulped a breath, her head filled with the evocative aroma of Venn. A scent she recognized from another time. The idea freaked her out. She shook her head, trying to dislodge the distraction.

"What were the visions?"

———————

Venn breathed in the confusion and panic emanating from her pores, and something else. Passion? He held himself in check, even though his desire to embrace her escalated into a physical yearning. The muscles along his arms, chest, and back tightened, his cock jutting upward. Completely aware of the rocky ground he treaded, he worked to keep control when all he wanted was to let loose.

What would make her remember? What would make her whole? What would make her his? "Emma. I know right now you're trapped between Amelia in a previous life and who you are today. Trust me."

She instantly seemed to recoil into herself. Clinging frantically to safe ground, he suspected. Her hands clutched the blanket, and her shoulders bunched at the neck. Her breathing turned irregular. She was caught in some sort of vortex between the past and present, and he wanted to release her. He wanted to cradle her in his lap and love her. He wanted to cover her and drive away everything else but the two of them.

"Yes, trapped," she echoed. "You nailed it."

Venn focused every bit of magic he possessed into his voice, wanting to make this easier for her. Accepting who and what you are sometimes hurt, especially when you grow up being different from your peers. He knew this had always been an issue with her. "Let's walk through this together, step by step."

The room filled with deafening silence as he awaited her response. Seth had warned him about preparing for a new life together, releasing what was potentially destructive and embracing the journey. She needed to also.

If she didn't accept him as a Guardian, she would never be his. It was not like he could change jobs the way humans could. Although, sometimes that's all he wanted to do.

17

Together. The word flamed in her head as her heart thumped faster and faster and her palms blazed. Venn seemed so calm, so still.

Her gaze slid to his hands. If he touched her, she'd bolt. Truly.

God, he'd put her to *sleep*?

Off-kilter and confused, she closed her eyes, trying to sort through her feelings of attraction and distrust. A montage of images from another lifetime fired behind her eyelids as if she'd hit the "rewind" button.

His wolf . . . her fingers buried in that lush, thick coat.

Her blood flowing into the ground.

An arrow. What of the archer?

Venn naked.

Shattering orgasms. Limbs entwined. Flesh warming flesh.

Gasping, she opened her eyes and met Venn's hot gaze. Unable to stay put a moment longer, she rose to move around. When she stepped by his chair, heading toward the windows, he clasped her wrist.

"Stop. You can't run from the connection we share."

"I'm not," she whispered, staring over his head, not daring to look into those golden eyes. She needed time to process it all. Her gaze landed on the statue of a wolf sitting on an end table—it was the one from his cottage that he'd brought home—she realized then the extent their lives were interwoven. He had always been part of her subconscious thoughts in some way, hadn't he?

He released her, and she took a few more steps, then paused, hugging her arms to her while the puzzle pieces melded into one composition. "We made love right here. I . . . I remember. On the floor, on a huge fur rug with the moon washing over us."

As every detail flickered in her mind, the next thing she knew, Venn's arms replaced hers against her ribs, slipping around her from behind. She leaned back against him, his solid chest achingly familiar. He curled into her then, kissing her ear, sending shivers down her neck and through her body. Turning in his embrace, she slid a hand into his dark hair, drew him to her. And as his mouth captured hers, she kissed him in desperation.

He emitted a low, throaty growl as he claimed her mouth and crushed her against him. Something touched her soul deep, building inside of her. She wanted Venn with everything she was now...and everything she was before. Even if she didn't know how that was possible. She met the thrust of his tongue, lap for lap, loving the way he kissed her with deep, frantic hunger.

His hands splayed across her back, sliding over her ribs, up to her shoulder blades, and down cupping her bottom, holding her closer, tighter. His lips sucked and drew on hers as he pulled back. She made a little sound deep in her throat.

He touched her heart in more ways than she imagined...the universe shifted with such a kiss, it had the sort of power that made tides ebb and flow, earthquakes shudder, and volcanoes erupt. And it transported her into a complex reality with the capacity to love beyond anything she'd known. Oh, how she longed to discover all Venn had to offer.

Slipping an arm beneath her knees and the other supporting her back, he lifted her and carried her to the bed. He paused to rain soft kisses over her cheek and jaw until he ended at her mouth again, and delicately fanned her lips with his tongue. Her knees grew weak as he set her down and began to slowly peel off her clothes. He eased the draped-neckline of her sweater lower over one shoulder, his mouth trailing where his fingers had been, kissing her and feathering his tongue. She inhaled a shaky breath. Ooo. With tension building in her tummy, she helped him shed her clothes, meeting his gaze and searching his ever-changing golden eyes.

When she stood nude before him, he made a low, guttural sound and allowed his gaze to glide over her in the most provocative manner, as if he were making love to her with only his eyes. She shivered.

Two could play this sensual game, and the thought excited her even more. She put her palm on his chest, right over his heart and felt its thudding beat. Then she bunched his shirt in her hands, tugging the fabric over his head. He had to tip forward in order to allow her to accomplish the task. Her arm grazed his warm skin, sending delightful shivers dancing through her. His pants were next, and she discovered to her surprise that he didn't wear undergarments. She let her gaze run over him, savoring her first glimpse of his honed chest that narrowed into a six pack, and dip lower, eyeing the fullness of his erection. Oh, he was magnificent.

He entwined his fingers in her hair, framing her face as he drew her closer. "My mate," he whispered into her mouth. "Emma."

As he kissed her, he took her with him down onto the mattress. Rolling them both into the center of the bed, ending with him on top, he braced himself on his forearm. With his other hand, he stroked up the length of her body, from hip to breast, pausing to trace delightful circles around her areola. Her pulse spiked, and her breath went ragged.

He plucked at her nipple, rolling it between his fingers, and as he did so, lowered his head to take its partner into his mouth. Ah, it felt so good, already tiny pulses were pinging through her sex. She hooked a leg over his hip. And he sucked and tweaked her nipples harder.

When he raised his head, she heard him draw a long breath through his nostrils. Coupled with the burning look in his eyes, he seemed primal, urgent, hungry. He slid his hand down her belly, burying his fingers in her curls. Caught up in driving desire, she parted her legs as he dipped his fingers into her secret folds. He began a slow rhythm, sliding them in long strokes in and out over her wet clit, then every so often he'd change it up, circling the bud until she pressed her hips into his fingers.

His touch sent shockwaves through her, and as she came, he kissed her and growled into her mouth. She felt the vibrations of his groan all the way into her throat.

He moved then, positioning himself fully over her and finding her opening, gently sliding inside her. She arched and curled into him as he entered her slick, ready channel, filling her with his thick manhood. And then they began driving in unison, a natural retreat and thrust that took her higher with every long glide, until the tempo increase, and they both were panting.

She climaxed, hot electric sensations, striking her core and pulsing into her limbs, into her tummy, into her chest. He came right at the peak of her strongest wave. She watched him throw his head back as he drove into her deeply, the cords of his neck straining. His massive torso shuddered. "Emma," he cried.

She dug her fingers into his shoulder, holding onto the exquisite sensations as long as she could until he collapsed into an exhausted, entangled heap.

When their breathing returned to normal, he muttered, "Oh, Jesus. That was even better than what we had once upon a time."

She winced. And as he curled her into his body, cradled in his strong arms, she wondered if there would always be that comparison. Or if there would ever come a day where it would simply be Emma and Venn.

18

Io cloaked himself as he impatiently waited in the corner of Mrs. Grant's hospital room. He'd flown around for hours contemplating his options. But he kept returning to the old lady as the best means of distraction. If Emma was worried about her grandmother, then she'd give less thought to Venn and be preoccupied enough to perhaps do exactly as Io instructed.

During the altercation in the park, he'd felt the strength of their bond. And, Satan's eyes, it worried him.

It was past midnight, and the new shift nurse had just exited following a routine vital-sign check. Io listened to the fading slap of footfalls from the hallway and waited.

Silence.

Satisfied he wouldn't be interrupted, he materialized. Mrs. Grant's eyes were closed, but he knew she wasn't asleep. A moment ago she'd expressed her desire for real coffee with breakfast.

Such trivial things to worry about.

Without making a sound, Io walked to stand beside the hospital bed. And Granny's peepers popped right open.

He smiled. "Good evening, Mrs. Grant."

"Visiting hours are over," she said, eyes narrowing on

him suspiciously. She turned her head more fully toward him.

Smart old bird.

"Those rules are for ordinary men," he said, and chuckled. And, of course, they don't apply to him.

She blinked and brushed the gray hair from her forehead, then made a pinched face and touched the IV tube in the back of her hand. "Oh, it's you, Mr. Price," she said, finally recognizing him. "The dedication. How is it all going? I'm so disappointed I'm going to miss it."

"Yes. Emma isn't happy about that. Least of her worries, though."

"What do you mean?" She tried to push up on one elbow.

"Never mind."

Mrs. Grant pursed her lips. "She's such a talented girl. That statue is going to be gorgeous in the park."

"Indeed."

"She's smart, too." Her eyes lit with pride.

"Yes, and that is just too bad."

Her almost-invisible brows lifted, like two mirrored question marks.

Io sneered. "I need you to give Emma a message for me."

"Oh?"

Losing patience with all this chitchat, he put on his game face—dark, sinister, evil. He leaned over, moving the call button out of her reach.

His voice deepened and warped as he began to transform from human form into a larger-than-life owl.

Granny inhaled sharply, her eyes round as poker chips. Her hand came to her throat as if she was having difficulty breathing.

Excellent. Scaring her to death. What an extraordinary plan.

Io extended his wings over her for theatrical affect. Yes, Mrs. Grant's face muscles twitched as she obviously made the connection between her accident and him. "It was you," she screeched.

He threw his voice out into the room, giving it an echo effect. "Yes. It was me. Venn and Emma are getting too chummy. So I've devised a way to alleviate that. And *you* are going to help me. Venn will find he's no match for me."

"What? Emma," she choked out. "Emma . . . warn—"

One of her monitors blared, and she glanced at it.

Fuck. This was taking too long. Io's feathers changed into a barghest's slick, black fur, and he let loose a vicious growl.

She clutched her head with trembling hands. As she did so, the IV tube caught on the bedrail and was torn from her skin, oozing blood across the sheets.

"Em—" Her body stilled, limbs collapsing, lungs expelling a final breath.

Another alarm blared, which to him sounded like . . . satisfaction.

19

The morning greeted Emma with a majestic radiance of blue sky and sun-kissed clouds. Perfect. She inhaled a dreamy breath. Absolutely perfect.

She lay with her head on Venn's shoulder, his arm wrapped from underneath her, cradling her into his side. Outside the floor-to-ceiling windows, the world returned to life.

At the moment she felt secure, giddy, loved. Her hand skimmed over the raised tattoo where it met his shoulder. She'd noticed it last evening but was too involved with their lovemaking to inquire further. "Turn over," she said, giving him a little push. "I want a closer look at the ink on your back."

"It's not ink. It comes from the Divine Tree." He rolled onto his side, presenting his back to her.

"Wow." She traced the pads of her fingers over the branches of the tree, understanding what he meant. The tattoo rose from the skin like welts or perhaps a brand, in shades of brownish-black and gray, the color of bark on an oak. "Has it always completely covered your back?"

"No. Over the years it's grown and spread."

She leaned in and lightly kissed along a branch-line above his shoulder blade. He moaned, and his tense muscles relaxed beneath her hands.

Her cell phone chimed a familiar rhythm.

"Let it go," he murmured.

She did and snuggled closer against him, slipping her palm across his ribs on a deep sigh.

"Mmm," he groaned.

A comfortable silence filled the air until the trill went off again. This time she could even hear the thing vibrating on the table. No way could she ignore it.

She scrambled over the mattress and snatched the disheveled sheet as she went. After a few quick steps, her feet moved from the plush rug beneath the bed to the cold marble floor. She shivered as she grabbed the phone.

With a swipe of her thumb to unlock the screen, she raised it to listen. "Hello?"

Silence greeted her. Perhaps they'd hung up.

In a playful mood, she turned to face the bed and her breath caught at the sight of Venn, lounging gloriously naked. He made a dramatic show of waggling his brows at her and clasping his hands behind head, obviously ready and willing for a bit of morning exercise.

"Emma." Her father's voice on the other end of the phone wiped the silly grin right off her face as if she'd been slapped.

"Yeah, Dad." She folded her arms over her breasts and searched for her clothes. Venn immediately lunged for his pants and donned them.

"Where are you?" her father asked. "You didn't come home?"

"What's up?"

"The hospital just called. Your grandmother has taken a turn for the worse."

Her thoughts slammed into a barricade as her pulse kicked up, stunned. "But . . . but she was doing so much better yesterday."

"I know. I know."

"I'll leave right now." With a numbness consuming her

entire body, beginning in her heart and ending at her fingertips, she hit the "end" button.

Venn was at her side in no time, taking her by the arm, guiding her sideways, encouraging her to sit down. "What happened?"

"He didn't say exactly. Something has gone wrong with Grams."

"I'll drive you to the hospital."

"Why didn't they call me? They have my cell number," she said, trying to hold it together.

"He's her son. The next of kin."

She shook her head. Grams had made every concert. Emma had always been closer to Grams than her father had. "The hospital didn't call him when she fell in the well."

"But he's here now."

"Oh. Yeah. You're probably right. I'm just not thinking straight."

"Well, naturally you're upset." He stood before her holding her clothes. She'd totally missed him collecting them. "Here are your things. Take a moment to shower and get yourself together. It may be a long day."

She found her legs shaky, and he helped her to the bathroom. He kissed her brow. "Everything will be fine."

Drawing on his strength, she nodded. "I hope you're right."

When they arrived on the ICU floor, Emma encountered Dr. Myer at the nurse's station.

"I'm so sorry, but your grandmother's status has changed. Let's go in here and I'll explain." With a hand on her shoulder, he guided her into a nearby waiting room.

A turn for the worse.

She took a seat and clasped her hands together so hard

her knuckles showed white. Venn sat next to her.

"Your grandmother has had a massive stroke brought on by atrial fibrillation. That's where the upper chambers of the heart have an irregular or rapid heartbeat, which can cause a clot to form. Although I must say I'm surprised in this case. Your grandmother didn't show any signs of heart related problems. I had thought we were out of the woods."

Emma shook her head as her stomach and chest tightened. If she heard the diagnosis, then it would be real.

He spoke of the type of stroke Grams had suffered, of being brain dead, back on the ventilator, and saying it was time to take a look at her living will. Emma nodded and swallowed hard, although there wasn't a drop of moisture in her throat. She heard his clinical words, then more words of apology, yet she felt like a kid in a carnival fun house, trying to figure out where the sound was coming from and which direction she needed to move in order to escape.

At some point, she became aware of Venn slipping his firm hand into hers as they stood. She thought she led the way but wasn't sure. Out in the hall, it seemed like a long way to Grams's room. Venn draped his arm around her shoulder and tugged her close to his side as they walked.

At her grandmother's doorway, Emma paused to dip her head in. She was not at all ready for this.

Her dad sat on the hospital bed holding Grams's unmoving hand. Emma couldn't go in just yet. She just couldn't.

The unfamiliar mood that emanated from her father shocked her. He seemed vulnerable, with a softness to him she rarely, if ever, saw. She clutched a fistful of Venn's shirt at his back while her father spoke.

"I should have told you yesterday," he said, still unaware of their presence.

Emma realized what was happening. Unfinished business and regrets. She inhaled slowly as a shudder of anguish ran through her.

Her father heard it and turned his head, the private moment broken. She entered with hesitant steps.

"Dr. Myer filled me in. There is no hope of her recovering." Her mouth trembled, and she sank her teeth in her lower lip, fighting for control.

"It's okay to let go," Venn said, giving her a squeeze.

A shaky breath escaped her lips.

Her father stood. "No . . . no. We just have to give her time."

"What?" Emma couldn't believe her ears. If ever there was a time she *wanted* her father to be right, this was it. But one look at Grams, and she knew her favorite person in the entire world had left them. She felt the emptiness in her heart. And Mr. Tell It Like It Is was smoothing over the truth. She glanced at Venn, who slowly shook his head. Their eyes met, and no words were needed for them to communicate. He knew, as she did, that her grandmother was gone.

"Dad, as much I'd love for her to get better, time isn't going to help anymore. Her brain isn't working." She paused, struggling with the next words she had to push out. "Grams has a living will. We have to honor it."

"No. No. There are ways to contest that. All I need is a few days." He stared down at his mother, sadness creating deep lines on his face.

"That's not what she would have wanted, and you know it. She wouldn't want to be trapped in a body, not really living."

He snatched his jacket from the back of the chair and then brushed past her toward the doorway, saying, "I best get to it. Dr. Myer already confirmed that we will have to move her to a hospice facility."

Emma followed him, grabbing his arm as he gripped the door handle. "No. Not this time. You won't have your way this time. You have a problem accepting things. But this time Mom isn't going yield to your demands, and I'm not going to run away in order to hide my special abilities, and Grams is not going to come back to life."

His jaw clenched, and he defiantly raised his chin, then fled into the hall.

She caved inward as if she'd been punched in the chest, all the tears and agony that had been building inside her letting go in a landslide of sorrow. With a wretched cry, she spun toward Venn, and he gently encircled her within his big arms. She mashed her face into his chest and sobbed.

———————

"Losing someone you love is never easy," Venn said, rubbing his palm up and down Emma's back. He'd nearly lost his mind when he'd had to go on living without her.

He held her while she came to terms with this new change in her life. He wished he could do more, wipe away her sorrow. Her shoulders shook, her rib cage hitched, her tears soaked his shirt. And like everything else Emma did, she threw her whole self into her grief.

His vision skipped around the room as she clung to him, taking in the picture on the wall of a blue-green ocean and palm trees, watching the rise and fall of Mrs. Grant's chest in sync with the whooshing sound of the respirator, and eyeing the elderly women's belongings lined up on the hospital tray. Things she would no longer need. And there, next to a pair of glasses, sat a feather.

He leaned in to get a closer look, even though the sickening bite in his stomach already told him what he needed to know.

An owl feather. Io had left a calling card.

Emma swiped at her eyes, and cool air replaced her warm body as she stepped back from him. "I need a tissue."

Venn shoved the entire box at her, blocking her view

of the feather. When she turned toward the bed, he snatched it up and crushed it in his hand. Energy swelled within him. At first he thought his rage had taken over, destroying any ability to control his powers. But then he realized it was something more. He saw a flicker of light off to the right, and the air warmed.

A wavering, semitransparent figure appeared at the end of the bed—Mrs. Grant.

What in blazes is going on? Her pissed-off mental demand for answers came to him from beyond the foot of the bed.

Venn did a double take, cocking his head sideways, and whaddya know, Grams's glow took a clearer form, her arms folded in a stop-messing-with-me stance. He'd been a Guardian for enough years, living through lots of weird shit, so he wasn't completely shocked to see her. The question that immediately hit him was, *Could Emma see her?*

He shot a guarded glance up the bed to Emma. No, he didn't think so. She seemed lost in thought.

He spoke to the older woman mind to mind. *You're not dead.*

Says who? I look dead. She motioned to the bed.

Point taken. He couldn't help the half-smile that tugged at his lips. Gutsy lady. Again he checked Emma for a reaction. She was reading over her grandmother's chart.

I guess this is what they call an out-of-body experience. Grams chortled, and she glanced at her granddaughter's bowed head and sobered. *This isn't about me. You have to protect her. Jacob...you know him as Io . . .* She shook her head, as if trying to comprehend the situation. *Io's some kind of monster.*

He wondered how much of himself Io had revealed to her. The poor woman.

I'll watch over her, protect her. Don't worry.

I knew there was something special about you. You have a noble aura, I told Emma. Mrs. Grant paused a beat. *She can't hear me, can she?*

He shook his head.

Mrs. Grant sighed, giving a troubled expression that

made him apprehensive about listening to what she would say next. *Io bragged about using Emma to kill the tree. He was going on and on, full of himself. He spoke of her ability to change metal. About using that somehow. I didn't really understand what he was talking about, but he said your name enough times that I know you are the one he's really after.*

Venn fisted his hands and sucked air in past his teeth. A slippery form of dread squirmed within him. There was something to be said about the old ways of attacking enemies before they attacked you.

The need to destroy Io burned within him. He glanced at Emma, and she caught his look.

"What's wrong?" she asked.

"Nothing," he lied, all the while trying to figure out how Io planned to use Emma. Should he tell her he could see Grams and was having a conversation with the woman? No. Not yet. Emma carried too many problems on her shoulders right now.

Did Io give any clues to his intentions? he asked Grams. Io was the ultimate tormenter, and for some reason, he was now out to prove himself the most dangerous and evil monster in heaven and hell.

Only that she needed to pay attention to him, not you. She sighed again, long and hard. *My death is my own fault. I allowed him to scare me to death. Literally.*

Venn admired this strong woman. She didn't place the blame on others. *That monster would scare anyone.*

She gave an accepting nod. *Well, he's after my Emma. Our Emma. How are you going to stop him?*

He squared his shoulders, let the muscles along his spine realign with the movement. *Emma is my mate. I'll die, relinquish my Guardianship, whatever it takes, before I allow him to harm her. No matter what it takes, I'll find a way.*

And send Io back to hell where he belonged.

"I'm ready to go," Emma announced, startling him. "Can we pick up Izzy and go to your place? I can't stand being around my father right now."

He pulled her into his arms, suppressing a groan and resting his chin on the top of her head. *Mine.* "You're always welcome at my home. I love having you with me."

"You know any good lawyers? I'll need help to stop my father. Grams wouldn't want to stay like this."

She's right about that, Grams said, her wrinkled eyes flashing with concern. *I can wait to be set free. But it would do my heart good to see Emma and her father reconcile before I go.* She sent him a what-are-ya-gonna-do-about-it stare.

Not asking too much of me, are you? Venn sighed.

Grams chuckled again as her shadowy form faded.

20

Her father's rented Lincoln Town Car sat parked on the front lawn. Muddy tracks marked the snow-patched grass where the wheels had missed a bed of daffodils by mere inches. Obviously, he'd positioned the vehicle as close to the house as he could manage. *Wouldn't want to get his shoes dirty.*

As Venn's SUV rolled down the drive and neared the house, apprehension rippled through Emma's middle. The crunch and snap of sticks and rocks beneath the tires only magnified her tension. She wrapped her scarf tighter around her neck. "Pull up at the side door, okay?"

"Sure." He did so and cut the engine. "Want me to come in or wait here?"

"Wait here, please." She paused before closing the car door and tried to smile, pleased that he hadn't automatically assumed she'd need his help. "You can be my getaway car."

He nodded. "You bet."

Inside the living room, her dad occupied the leather recliner where Grandpa used to sit. The seat was tilted back, and he spoke legalese over the phone. Scrambling for that durable power of attorney, most likely. He didn't waste time, did he? The instant he saw her, he righted the chair with a *pop* of the mechanism.

Emma made a beeline for the stairs. As her loafers tapped the rhythm of her ascent, she felt a small victory bloom in her chest. Two minutes into the house and so far, so good.

No questions. No overbearing pressure. No demands.

In her bedroom, she dropped her small suitcase onto the bed and packed it with the things she'd need for the next couple of days. Really, she couldn't think beyond that.

Izzy bounded into the room, tail wagging furiously, his nails clicking on the wood flooring as he entered. He pawed at her legs, begging to be picked up.

"You miss your momma, don't you?" She scooped the dog into her arms and accepted a few wet laps on her chin, curling the furry, wiggling animal into her chest. Circling her fingers in Izzy's coat, she added, "Me too."

A few minutes later, she was set to go, suitcase ready and Izzy tucked in the crook of her arm. Now to make it past the guard once again. She'd gotten in without a fuss, but getting out would require a fight. It always did.

You're being foolish, a little voice inside told her. Facing her father shouldn't be such a big deal.

She drew herself taller. This time it wasn't about her, though. Grams deserved her dignity.

Emma skidded to a stop at the kitchen door, where her father was standing at the counter. She squeezed the handle of the suitcase a little tighter as he dumped a shot of whiskey into a glass of Coke. If ever there was an occasion for a drink at two in the afternoon, this was it. For once she couldn't fault him that.

His gaze darted up. His surprised expression indicated he hadn't heard her approach. He straightened, and his free hand went to his loosened tie, as if realizing his uncharacteristically unkempt appearance. Dark finger-combed hair fell over his forehead. His eyes gleamed, haunted. He clenched his square jaw.

"You're leaving?"

"Yes." For a second, her fear of him turned to sympathy.

"No need." He sipped his drink. "I've already made arrangements. Mom will be moved to Glen Meadow tomorrow."

A spurt of anger supplanted her fear. *He thinks he's won. He thinks I can't do anything about this. I can. I will.*

Emma closed the distance between them, plopping the suitcase on the chair as she passed it. Stopping when they were toe to toe, she tipped her head up to meet his smug gaze. "That is not what she would have wanted, and you know it."

His blue eyes flashed. "She just needs time to recover."

Emma was gratified her voice remained steady, even though she shook inside. "No. She has died. And I will pull the plug myself if I have to."

"You can't. You wouldn't."

"Watch me."

Her father's face turned beet red. He gulped a long draw of booze, and she noted his hand trembling on the glass.

She turned, plucked her suitcase from the chair, and marched toward the exit. At the door, she glanced back and felt a slice of alarm at the emotionless expression in his eyes. But she remained focused on her grandmother. "My lawyer will be contacting you."

He took an intimidating step forward. "You know I will get what I want."

"Not this time." Emma walked out, straight to the open car door Venn had waiting, where he took her bag. As soon as she sat down, the shakes rippled through her.

———

Venn pushed the heel of his hand against the car door and glanced to the ground, where the snow was tamped down by his pacing. He had not been able to wait inside the SUV. It had proved too confining, another barrier between him and Emma should she need his help.

But she had managed all on her own. A grin tugged at the corners of his mouth as he walked around the vehicle and set her suitcase in the back. His mate had fire. With his beyond-human hearing, he'd heard every word between father and daughter. And she hadn't backed down.

He slid behind the wheel, reached over, and squeezed her hand. "You did a fine job."

She exhaled a quivering breath. "I did, didn't I?" After a moment, she turned her head. "You could hear me?"

"I'm a bit more than your average guy, remember?"

"Yes, you are." A sassy twinkle lit her eyes, if only for a moment, and he was pleased to see it.

"We *are* talking about hearing, right?" he teased.

"What else?"

What else, indeed.

On the way to his place, Emma finally gave in to her exhaustion. With her head on the headrest, she fell asleep, Izzy curled in her lap.

Venn drove, swiped his free hand down his face and rubbed two days' worth of beard. They had left his place this morning in such a hurry he hadn't shaved. Again. So much had changed in the course of a day.

Last night had been exquisite. His body responded to the memory, his erection hard and full against his zipper. And she'd wanted him as much as he'd wanted her.

He clenched his jaw, eyeing her between watching the road. He touched her cheek and tenderly pushed a lock of hair off her forehead. *Mine.*

Io had killed his mate's beloved grandmother. The demon had despicable plans even Venn hadn't anticipated.

He gripped the steering wheel harder, with the urge to strangle Io, as he pressed his foot against the accelerator. A slip of fear that ran through him, no matter how hard he tried to suppress it. He damn well better keep her safe.

Venn growled to himself. Desperate. That's what he was.

Argh, he loathed the position.

Io excelled as a manipulator. And didn't evil fiends all have hidden agendas?

But how do I protect someone who doesn't want protection? Doesn't realize the danger? And even though he didn't know the answers to those questions, he knew he could remedy at least part of the problem. He needed to tell her the rest of the story. That Io had killed her before and would probably try to do so again.

But he couldn't sneak her out of town and leave the tree unprotected. He couldn't lock her up, couldn't hide out forever. No, he had to tell her the truth and risk her turning away from him altogether. Just because he knew and felt that intense mating bond didn't mean she did.

Still, there was another part of the equation. Venn replayed Mrs. Grant's words. She'd said Io had rambled about using Emma to kill the tree, something about her alchemist abilities. But how did they relate to each other?

Did Io know something he didn't? Did he have a secret weapon of some kind?

Then the lightbulb moment he'd been searching for occurred.

He had his own secret to draw upon, a connection he shared with the ancient oak. A source of untold preserved information. A friend like no other. Custos.

Perhaps the Divine Tree would give him answers. He was well aware that there were things Custos would share with him, and other things he couldn't or wouldn't. But he wouldn't know until he asked.

The strategy lightened his heart. He'd consult the oak tonight. Satisfied to at least have a plan, he stubbornly veered away from his inner wolf's warning that any bargain would require a sacrifice.

Venn pulled into his garage and took the key from the ignition. He sat there another minute or two, though, watching Emma sleep. Her mouth was parted the slightest bit, and she looked so kissable. God, he wanted to kiss her, hold her, love her.

He gently shook her shoulder. "Hey, sleepyhead. We're home." How he wished this really were her home.

She groaned, peeked about, then bolted straight up in her seat, rousing the dog. "Oh, I fell asleep."

Izzy yipped and walked his front paws up her chest. Venn envied the dog, remembering the soft feel of her breasts against his face.

"You needed the rest." He got out, came around the car, and opened the door for her.

She stepped out with a squirming Izzy, and he grabbed her suitcase from the back.

She walked a few steps, then stopped abruptly, staring at the ceiling. "Oh no," she muttered in a disgusted tone. "I'm not thinking straight."

"What?"

"I should have driven Grams's car."

"Driving and sleeping isn't good for your health, you know."

Her face softened with a tired smile. "I can't have you driving me all over the place."

"Why not?"

"Really. You must have better things to do."

Nothing is as important as keeping you safe.

He gestured behind them, to the far side of the SUV, where the four-car garage housed a Corvette, Mercedes, and a Lexus SUV. "Take your pick. I have cars to spare."

She looked over her shoulder. "You'd trust me with one of those?"

"Of course, I trust you."

"I don't know why." Her eyes glanced upward. "Can't you see this big cloud hanging over me?" She shook her head as he guided her toward the entrance. "I mean . . . my apartment catches fire, my grandmother has an accident and—" she faltered, then swallowed "—and dies, and my thorn-in-the-butt dad, well, we haven't seen the best—or should I say worst—of him yet."

He shrugged and ushered her inside. "I'll take my chances."

"Brave man."

"Speaking of your father . . . You asked about a lawyer. I've called my friend Kianso and left a message. He'll be returning my call."

"That's great." They entered the kitchen. "Mmm. Something smells delicious." Izzy yipped, and Emma held the animal tightly.

"Dinner."

Emma glanced around. "Is it safe to put him down? What about your wolves?"

"They're dogs." Although he had bought them because of their wolf heritage. "I called Henry while I was waiting for you and had him lock the pair of them in my suite. So Izzy isn't in danger." He gave a half-smile, adding, "They wouldn't hurt him regardless. They're very obedient."

She nodded but didn't set the dog down, yet.

"I'll show you to your room. It's across from mine," he said with controlled emphasis, and his heart clenched a little, totally wanting her in *his* room. In *his* bed. In *his* life.

Forever.

21

Venn worried over Emma as he went downstairs and into the kitchen. Her energy level read as a glimmer, a meager wavy line.

"Is everything okay?" Henry asked.

"She's exhausted, and rightfully so. She'll eat dinner in her room."

Venn explained what had transpired during the day while Henry went into action, preparing a tray for her. The butler even added a small bowl of water and food for Izzy. He passed the tray to Venn, who took it upstairs.

"Room service," he murmured, knocking lightly on her door. "I know it's late for dinner, but you need to eat."

She opened the door and let him in. "Thank you," she said. He set the tray on a footstool that also served as a coffee table. Then she was right there with him, slipping into his arms and hugging him, resting her cheek on his chest. "You really know how to take care of a girl."

He slid his hands up and down her back, aware of her tempting curves, aware of the protective tug in his chest, aware of the desire that gnawed at him. He separated from her with the same regret he always had at their parting. "Eat."

As she sat and dug into the food, he took the bowl for

Izzy and set it on the floor. "Henry will feed him more in the morning." He scratched the pup's ears.

Emma nodded and offered Izzy a morsel of her roast. "Thank you, again."

"If you need anything, just ask."

He smiled to her and left her alone to rest. He went to his room, instead, where he paced restless steps along the windows. Henry brought him dinner and left it on the coffee table.

"Sir, may I suggest you take your own advice and eat something?"

Venn nodded his thanks, then made his way to the tray of food, more to appease Henry than due to hunger. "I will be going out shortly. Please keep an ear open for Emma."

Henry pressed his lips into a firm line. "Of course," the butler said, and left.

Although Venn was certain the roast tasted superb, it could have been bark for all the attention he gave it. He cleaned his plate because he needed to feed his beasts, not for enjoyment's sake, all the while tuned in to Emma across the hall.

With the gurgle of water, his hands itched to wash her. With the moan of the mattress as she lay down, he groaned. With the rustle of sheets as she likely settled beneath them, he closed his eyes and imagined her right next to him.

It seemed like a long time before the house was quiet but for the sounds of Emma's deep REM sleep coming from her room.

It was time for Venn to make his way to the tunnel and seek the wisdom of the Divine Tree.

There were times—not many, but a few—when Venn hated going down into the tunnel and underground. He felt like the earth would give way and he'd become buried beneath its crushing weight. As he heard the echo of his steps reverberate off the stone walls, he realized this evening was one of them.

What if Custos didn't have a solution? He slowed his steps, thinking. What if Emma had to die once more and they were doomed to repeat the vicious cycle over and over again? He stopped, his hands sweating, his heart thudding in his chest. What if Custos told him there was no way to save both Emma and the tree?

Reaching for the light, he turned it off and stood utterly still in total darkness. He closed his eyes, opened them. No change. It was difficult to understand which was up or down, left or right, except for the reference to his own body. And that was how life was without Emma. Empty and dark. He had purpose as a guardian, but no light, no love.

There had to be a better answer than losing her again.

His hands shook as he turned on the lamp and resumed walking. He entered the tree, undertook the anointing ritual and wound his way down into the catacombs.

Once inside, he traveled to the center of the room, to a platform created by knotted roots upon which sat the Crown of Knowledge. The uneven combination of high and low wooden spikes, formed in the shape of a crown, shown with a glow of gold and the essence of light. Each spike stood jagged and sharp and irregular, pointing upward, and as far as he could tell, made of a unique substance that was a cross between live and petrified wood.

The tree's usual groaning and scraping sounds, like a house settling, made him feel at home. He chose a spike at random in the circle. Paused. Inhaled.

"How can I help you, Guardian?" The tree's ancient, raspy voice startled him.

"I need answers." He set his jaw.

"You know you should not," Custos admonished.

"I'm well aware of the rules." He also knew this was the only way to obtain information beyond that which the tree would willingly share. And by law, there were limitations as to what could be shared. Venn rolled up his sleeves.

"Guardian, don't," the Divine Tree warned.

Venn positioned his hand over the spike and forced it downward, stabbing his hand with the point. Splinters pierced his skin, each digging far deeper than the inch of flesh it penetrated until tendrils of energy and heat wound through him and converged with his mind and heart and gut. He gritted his teeth at the pain, like a million bees buzzing within him, stinging.

And then he grew numb. Euphoric. The trip of all trips. *Must focus.*

He must remember his purpose. Remember back to the day of Amelia's death. Find a way to save Emma.

Slowly, his memory settled on the day in the park and his final moments with Amelia, as clear as if they were happening in that very moment. No, doubly clear, for he was both spectator and participant.

He silently thanked Custos for directing him to this particular moment. But how long could he hold on? For a time he would be suspended between the two worlds, and he didn't have that long to get the job done. The muscles in his forearm twitched violently in a spasm. What if he didn't seize the right details? His distractions were great, for as much as he needed this information, he was also desperate to get back to Emma.

Pinpricks of light cartwheeled across images of Emma as she was in her previous life. His heart tripped over itself like a stuttering lad, anxious to relive the delight she wrought yet fearful of the shocking outcome.

Her lips pulled into a teasing smile as she accepted the peach he'd plucked from their picnic basket. She sank her teeth into it with sheer joy, the juices running down her delicate chin, and then she passed it back to him. He could smell the sweet bright aroma, taste it as if it were the first peach he'd ever eaten.

He ate from the precise spot she had partaken of and passed it back to her. She repeated the ritual, and on taking his turn again, he could taste Amelia's flavor laced with peaches. Exquisite.

Venn squeezed his eyes shut and breathed in.

On a level separate from that of his trance—in the "real world"—a gust of cool air brushed the back of his shoulder. Venn ignored the sensation. He needed to stay with the memory. He needed whatever information the tree was about to impart.

He tightened his hand on the wooden shard. His palm grew wetter as blood oozed between the joint junctures and trickled over his knuckles.

Amelia stood. "Let's dance. Here, on the green carpet of grass. You are my knight, and I your lady." She stepped from the quilted spread and waltzed in a circle, her skirts billowing outward. With a theatrical show, she faced the tree and dropped to a low curtsy. "My king."

Venn's eyes widened at a detail he'd forgotten. They had been speaking of the Middle Ages. Of knights and kings and dragons and castles and ancient traditions. A time he had actually lived through that didn't possess nearly the romance she'd imagined.

As she turned back to him, her smile was infectious. He was ready to join her play.

Another wisp of cold air struck his back.

Again, he ignored it.

He swallowed hard. Next, she would die. As impossible as it was not to close his eyes, as much as he longed to deny and separate himself, he stood firm with the task of reliving what he knew would come. He deserved the agony. To torture himself once more. To make certain he didn't forget he'd failed to protect her. To make certain he didn't forget how deadly Io was. As if he could actually forget.

Emma's eyes met his, her face warm, loving, playful. Then the arrow sailed from out of nowhere and pierced her breast. Stunned incomprehension erased her lovely smile as she glanced down at the arrow, then up at him.

The seconds elongated. Her eyes were huge, sorrowful, and eventually perceptive as she realized her fate.

"Nooo!" The guttural, wounded scream burst from his lips and oddly echoed within the tree as if it happened in real time.

He saw himself dart to her, faster than humanly possible, as he caught her before she touched the ground. He knelt and cradled her in his arms. There was no healing her. The blade of the arrow jutted from her back, having gone clear through. Her blood flowed from the wound.

Terror clutched his heart. Helpless, he smoothed her hair and declared his love.

Helpless, he bargained with the Divine Tree, with God, with Fate.

Helpless, he watched her die.

But why?

Must have answers.

He grabbed another spike, with his left hand this time, and shoved downward once more. Maybe the more surface involved, the deeper he'd be able to tap into the tree's knowledge. At this rate, his entire body could end up pierced.

"Venn, stop. You're not allowed to use the tree for your gain," Seth uttered in a biting, disapproving tone.

The gravelly warning hurled from behind made Venn stiffen. Had the archangel followed him, or was it his natural, impeccable sense of timing that brought him here? "Go. Away," he said through clenched teeth.

Tears wet Venn's eyes, just as tears had wet his cheeks

those centuries ago. Only now, looking at it from afar, he noticed an odd phenomenon. Something he had not detected in the agonizing moments following Amelia's death.

On the red-stained ground beneath his mate, the roots of the tree moved and grew and multiplied.

The Divine Tree released a rustling sigh, filled with awe. "You see, Guardian. *She* anointed *me* with her blood. And in the process, it changed all three of us."

The statement was shocking, but more than the declaration, it was what the tree didn't say that bothered him. Had a bond formed between the oak and Emma? Was that admiration in Custos's voice?

"Well, Shakespeare's eyes," Seth choked out. "So that's what's different about Emma."

Venn jerked his hands free, disregarding the burn and throb and blood, ignoring the pain-in-the-ass angel. An immutable measure of jealousy swept through him like the north wind of the old country.

All along the tree had something Venn had not: a part of Amelia.

The sour taste of resentment spread into his gut, quickly and illogically. His heartbeat amplified in his head, and his beasts clawed to get out. He needed to calm down.

"I wanted her to return, also," the Divine Tree divulged. "Sad. So much knowledge and no power."

"So that's why you requested that I bring her back. You used me," Seth muttered with annoyance to the tree. Then he tossed Venn a piece of cloth that had mysteriously materialized from out of nowhere. "Here. You're bleeding all over the place."

Venn nodded his thanks and dabbed at his hands, still trying to absorb the information.

"Let me get this straight. You wanted to bring Amelia back, so you persuaded Seth to make it happen," Venn asked Custos, incredulous. Then he turned to Seth, "And since archangels have special privileges and powers you—"

"I did it for you." The angel jabbed his finger at Venn. "Custos made the suggestion."

A rumble of laughter shook the oak. "Favorites."

Seth scowled.

Venn had known for a long time that he got along with Seth better than most of his brothers did. After their bumpy beginning, they shared the chemistry of good friends.

But the tree . . . How was it that it laughed and expressed emotions? Why hadn't he noticed that before?

Was it possible the tree had . . . feelings? Had Custos kept that hidden all this time?

Venn met Seth's stare as the questions settled on him with angst-ridden uncertainty. He needed time to sort this out, and maybe Seth could help. How could he use the information about Amelia's murder to protect Emma? With a groan, he stretched his sore muscles.

"I still don't know how to stop Io? There must be a way."

The tree rustled and shook, saying woefully, "How do you capture the wind? Or kill the rain? How do you control the tornado? Or harness a hurricane?"

"You're saying that it can't be done?" Venn asked, trying to keep his tone level.

"Not under normal circumstances."

Seth shook his head.

He looked about. Here, inside the Divine Tree, was not the place for that discussion. The air suddenly grew warm and clingy, claustrophobic.

What should he say to the Divine Tree? *Thank you for sharing. Forgive me for breaking Guardian Law.*

With the cloth Seth had given him, he cleaned his blood from the spike as best he could. But the tree stopped him, saying, "Don't. You have done enough."

Venn decided not to dwell on the tree at the moment

as he guided Seth to the exit hall.

When he arrived at the tunnel arch, he paused and turned back. Staring at the place where his blood stained the spiky crown, he wondered if his bond with the oak was also changed, deepened. It stood to reason that if Amelia's blood forged a connection, then his might have, as well, or perhaps it already had centuries ago and he'd never realized it. From the beginning Guardians were amalgamated to their trees. So it was difficult to tell.

"Custos," he called out. "Thank you, my friend, for allowing me to share your knowledge."

"You are welcome." The voice practically glowed with satisfaction.

———————

"I'm starving," Seth announced when they were in the tunnel near the garage.

"No surprise. You're always hungry. I take it you want company?" Venn said, despite the fact his stomach didn't feel too happy. He checked his watch. Eleven-thirty.

Seth straightened. "Lasagna at Marco's?"

"Too late."

"Bella's?"

"Also closed."

Seth's wings sagged. "I'll never master human time. I bet they're eating breakfast in Florence right now."

"Probably. Come on. We'll find something."

Venn's initial idea was to head home, where Henry could whip up a delicious snack. Only Emma slept there now, which increased the likelihood of her walking in on their conversation.

Seth and Emma in the same room . . . not what he had in mind.

She wasn't ready for that conversation, yet, and neither was he.

Then he remembered that the diner near the hospital was open all night. No gourmet cuisine, but at least it was better than a fast-food joint. And he'd buy the angel whatever he wanted in order to get him involved in some serious brainstorming.

With his wings hidden, Seth looked like an aging rock star, a little rough around the edges, his black braids tied at his collar. Venn led the way to a dimly lit booth in the back corner, as far as he could get from other customers. In fact, there wasn't anyone else on this side of the restaurant.

Perfect.

After a glance at the menu, Seth ordered a plate of way too many eggs and a lot of pork. Then again, neither of them had to worry about their health. One of the perks of immortality.

"Why are you here, anyway?" Venn asked. "Am I in trouble again?"

"You've been the difficult one from the beginning." Seth slid the saltshaker between his palms, passing it across the table like a hockey puck. "What do you think is happening with the tree?"

Venn blew out a frustrated breath. "Like I have all the universal knowledge that you're supposed to possess."

"I think you're getting me confused with the Divine Tree." Seth raised an eyebrow. "We both saw something in that chamber. Let's exchange notes."

Venn nodded. "Obviously, Emma's change has to do with her blood seeping into the Divine Tree's roots. Custos said as much. So perhaps her talent of manipulating metal, one Amelia didn't possess, is the result of a connection to the tree."

"It explains why Emma changed the tree but not the other way around," Seth added quietly.

"Somehow during her reincarnation, she received alchemy powers over metal."

"Did you catch how the roots grew and altered beneath

her?" Seth asked.

"I did." The scrape of the shaker along the tabletop grated Venn's nerves like sandpaper. "Will you put that away?"

Seth pushed the container aside, folded his hands, and propped his chin on them, leaning elbows on table. The pose looked quite angelic. If a pirate could pull off angelic.

"So her blood formed a bond between them," Seth stated.

"Is it possible that she has a connection with the tree that's similar to the Guardians'? Meaning, if she dies, the tree dies."

"And therefore *you* die, as well."

"Now there's an idea that would ring Io's bell." Venn glanced across the room. What exactly did Io know? "That kind of theory is too dangerous to even speak of."

The waitress returned with coffee. Seth leaned back in his seat until she left. "Right. Then how do we discover the scope of their relationship?"

"I've explained to her my role as Guardian. She knows about the tree, my shape-shifting, immortality, everything—except where Io is concerned."

"Perhaps you'd better tell her the rest soon."

He was dreading that conversation. Everything depended on the outcome. It could bring them closer together, or she could flee. He wanted to believe her soul would recognize the truth, but when it came to dealing with demons, things could get pretty mixed up. Including your head.

His thoughts turned to the bond they each had with Custos. Somehow Emma's blood had made the tree's emotions come alive. Venn would bet on it. And then the tree had a part in Emma's reincarnation. An action that led him to believe it liked Emma. Or perhaps loved her. And he wondered how far those sentiments went. How far would it go to please her?

The waitress brought their food, and Venn followed Seth's lead and dug in. "I'm not sure what Io's intentions are, but this could be bigger than I thought," Venn said between bites.

On a TV positioned just below the ceiling in the corner, a world news reporter's voice saddened, growing heavy with extra emphasis regarding the horror of the current story. Seth pointed his fork toward the television. "Hear that? They're after a child trafficking ring." He shook his head, ate a slice of bacon and licked his fingers. "Sick. This evil shit is killing us. Got to stop it."

. 22 .

It was three in the morning by the time Venn directed Seth to the kitchen refrigerator and opened the door. "Help yourself. Henry gets off on culinary creations, and I'm sure he'll appreciate a connoisseur in the house."

Seth's eyes lit at the sight of labeled containers. "Heaven."

Venn grabbed a bottle of water. "You should know."

They shared an offbeat snicker.

Angling the bottle up the stairs, Venn said, "The suite to the far right has your name on it."

"Thanks. I'll hang here for a bit. If that's all right."

"Suit yourself."

As he climbed the stairs, he heard the *chink* of corning against granite. He grinned. That archangel had a bottomless stomach and an overflowing heart.

When Venn reached the upper hall, he paused between Emma's room and his own. The thought of slipping in bed beside her tugged at him, but she needed her rest. Resisting the temptation, he opened the door of his room to a surprise. Emma stood at the vast group of windows, with Izzy wrapped in her arms.

A sliver of moonlight slipped in through the window, forming a misshaped triangular pattern on the floor near her feet. "I hope you don't mind. I couldn't sleep." She set Izzy down. "I adore this view and—"

"I'm glad you're here." His heart banged against his rib cage, coursing blood throughout his body, including down south. In a few strides he stood behind her, slipped his arms around her waist, and encouraged her to lean back against him.

They stood there, absorbing the silent scene unfolding outdoors. The wolf dogs were wandering near the tree line of the woods, sniffing. Venn could sense their communication over a rabbit. He'd allowed them to roam more freely with the threat Io represented. If something were amiss, Venn would know through his pack.

A glimmer of fear sliced through him at the thought of Io being that bold.

"Tell me," Emma said. "There's something you need to say."

"We'll get to that in a moment."

She turned in his arms to look at him, then wound her arms round him like a vine on a trellis. With a sigh, she rested her head in the hollow of his shoulder. "You're good at avoiding things, you know."

"What's keeping you awake?" he asked.

"So many things."

"Your grandmother?"

"Yes. But also I have this huge sense of foreboding . . . I don't know why." She shook her head, confused. "The vision I have of me dying morphed into a dream that woke me. But this time it was different. This time you and Grams were there, telling me to run."

She shivered, and he took her hand, leading the way to the love seat in the sitting area. He gathered her into his lap, kneaded the length of her elegant neck, and then her shoulders. "Perhaps if I explain a few things, then you might understand what's going on."

The gibbous moon shone through the windows, and given the lower angle of the sofa, it was visible from where they sat as it eased behind a cloud cluster. He ran his hand over her shoulder and up her neck, moving her fiery hair away from her face with his thumb. "It's time I tell you everything."

She eased away from him until her back nudged the armrest. She folded her legs so she could loosely wrap her hands around shins and pushed her toes beneath his thigh to warm them. She was going for being in control and relaxed, but that was such a lie.

His chest rose and fell as if he were bracing himself, as if on the intake of air he could smell the scent of her emotions, perhaps the aroma of her unease now. Ever since she'd learned he was a shifter, she'd understood he possessed animal instincts that set him apart from other men.

As Venn spoke of archangels and the tree of life and Immortal Guardians, the spring within her rib cage coiled tighter and tighter.

"Emma, I believe you've struggled with this your entire life because it's part of you. You are Amelia reincarnated."

His words took life in the strangest way, touching her heart and discharging that mechanism holding her life in place. "Yes. I've felt her connection for a long time. But I just wasn't sure about who she was." She paused, swallowing. The core of frustration at being abnormal spun away in an exhaled breath of acceptance. She'd come to terms with her differences some time ago, but still, it was easy to slip back into doubts.

"So I am Amelia reincarnated?" she whispered hesitantly, her tone saying she didn't quite want to believe it, yet understood that what he said was true.

"That's right."

To an ordinary person, this would all seem farfetched,

but to her it made perfect sense. It explained why she was different, why she had visions and dreams, why she'd felt connected to Venn from the very beginning.

Even still, her heartbeat escalated and thrummed in her ears. With slow blinks, she summoned glimpsed images of Amelia and Venn at the river cottage, of them making love, of them riding at the country estate, and each was like a memory with a cluster of sensations and smells to accompany it. The images wove together with memories of the tree and of her dying. A glimpse of *her* life as Amelia. It was all too much.

Run. The instinct weighed on her, nearly irrepressible, and she fled the sofa and the warmth of his nearness. At the massive windows, when she could go no farther, she stopped. Only the glass prevented her escape.

To her amazement, Venn didn't chase her. He remained where she'd left him. He gave her space and time to process.

Little by little the truth filled the empty holes in her soul. The odd things in her world became clearer. The reason her life was so bizarre in the first place. The dreams and visions and her hot hands. With the last thought, she glanced at her palms.

"Did Amelia have the same talent for melting metal?" she asked.

"No. That seems to be uniquely your talent. Although, I believe it has something to do with your bond with Custos."

A slip of unease blossomed in her chest, and she touched her fingers to her sternum. At least that was something uniquely her own. "Custos?"

"The Divine Tree."

She nodded in tentative recognition. The first day she'd returned, there had been a strange yearning when she'd arrived at the tree.

At last, she held her hand out to Venn in silent acceptance. In no time, he was there, wrapping her in his strong arms. Corded muscles flexed beneath her hand as she palmed from bicep to shoulder. His fingers tantalized her as he eased the hair away from her forehead and slipped the strands behind her ear.

She slowly turned in his arms, anticipating his full embrace, searching the reassuring familiarity revealed in his eyes. He pressed his lips to her brow. A feeling of coming home soothed her tattered nerves. As his mouth brushed her cheek, a hot flush of excitement fanned her core and made her legs go weak. He kissed her long and hard, and with more passion than she'd ever thought possible. A blaze ignited within her that only he could trigger. Only Venn. It exploded, a spontaneous combustion, a flame of woven energy, like the way body and soul and minds intertwine.

And she wanted all of him—hot wild sex, his secrets, his acceptance, his love.

With that one spectacular kiss, they shared an awareness that she *knew* transfixed him, too. She felt his body quake, a hungry growl of impatience rumbling in his throat, and he tugged her tighter against the length of his body. She answered his possessive pull by burrowing her fingers into his taut, muscular back. As fire consumes oxygen and intensifies, the exchange established a deeper connection that she could literally feel in every cell of her body, as if she'd taken a part of him into herself.

When the kiss ended, she opened her eyes, knowing that as solder melds to metal, part of her was bonded to this Guardian. The question was, what did that mean for their relationship? For their future? He was immortal, after all.

Relationship. She let the word roll around in her mind. It was the very thing she avoided much of the time. She gazed out the window at the coming day, as pink lightened the sky and streaks of morning-kissed clouds fashioned an iridescent canopy above the trees.

Her pulse gradually calmed. Venn slipped an arm

around her back and along her waist, and she hugged him at her side with both arms. She rested her head on his shoulder. The sky turned a shade brighter, and she followed the lines of the trees to admire the magnificent landscape. She could see a pair of wolves near the fountain below, gazing up at her with intent, glowing eyes. Expectantly, she thought.

"You have wolves?"

"Yes. They're a special breed. That's Glen and Loch."

On the lawn, standing alongside the wolves, stood a tall, rugged man. A security light seemed to spotlight him.

"And who is that?" she asked.

Venn glanced after her. "Seth. The archangel who set me on this path."

It should surprise her, but it didn't. She wasn't sure anything could anymore. "Oh. An angel? That guy who scowls a lot? He looks very angry."

"Yes. No doubt he is."

Venn and Emma showered and dressed and were in the kitchen as the sun crested the trees. Seth shuffled in moments later.

"Coffee?" he asked as she set her purse and phone on the table.

"Please."

Henry entered the room, heading straight to the fridge. "Are you up for a hearty breakfast?"

"I believe we're going for something quick." Venn gave Emma a questioning look as he set coffee and cream in front of her.

She nodded in confirmation.

Henry removed several items, grabbed some plates, and took it all to the table. He unwrapped a loaf of banana bread, then offered a slice to Seth. The angel declined.

Venn realized the depth of Seth's ire when the angel refused the food. Wisps of steam rolled off Seth's wings, which he couldn't retract while angry. Venn had forgotten that detail. It had been centuries since he'd witnessed the likes of this temper tantrum. All because he didn't do as he was told and share everything with Emma about Io's true purpose.

He surmised Seth's irritation had been boiling while he and Emma had been preparing for the day. Now the geyser was about to blow.

Emma sat at the table, nibbling a bagel like a nervous mouse, her eyes round and watchful. Obviously, she wasn't sure about this angel business.

Seth paced the kitchen, then advanced into Venn's personal space. "You ass. You omitted the most important detail of the story."

Exactly, and now the angel intended to ruin things. "What's the point? She has no defense against him," Venn growled, expelling some of the frustration over how to keep Emma safe. He glanced sideways to catch her shocked expression. He struggled to regain control of himself and added in a low voice so she wouldn't hear, "She's suffered enough over her grandmother. I'll not add to it."

"You must."

"No."

"It has to be done."

She'll hate me. Venn understood all too well what Seth wanted him to do. However, telling Emma that Io had caused her grandmother's death seemed cruel and pointless. "Damn it, knowing will make not a whit of difference."

Seth blew out an irritated breath and mumbled under his breath. "It will save the tree. She needs to decline whatever plan Io has in mind. She can't make the right choice if she's not informed."

"Damn you." Venn smacked his cup down on the counter so hard that coffee sloshed over the rim.

Henry hesitated mid-stride as he neared the table.

"Guys," Emma rose. "While I can't say I understand your dilemma, I know one thing for certain. I need to speak with a lawyer who can stop my father. So I'm going to just . . ." Her voice trailed off, clearly uncomfortable.

Venn shoved his hands in his pockets, checking for his cell phone. "I have that covered, remember? Kianso will meet you this afternoon wherever you chose. All I have to do is let him know."

She smiled and crossed the few feet to him. Placing her hand to his cheek, she kissed him. "Thank you. I can meet him at his office."

"No problem."

Seth turned away, and she gave a slight smile. "If you'll excuse me, then, gentlemen, I should stop by Grams's house and see if I can find a copy of her living will."

"I'll meet you there. If need be, I can distract your dad while you look."

She glared at him. "No. You've done too much already."

"I hate the thought of you being alone."

"I'll be fine."

He clamped his lips shut, resisting the urge to hold her back. He had every intention of following her.

A few minutes later, he watched her pull out of his garage in the Mercedes. He couldn't care less about the car, but the tension resonating within him was all about her safety. Io most likely wasn't watching Venn's place; his wolves would have alerted him if the beast lurked near. So he tried to convince himself all was well but didn't succeed.

Something was off. He couldn't put his finger on what, though.

He returned to the kitchen where Seth lounged against the counter with his arms folded over his chest. His glare had the force of an earthquake shaking the room. With Emma gone, the archangel no longer held himself in check. Unfazed, Venn set his coffee cup in the sink.

"Okay. Let's do this." The intricacies of dealing with an irate angel didn't escape him. Seth could make one's life damn miserable. Even a Guardian's. On the other hand, Seth couldn't do anything that would hinder Venn's position as protector.

Seth made a show of expanding and relaxing his wings, which resembled taking a long slow breath. So theatrical.

"You can't fathom the drama I can wield," Seth bit out.

"Seen you in action, man. I know." Venn moved closer and folded his arms, prepared for a face-off. "What's the deal?"

"Open your eyes, Guardian. I think your plan is to do nothing so Io will leave her alone. And then whatever Io's plan is, it will succeed. You can't choose Emma over the tree. Too many other people are bound to die."

"I'm not." Still, he erected a barrier to his thoughts in an evasive move. He planned to keep both Emma and the tree. He just wasn't sure how yet.

"Right. Which is why you're shutting yourself off from me," Seth said, then waved a hand. "Never mind. The point is, you must tell her about Io so she can thwart whatever plan he has her involved in."

"Trust me. I have it under control."

"God, you're blind." Seth shoved his hand past Venn, grabbed a stack of banana bread slices off the plate, then poofed it with a few sparks of light. "Tell. Her. About the demon."

Venn fisted his hands at the last bright flicker. Interfering archangel. Couldn't he see that Emma was like a starved person: Feed her too much or too fast and she'd puke it all back up. It killed him to go slow with her when all he wanted was to have her accept their relationship and return his love. That wouldn't happen if she knew about Io, knew that it was because of Venn and the tree that her grandmother was dead.

No. There would be time for her to deal with Io, and

she would not do so alone. Not if it were the last thing Venn did. With that thought, he impatiently changed into his wolf form to book it to the Grant home.

———————

Io caught the essence of Emma as he flew in his owl form and followed that imprint until he found the car she drove. From afar, he tracked her, realizing she was going in the direction of her grandmother's place. And, for once, Venn was not with her.

He landed on a nearby lamppost when she finally parked. She remained in the car, though, and he screeched long and loud, but she didn't even look his way. That she paid him no mind irked the hell out of him. Didn't she know he held the power of life or death over everything she held dear?

He heard the snap of the brush below and winged his way to a high, dense pine. The wolf loped from the forest shadows and approached the car. He should've known Venn wouldn't be far behind.

. 23 .

Arriving at her grandmother's house, Emma switched off the ignition and sat apprehensively in the car with her hands gripping the steering wheel. She stared out the windshield at the evergreen tree in the center of the yard. It reminded her of Grams, who grew pecan trees but loved tall, dignified pines the most.

Emma had the incredible urge to clutch the prickly needles in her hand and inhale their clean fragrance.

She drew a long slow breath. The enormity of the tasks ahead weighed on her. The alone time during the drive had allowed her mind to wander from the delectable feelings she was experiencing with Venn to the weirder-than-weird angel and mystical tree, to her father's hard-nosed repudiation. God, her life had always possessed an element of the strange, but instead of improving and moving away from that, now she was being sucked down a whirlpool, dousing her inner flame.

She needed to get on with it.

Praying that at least this next task would happen without too much difficulty, she exited the car, walked around the front bumper, and stopped short. From the shadows of the trees, golden eyes stared back at her. The thought of it being Venn was spontaneous; the spark in her heart told her it was him. "You're incredibly fast."

He altered into a man while advancing toward her. Yes, her support team had arrived. He immediately draped an arm around her as he guided her to the side door of the house. "You'll get used to that."

His warm hand squeezed her shoulder. Well, she could definitely get used to his touch, which was often possessive, gentle, and endearing. Some of her tension evaporated in an instant.

"Aren't you worried someone will see you change?" she asked.

One magnificent, solid shoulder rose and fell in careless disregard. "No windows on this side of the house. Plus, I can sense when others are near."

"Oh," she said, realizing he absorbed far more about their surroundings than she did.

Her father's car wasn't in the drive, but she didn't know how long that reprieve would last, so she didn't have time to dally. As they walked through the kitchen, the grandfather clock chimed ten o'clock.

Her grandmother was extremely neat. The floors had to be swept so not a speck of sand was tracked in, all the knickknacks gleamed without dust, and her bed was made first thing every morning. Her one failing had been paperwork. Tucked in an alcove off the kitchen, a computer sat on a desk surrounded by stacks of envelopes, decorative boxes of varied sizes, notebooks, and clutter. A filing cabinet ran up each side of the desk.

"I think she would have kept important papers upstairs," Emma said as she looked at the mess. She turned to trek up the stairs, Venn close behind her. There was a measure of comfort in having him along, yet at the same time, she wanted to absorb the essence of her grandmother, which on some level he distracted her from. It felt strange walking through the house knowing that she would never hear Grams fussing in the kitchen again or calling Izzy and scolding the little dog she'd loved so much.

When Emma walked into the spare room—the project room, her grandmother had dubbed it—her heart sank. "He's already rifled through this," she said, swiping her palm over her brow. The boxes and file cabinets had obviously been moved. Some were stacked on the sewing table, and files were strewn about.

"We should go through it, anyway. You don't know if he found what he was looking for."

She nodded. "You're right."

Emma realized immediately the enormity of the task. Grams saved *everything*.

Nostalgia washed over her when she came to a folder of mementos she'd sent her grandmother. Pictures of Emma at a chorus concert, of her high school art projects and awards, of homecoming, of Paris. There was even a copy of the children's book that she and her dad used to read with Grams, *Forever My Child*. She closed the folder, choking back salty tears. She didn't have time to cry; her father could be home any minute. She swallowed hard and pressed on to the next folder.

She and Venn fell into an effective rhythm of going through an envelope or folder and setting it in a "checked" stack over in the corner. She also made a stack on the sewing table of stuff she'd like to go through again at her leisure.

One large, yellowed envelope caused her breath to hitch as she pulled the contents out.

"What is it?" Venn asked.

"My grandfather's things." She thumbed through the items. "His discharge papers from the service, some medals, pages of family genealogy, and a picture of my grandparents' wedding." The connection to the past was palpable, a transparent thread perceivable and distinct like stitches over a wound that had been stretched too far. Emma palmed the back of her neck and put the envelope in the sewing-table pile.

"That's it," Venn said, closing the last folder. "We've gone through everything in here. Where else?"

It meant a lot to her that Venn didn't immediately give up. "Let's check her room, then we'll move back downstairs."

Emma wasn't prepared for the onslaught of emotion that struck her when she entered Grams's bedroom. The fragrance of Chanel No. 5 hit her like a frying pan to the nose, causing a gripping pain in her chest, eliciting instantaneous tears, regret, and a longing to have those spry arms embrace her in a zestful hug. But that would never, ever happen again.

Oh, God.

She gulped air in an effort to control her reaction, and Venn was right there, gathering her in his strong arms, running a soothing hand over her head and cheek, and crooning words of comfort. And for once in her life, after all the years of trying to bind and hold in her feelings so she didn't do something inadvertently stupid like melting her grandmother's key fob—the flash of memory of that latest slipup brought a blitz of fresh tears—she let go.

But she didn't just weep. No. A guttural sound tore from her throat. Energy simmered and boiled from within her heart, frothing outward like molten lava, spilling into her limbs. Her hands grew extremely hot and glowed red.

Venn didn't shush her or try to make her stop. Instead, he held her to his chest, even though his flesh must have burned from where she wrapped her arms tightly about him. Then the strangest thing happened as she drew back to look into his eyes. He captured her mouth with his ready lips, in a kiss that wasn't sensual or sexual in nature but that drew her pain from her and absorbed it within him. Oddly, she sensed what he was doing by drawing the agony from her, in the way sucking snake poison from a wound relieves the hurt and pressure. It was a lifesaving tactic.

Moments later, she pulled back, fully aware of what had transpired. She drew an enormous cleansing breath, feeling refreshed, at once able to see clearly once more. "How did you do that?" she asked.

"I don't know. I've never done it before."

"It was amazing."

He shrugged. "You were in such pain. I had to do something. It was a gut reaction."

She inhaled deeply. "Well, it worked."

He smiled at her and kissed her forehead gently. "Good."

"Let me take a quick look in the closet and we'll be done up here."

"Okay." He nodded and stepped away from her.

"Ugh. Your clothes," she said when she looked back at him.

He glanced down his chest as she took in the charred remnants clinging to his skin. "I have plenty of others." And he plucked the fabric away, taking a bit of flesh with each piece. Before her eyes, though, the lesions immediately began to dry up and heal, until they disappeared completely. With cautious strokes, she smoothed her fingers over his pecs and ribs, where not a mark remained.

Her eyes slid up to meet his, her voice still thick with tears. "We truly are meant to be together, aren't we?"

"Yes. We are."

Venn tensed, the muscles in his back bunching.

"What's wrong?" she asked, worry creasing her brow.

"If you're going to check in here, I suggest you hurry."

She didn't question him but went straight to the closet. If Grams hid anything in her room, this is where it would be. So Emma dug around, opening every hat and shoe box.

Nothing.

When Emma turned from the closet, she found Venn staring out the window, his palms braced on either side of the frame, as if he were ready to hurl himself through it at any second.

"My father's coming?"

He turned his head, and their eyes met. "Yes."

In tandem, they rushed toward the door and ran downstairs. Emma moved straight to the desk and made a quick last-ditch effort to rummage through the items there. Venn entered into the kitchen and headed for the door.

"Don't hurt him," she cried.

"I just plan to stall him," he said as he exited the house.

She glimpsed him change into a hawk and flap his powerful wings up into the sky.

A shriek cut through the silence. Emma didn't dare take another second to contemplate what might happen out there. She refocused on her task at hand. If she didn't find a living will, what else could help her case?

She heard a car door slam shut at the front of the house. Her gaze swept the area near the laptop as her father fussed and cursed from outside.

Her heart raced, and wisps of steam emanated from her palms. She gathered the laptop, an address book, and her grandmother's purse into her arms and fled outside to Venn's Mercedes.

After depositing her armload on the floorboard of the car, she glanced around. The scraping sound of her father's feet losing purchase directed her attention to him, in time to see him backpedal and fall to the snow-damp earth.

"I'm going to get my rifle and shoot that bird," he bit out. "Watch out," he warned his daughter.

But the hawk flew past Emma without any notice. It dove after her father every time it flew past.

"What the hell." Her dad stood, frowning.

Venn must have thought his aggressive attack had served its purpose, because after a final menacing flyby, he perched atop a tall post that sported an old-fashioned, black dinner bell.

"I was looking for Grams's living will, Dad," she told him, holding her chin up high.

He stood, brushing dirt off his jacket, and glared at her.

She glowered back. "Dad?" He gave her that courtroom look that she detested. "Did you find it? The place had already been gone through, so I know you were searching."

"Why are you fighting me on this?" It wasn't a question he really expected an answer to, and she knew it. He shook his head. "Yes, I found it, and a lawyer is working on having it voided as we speak."

Emma gripped the car's metal door handle, ready to jerk it open and leave. The material turned pliable beneath her fingers, but she tried to ignore it. There was no point whatsoever in arguing, or pleading, or trying to persuade her father to change his mind. She'd learned long ago there was no swaying him.

"You never trusted my judgment," she said, instead. "Maybe it's because I'm different. Or perhaps I'm just not the daughter you had hoped for."

"Emma, please, listen to reason. We have to give her a chance to heal."

She glanced down, horrified as she realized she'd melted the handle right off Venn's beautiful car. Without skipping a beat, she marched around the car, opened the passenger-side door, climbed across the seat and console, and slid behind the steering wheel.

Fury rushed through her as she stepped on the brake and pushed the car's auto button to start the ignition. Damn him if he thought she was going to cave to his whims. Grams deserved her dignity, and her wishes *would* be respected.

Venn flew above the Mercedes as Emma drove. He gave her the space he thought she needed to cool down. The escalation of her metal manipulation concerned him. He'd watched how effortlessly she'd fired up the handle of his car and had experienced firsthand the heat that came from those hands. He needed an explanation for what was happening to her, and even though the Divine Tree had given him some clues, the answers were far from concrete.

Did she notice the intensifying level of heat in her hands? He wondered if it had anything to do with her relationship with him, or the tree, or Io.

Exactly what was going on between Emma and Io, anyway? Did Io realize the connection between Emma and the tree? Even the thought made Venn's blood run cold with fear. The potential danger to Emma multiplied astronomically if Io learned he could actually reach the tree or him through Emma.

He sternly reminded himself that this was about more than the pain of losing her, as pronounced and horrible as that would be; it could mean the death of the Divine Tree. Which meant the lives of far more people were at stake, and that the course of humanity would change for the worse. He couldn't allow that to happen.

After several miles, Emma pulled the car off the road and stopped. Venn banked in a tight circle, then dipped low to the ground, transforming from hawk to human as his feet hit the ground running. He came to a halt alongside the passenger-side door and jerked it open. "Are you all right?"

Emma rested her brow on the backs of her hands as they still gripped the steering wheel in a strangled hold. Seconds passed, and she didn't respond, and even though Venn could hear her labored breathing and smell the scent of her anxiety, he also knew she was holding herself together.

"I feel as though every atom inside me is on the verge of imploding," she said softly.

"I understand. Believe me. The circumstances were different, but . . . when you died, I—"

Her head reeled back. "Then, yes, you get where I'm

coming from. To me, she's already gone. And it hurts so much."

It was a morbid link they shared—a loved one dying—but he'd endured the same type of agony and confusion she must be feeling at this moment. And he wouldn't wish it on anyone.

"I'm sorry to say, it will be a while before things improve." It had been a long, long while for him.

She reached out for him, and he clasped her hand firmly within his. "Thank you for being here," she whispered. With a sad smile she reclined against the seat and closed her eyes.

He longed to hold her in his arms and stroke her hair and tell her everything would be okay.

Every now and then a blast of air shook the car as a vehicle flew by them, heading toward town. But Venn merely sat there, waiting for Emma to recover. Finally, she dragged her hand from his, straightened, and regarded him with a quizzical brow. "I grabbed Grams's address book—thought it may give us her lawyer's contact information. I also got her purse and her cell phone. Plus, the computer. Surely, somewhere in all that, we can figure out where she may have kept her important papers."

"Excellent. You're pretty good at this."

The dry glance she shot him revealed his attempt at humor had missed its mark.

She took a deep breath. "Where do you suggest we review this information?"

"Kianso Oka's law office. He is expecting us."

She nodded her agreement, put the car in gear, and took off. "Sorry about the door handle," she said, shaking her head.

"We'll have to work on those hot hands."

"My grandmother used to say almost the same thing."

He grimaced inwardly, not wanting to return to that sensitive subject before he had to. "I can see why. But don't worry. I'll have the repair shop pick it up and fix it."

For a while, he directed her toward the law office while also thumbing through the address book. "I found an address and phone number for her lawyer," he murmured. Perhaps they'd caught a lucky break.

He didn't know if it'd be the right one, but he was staying far away from dangerous subjects like hospice centers or turning off life support. They would be dealing with all that soon enough.

24

Law offices generally emitted a lemony, polished odor Emma instantly associated with her father. The reminder gripped her stomach and caused a queasiness to set in as soon as she entered the sun-filled atrium foyer. Without actually intending to, she moved closer to Venn.

He introduced her to Kianso Oka, a man in his mid-thirties with dark hair worn in a flat, cropped hairstyle. He had a roundish, yet rectangular, face, pinned-back ears, and wore glasses. His eyes crinkled with mischief as he greeted them. His brisk handshake and easy manner melted her tension away instantly. No stuffy pretense with this guy.

"I'm sorry about your grandmother," he said.

"Thank you. And I appreciate you meeting with us."

His mouth pulled into a tight-lipped smile. "Let's go in my office."

When they were inside and seated, Emma set her grandmother's items on the desk. Venn added the computer, saying, "I've already filled Kianso in on what has transpired up until this morning."

She nodded. "My father told me today that he found my grandmother's living will and gave it to his lawyer to have it overturned. In the meantime, my grandmother has been moved to a hospice facility. The hospital wouldn't honor her DNR request because they're afraid of being sued by my dad. Can I stop him?"

Kianso tipped back in his leather armchair and rocked several times. "This is a very tricky situation, and the medical community, although they don't like it, usually will surrender to the person advocating life. The bottom line is that a dead person can't sue. Your best recourse is to convince your father to change his mind."

Emma's heart sank. She glanced between the men, setting her jaw firmly, and came to a decision. She would pull the plug herself if she had to.

"I had hoped that something in her estate planning or living will would take precedence over my father's wishes."

Kianso frowned. "I've seen acrimonious family feuds go on at length before an issue like this is resolved. Unfortunately, it happens. So you need to prepare yourself."

"Mrs. Grant's lawyer is Richard Payne. Will you contact him and determine what, if anything, can be done to stop her father?" Venn asked.

Emma gasped and looked at Venn. "When did you discover who her lawyer was?"

"As we were driving. It was in the phone directory, like you suspected."

"But you didn't mention it."

"I said I'd found it. Maybe you were distracted. I didn't think we needed to discuss it yet. And, let's face it, after dealing with your father earlier, you needed a break."

Venn's words sank in, causing her anger to rise. "Please don't keep things from me. I don't need you to baby me because you don't *think* I can handle it."

"That's not what I meant. It's just that dealing with your grandmother's death must be overwhelming."

"It is," she admitted. "But I'd rather know what's going on."

"Got it." Venn's pursed lips pressed thinner.

A silence fell between them, and she became aware of a

soft ticking sound in the background. Her gaze skimmed the room until landing on a mantle clock with an inscription plate on its base. She sighed. "You know, it's time I stopped running away." She tilted her head as if considering the impact of what she'd just said. "I need to confront my dad and find an actual way to convince him. And not give in until he agrees to let Grams go in peace."

Kianso organized the items on his desk into a neat stack. "What do you think will get him to change his mind?"

"I don't know." Emma's stomach clenched at the thought of the days to come.

———————

The tension between Emma and Venn was still palpable as they exited the law office and got in the car. Part of him knew she was right and that it was best to finally have it out with her dad, but the protector in him totally balked at the idea.

Don't keep things from me. Emma's words resounded in his head, and he cringed inwardly. The information regarding Io still remained his biggest secret. He was worried enough about her blaming him for what happened to Grams, but now he feared she'd also resent him for keeping the whole truth from her.

Venn glanced from the road to Emma as she stared out the window, her brows pushed together deep in thought. He wished he could read minds. Maybe then he'd know what to do.

"So now what?" he asked.

Emma shook her head, then bit her lip. "This is the hardest thing I've ever had to do in my life."

"I'm sorry."

She blew out a trembling breath, and then another. "I think I should get Izzy and go back to my grandmother's."

"What? Why?" As long as she was at his place, Io wouldn't bother her. It was probably the reason the demon hadn't contacted her lately. Venn considered Io's cunning—by killing her grandmother, he'd ensured that Emma and Venn's relationship was on hold. What sort of bond blossomed in the midst of death?

"Can we stop by the park on the way?" she asked.

Venn's head snapped around, and he tried to read her eyes. "Of course," he replied, but as he steered the car in that direction, his beasts tuned in to his edgy disposition. Emma's request held a hidden significance, and now that he knew Custos had a special connection with Emma, a spark of irrational jealousy ran through him. But wasn't that like being jealous of his father, or brother, or friend? He forced the feeling aside.

"It was foolish to think I could escape my father. I've been trying to run away from who I am for so long, I guess I didn't realize what I was doing."

Venn slowly pulled the car into the park's lot. "I can tell you who you are: You're my mate."

Her back stiffened. "Mate?" She looked confused and unconvinced as she stared down at her hands. "I have to say, given my parents' relationship, I never really believed in love."

"No matter what you call it, we are destined to be together."

Emma appeared to ponder the idea. "It's nice to know that no matter what happens, I always have you." She stared across the car at him, her eyes searching his.

Her proclamation struck him in the chest. It didn't seem like the right place or time to be having this conversation. He reached over and cupped her cheek with his hand. "Yes, you always have me."

He leaned in and tenderly kissed her. His wolf and his hawk stretched out with a sigh, in languid contentment within him.

He followed Emma's lead as she walked over to the

tree, and he could tell she was struggling to sort through things, perhaps striving for a communion of some kind. Or perhaps simply an understanding.

For Venn, life had been as it was for so long he'd forgotten how confusing it had been in the beginning. Now, he didn't want to confront the triangle between them too closely.

Emma walked straight to the tree and placed her palm on its coarse bark. She closed her eyes and breathed as if meditating, as if drawing strength. When she looked at him again, she stretched her other palm out for him to take.

And as his fingers locked on hers, a mix of soothing calm and dizzying heat washed over him, reassuring him in a way he didn't expect. It was as if he could *feel* light and darkness and the mix of the two into smoky grays. And it was amid the grays that they stood in thrall, as along with Custos they formed a fragile triangle.

Directly, Venn's heart pulsed an ancient rhythm of oneness and he desired to share every aspect of his life with Emma. He hugged her to him so their bodies touched all the way down the front from chest to hips. She met his gaze. He nuzzled his nose to hers, brushed his lips lightly over her mouth. "Would you like to see inside the oak?"

"Really?" She grinned widely. "Can I?"

"I'm not sure, but let's find out." He led her by the hand away from the tree.

"Where are we going?"

"There's an underground entrance via the garage across the street. That way I have access to the Divine Tree without having to go back to my house or through the above ground portal—which I don't think you'd be able to use."

"Oh," she said quietly. "This is convenient."

He unlocked the garage and they went inside. A dark brown door at the back led into what looked like a storage room. And within there, he pushed on a panel, opening a concealed door.

"From here it's much like it is from my house. Only shorter and steeper because we don't have as far to go."

He grabbed a flashlight from a wall-mount and slipped his arm around her waist in order to guide her. Five minutes later, they stopped at the underground entry.

She tilted her head back, looking up at the etchings of wolf and hawk adorning the entrance. "This is amazingly beautiful," she exclaimed.

Venn demonstrated the anointing ritual. Then he held Emma's wrist up, lifting it beneath the root. "The mate of a Guardian. Benison."

"What does that mean," she whispered as a drop sap dripped onto her wrist.

"Blessings."

"Ooo, that burns a little. Like menthol."

Concern caused his brow to bunch. Average men were not meant to enter the tree. He was betting on her connection to allow her admittance and hoping he wasn't overstepping his bounds. As far as he knew, no one had ever crossed the threshold of a Divine Tree except for the Guardians and Seth. He held his breath and heard his own heartbeat inside his head.

A few seconds later the door swung wide. Venn released a sigh of relief. He moved inside, bringing Emma along with him.

Emma had never seen anything like this in her whole life. Sure, she'd visited the Sistine Chapel and the art wonders of Europe but nothing, nothing compared to the natural beauty inside of this Divine Tree.

"Oh, Custos, you're beautiful," she said awed.

The walls were fashioned of golden hues of wood with

its grain and growth rings showing through in a continuous movement of lines, an artistic piece in and of itself. Emma ran her hand along the wall, admiring the smooth texture worn by age. Venn led her up a winding knot of stairs and into a living area. The inside looked more spacious than she would have thought, grand even. The place was like an upscale efficiency apartment. A large burnt-red sofa and recliner chair took up most of the space, with a few end tables strategically placed. A medium-size alcove that reminded her of a massive limb housed a kitchenette. "This is magnificent," she said, taking it all in.

Seeing it like this made everything so real.

The magnitude of this place hit her like a fist to the chest. The idea that the Divine Tree had existed for centuries and Venn along with it was nearly impossible to grasp.

"I recently refurnished it. There are so many modular options available today that make it easier to get furniture in here."

She let her gaze sweep the room again, noting that as fantastic as the Divine Tree was, Venn commanded her attention like nothing else. Her awareness of him made her heart flutter and her loins clench with desire. His tall figure and strong, muscular shoulders made him seem even more powerful in the confined area. She swallowed as she sensed him watching her. His gaze collided with hers, lingered.

A long silence hung between them as he undressed her with his eyes, his gaze skimming hotly over her body. Every touch-mark left a sizzling impression, on her ankles, her knees, her thighs, the V between her legs, her hip bones and navel, over her breasts, on the pulse-point of the neck, and finally to her face. The slightest breath escaped her mouth, and she felt the dampness between her thighs increase.

He lifted his hand, cupped her face and ran his thumb

over her lips. "You realize that you're in here because of your connection with the tree? And your connection to me."

The pad of his thumb danced over her lower lip, sending little sparks through her. "I know. And this feels so...right."

On a groan, he claimed her lips in a slow, sultry kiss. She slipped her arms around his neck and threaded her fingers in his thick, dark hair. His free hand wrapped around her and grasped her bottom, urging her against his steely ridge, where he ground against her sensitive mound.

The kiss held the magic of the universe, tumultuous and fiery, sweet and slow. And he kept kissing her as he removed her clothes, until the very last second when the contact broke in order to slip off her pants and undergarments. She undressed him, savoring the feel of his smooth skin beneath her palms. When they were both naked, he captured her mouth again, as if he couldn't get enough of her.

His hands cupped her breast and plucked her nipple delicately. With light stokes he moved his fingers over her midriff, then ever so slowly over her tummy, until he reached the curls covering her sex. She gasped into his mouth as he dipped his fingers lower and stroked her clit. And she curled her hips into his touch, as her excitement ran higher.

He moved her over to the couch, barely missing a beat, where he sat and tugged her in front of him. "You're so gorgeous," he murmured, then lifted one of her bare legs to gain better access, positioning her foot on the sofa. He nuzzled his face into her curls, using his tongue where his fingers had been, lapping and twirling it over that most sensitive spot. She moaned deep in her throat.

The questions that plagued her about the kind of relationship he'd had with Amelia completely melted away. It didn't matter. She was the one he was making love to now. She thrust her hips as the delicious sensations built, and she clutched his shoulders and dug her fingers into his muscles as a climax washed over her. Her legs quivered, and she threw her head back, "Ooh yes," she groaned, rocking on his talented mouth.

Breathless, she pulled back. "I want...I want to have you in me, now," she purred, her voice so thick she was surprised the words could make it out. She placed her palm on his chest, pushing him backwards on the sofa. His manhood jutted up, ready for her. She straddled him, taking him in her hand, rubbing his smooth tip over her clit. When he growled, she slid down on him, taking him slowly inch by inch, taking all that delicious power into her.

His face looked strained and beads of sweat dotted his brow, the essence of a male in the throes of passion. "Urrr, so good," he moaned. Then he took hold of her hips and guided her up and down, setting the rhythm that brought her so close to soul-shattering pleasure. She slid perfectly against the long angled thickness of his shaft, taking him deep, her muscles pulsating on him, demanding even more. The pounding tempo increased, until they both cried out in unison with their release. In the end, his strong hands held her in place—she was so boneless she thought she'd topple to the floor. Instead, she collapsed onto his chest, in utter fulfillment, in happiness.

"That was incredible," she murmured through raspy breaths.

He looked at her, and she smiled. Her heart had never felt anything close to this resplendent euphoria in her entire life. She felt sunny, her mind clear as a blue sky, and her body floated on a bubbling stream of delight. She rolled sideways and arched backward, absorbing the impressions the Divine Tree poured over her. And they were all of Venn, about the powerful, loyal protector he was.

The magic of the tree had drawn her although she

hadn't understood precisely why. She felt its enduring strength, its beauty, and its wisdom. Its branches of energy, dancing in the sky. Its roots secure, deep within the earth.

She had come to the tree out of intuition, to discover her true identity and her connection to Venn, the entanglement of their lives.

As they dressed, she wondered if he would ever bring her here again. She hoped so.

Their lovemaking had been a much-needed break from reality. In more ways than one.

Upon leaving the lawyers, the weight of it all had seemed overwhelming. Not even the prospect of a relationship with Venn had lifted her spirits. And so, instinctively, she knew she needed to come here to the oak.

And she was so glad they had. Deep within her, the supernatural essence she'd always possessed blossomed.

Dressed, Venn pulled her into an embrace much like that of when they'd begun. Only this time he held up his hand, matching it to her smaller one and interlacing their fingers. He kissed each knuckle, then opened her hand palm up and flicked his tongue over her heart-line. Have you ever noticed how the lines form an imprint of a tree?

Relaxed, she shook her head.

"We should go," he said gently.

"I'm not ready."

"Seth is expecting us," he pressed.

She didn't want their incredible joining to end, but she knew she still had much to do. Yes, beginning with her grandmother's memorial. "Okay," she agreed. "How about we eat back at your place when I collect Izzy?"

Even though she wasn't quite ready to leave the Divine Tree, she inserted a spring into her step, certain she was on the right course. Her dad would change his mind. Grams would find peace. Venn had reinforced his mate status and she was learning more and more about the reincarnation deal, which was kind of awesome when she thought about it. How many people got the chance to see who they were in a previous life?

The one thing she didn't quite get was why Jacob Price's image had come to her so many times in the impressions the tree poured into her. Very strange. But she sensed the association had to do with her grandmother's supporting Emma to complete the project that brought her back to Georgia in the first place. Yes, that would bring closure to this whole dreadful mess. She didn't want to think beyond that. She couldn't.

25

Loch and Glen, Venn's wolf dogs, were as restless as he felt. They dashed in circles, whipping their tails against his legs. They darted back and forth between Emma and Seth. Emma thought it was because she was holding Izzy, but Venn knew the truth. It was due to her interaction with Custos. The Divine Tree's influence left an imprint that nearly glowed.

Henry handed Emma a packed, soft-sided cooler. "For dinner I prepared curry chicken. There should be plenty for several people should your father like to eat."

"Thank you," she said graciously. "You really didn't have to go to the trouble."

"It's the least I could do." The servant returned to clearing the table as he had been when Emma came downstairs with the dog.

"Where's mine?" Seth murmured.

"Not to worry, you won't go hungry," Henry admonished.

Seth grumbled under his breath.

At least that was one thing that remained normal. Well, as normal as an archangel could be, he supposed.

Emma and Venn walked out of the house, and fifteen minutes later, they arrived at the Grants' home. He hadn't been out and about town as much as he had the past several days in probably over a year combined.

Emma set Izzy down in the kitchen, and the pup seemed thrilled to be home. He ran around with her nose to the ground, looking for something. "I think he's searching for Grams."

"You could be right." As the dog flitted by him, sniffing around the tables, Venn glanced out the window. "Your father's car is here. Do you think he's upstairs?"

Emma meandered into the living room. "I suppose so."

Venn was about to turn from the window when he caught sight of the ugliest great horned owl he'd come to know.

Io.

Fuck.

He glanced over his shoulder in the direction Emma had gone. The muscles along his shoulders and spine clenched. Should he go support her in her petition to her father, or go take care of his enemy outside? He sighed and reached out with this senses to confirm where Mr. Grant was—upstairs sleeping..

With that insight, he headed for the woods. Catching Io's scent, Venn hit the tree line at a full-out run. Anger bubbled up inside him with every step. He hadn't paid Io his due for taking the life of his love's dear grandmother, let alone everything else the bastard was trying to do to Emma and Custos. He owed Claire Grant that much.

Yet even as he closed in on his enemy, he realized a greater battle than breaking every bone in Io's body. This fight would require calm, intelligent thinking. If he beat the shit out of the demon, then how would he discover Io's specific plan to use Emma?

No, Venn must learn the full measure of what was going on in Io's filthy, sick mind.

When Venn stood beneath the tree where Io perched, he stopped.

She's changing, Guardian, came his enemy's voice in his mind. *What of that?*

"I don't know what you're talking about."

If I see it, so must you. The Divine Tree has intervened in some manner.

"No," he lied, clenching his jaw against his anger.

Do not deny it. I saw the glow radiating from her with my own eyes. Io chuckled mean and deep, his feathers standing on end.

"Stay away from her," Venn roared, having a difficult time staying with his plan. "She is of little consequence to you. Go back to your underground fire pit."

Again, Io laughed. *Haven't you noticed her transition? She fires up metal now without thought.*

"So, she's talented."

It's more than that. Much more.

"You're imagining things. Wishful thinking on your part."

Io stretched his great wingspan and then flew a circle over Venn's head. He landed in-your-face close to Venn, changing into human form as he confronted him. "The metal she touches changes, Guardian. It possesses unique properties. Properties that—" Io stiffened and retreated several steps.

"That what?" Venn advanced.

But a shroud had already dropped around Io as he must have realized he'd been about to spill key information. "Never mind," he sputtered, "It has no beginning and no end, and once gone you never get it back. Sadly, you won't figure it out until it is too late."

"That remains to be seen," Venn said with more confidence than he felt. "I think you're too full of yourself."

Io snarled, and Venn's beasts could no longer contain themselves. And the Guardian longed to oblige them.

"Stay away from Emma," Venn growled. "She's

suffering enough over her grandmother, thanks to you."

"The pleasure was mine."

"I will kill you if you touch her."

"If you kill me, then Seth will have to take my place. Did you know that?"

Venn forced his face to remain a blank slate, but he hadn't known that at all. He was aware they were brothers and had assumed that was the reason Seth had always forbidden Io's death. Not because he'd have to take the demon's place.

Io smirked one too many times, and Venn launched forward. Even if he couldn't kill the beast, he could at least cause some damage and pain.

In a whirl of feathers, first one man transformed and then the other, the owl taking to higher ground, trying to get away from Venn's sharp beak and razor claws.

Shrieks and cries rendered the silence as they attacked each other like sword fighters, lunging and parrying and thrusting at each other until they were both marred with bloody gashes. Venn kept advancing and striking, without letting up. Finally, Io executed a sharp dive toward the earth and changed into his barghest form at the last minute, taking off at a run when he hit the ground. He kept running and growling that vicious growl, the sound of Venn's nightmares.

From his bird's-eye view, he watched Io flee for a good long time before the demon was no longer visible. Then he flew back into the cover of the forest and changed, feeling the sting of every cut and bruise and contusion as his skin righted itself. As he assessed the damage, he realized there was no way he could return to the Grants' house until he was healed.

Indeed, a flaw in his plan, he realized as Emma's voice came to him on the breeze.

———

Emma was sitting in her grandmother's favorite mauve-colored rocker, tipping back and forth and listening to it squeak, when her father came downstairs.

"I'm surprised to see you," he said.

"I'm surprised to be here." It was the sort of tit-for-tat exchange she was in the mood to give. Her discombobulated feelings and irritation from earlier this morning had changed to focused determination. Venn and the oak had renewed her strength and resolve, and given her such a sense of peace. She didn't understand the reason for the change, but she felt its result.

This is the way it's going to be.

When she'd come downstairs after discovering her father asleep, Venn hadn't been in the house. With the car still in the drive, she'd assumed he'd taken off in the same way he'd come to her the other day—in the form of wolf or hawk. And she chose to think that meant he believed in her, too. Although it would have been nice if he'd given her a heads-up he was leaving. However, in her confident state, his departure didn't bother her one bit.

Her father ambled into the room and took the other rocking chair. "Are you staying this time?"

"For now. It's time we talked. Really communicated."

"Okay. I'm listening," he said, his face drawn and hollow.

Emma almost felt like she was taking on the role of the parent. She couldn't pinpoint how she knew that role reversal came about, but it was definitely in play here. "There are certain things we agree on. One of them is that Grams is eighty-five years old and has lived a good life."

Her dad nodded. "Yes. She lives the way she chooses."

Emma felt a calmness wash over while something simmering inside her at the same time. And now it seemed as if the two elements were combating each other, like oil and water. She inhaled deeply and let the breath out slowly. "I remember when she decided to vacation in California a few years after Grandpa passed. You didn't want her to, did you?"

"No, it's not that. It was the driving cross-country on her own I didn't approve of."

"But she found a friend to tag along, and the two of them had a grand time." Emma smiled, recalling the pictures of Grams and her friend with a couple of hot men in Las Vegas. She didn't mention that memory to her dad.

"She was often too wild and outrageous," he admitted.

"Dad, people have to be who they are deep down inside, not who others want them to be."

"I know that."

"Do you? How often have you tried to change Grams, or Mom, or me? You see your way as the only right way."

His brow pinched. "I know I'm a hard-nosed SOB."

"You can be. And I'm not happy the way we've drifted apart these last few years."

He looked at her for the very first time since he sat. "Neither am I."

"But like Grams, I have to live my life my way. And I need to be accepted for who I am." Suddenly she wondered how the subject segued from her grandmother to her. "You know I'm speaking of my dreams, and"—she glanced down at her palms that even now were turning red—"my talent with metal."

The movement of his rocking chair halted. "That still going on?"

"Yes. I'm dealing with it better now, understanding it more." She hesitated, unsure how far she should go with this. Swallowing the lump in her throat, she decided today was a fork in the road for them: Either he accepted her or he didn't. She wasn't going another moment pining for his love and approval. "You made me feel like a freak, you know. But I am who I am."

She paused in her rocker, too, and the stillness in the

room gave her goose bumps. She awaited his response.

"I know. I've fought it, but . . . I know you can't change," her dad said with a miserable catch in his voice.

Out of nowhere, her grandmother's piano thrummed a single key.

Emma smiled to herself. Grams used to say it was Grandpa's spirit trying to put his two cents in. But Emma chose to believe it was Grams this time, giving her a nudge. "Dad, you know we need to honor Grams's wishes regarding her living will. You said you took it to your lawyer. Which means you saw it with your own eyes. She didn't want to be kept alive by machines."

He pressed his lips together and shook his head. "I can't . . . do that."

Emma leaned forward in the rocker, setting both feet on the solid ground, resting her elbows on her knees, and intertwining her fingers. Her voice was amazingly steady, considering what she was proposing. "We have to. Right now she's lingering in between. She's already gone, but we haven't set her free."

Her father stood rapidly, almost losing his balance. "No. There might be a chance for her. It happens." He moved toward the kitchen.

"You're only dragging out the inevitable. Believe me," she said, her voice trembling as her defenses began to deteriorate. She swallowed and breathed through her nose. With the slightest bend of the truth, she added, "With the way you *know* I am, the things I see, I can emphatically tell you, she's gone."

He flipped his hand at her dismissively and continued running away into the kitchen. Emma rested back in her chair and squeezed her eyes shut. This whole debate was so incredibly painful.

After a moment, she got up and followed him. He stood at the sink with his hands braced wide on the counter and stared out the window.

"Think about it, Dad. But with you or without you, I

will see Grams's wishes honored. I've arranged to meet at the hospice center at nine o'clock tomorrow. My lawyer has obtained a copy of the living will. I hope you will be there. During trying times such as this, family really should stick together."

He stared over her shoulder at her with that same tight-lipped expression from earlier, and she exited the side door without another word. She glanced around for Venn or one of his beasts. When she saw nothing, she headed to the garage out back and fired up her equipment. The urge to work, to create, swirled inside her.

The last time she'd worked on this piece, Grams had been doing the wash, fussing around the house. Now she was gone. For a reason Emma couldn't explain, she felt a tremendous sense of peace. She wondered if this was wholly due to the Divine Tree, or maybe her Grams watched over her with a guiding hand. Or maybe it was her reincarnation that directed her to believe in such phenomena as guardian angels. Perhaps that's what was happening now. There were so many things she couldn't explain in life.

Taking up the barbed wire, she began adding shape to the neck and chin. As time progressed, she got lost in the process, allowing her passion and awareness to surface and her hands began to get hot. Eventually, she put aside the torch and started to fine-tune the piece with her fingers. The metal glowed white-hot as she bent and shaped and fused the wire into the shape of a wolf.

Venn.

God, when would there be time for them?

26

Waiting at the edge of the forest as long as he could stand it, Venn finally deemed his wounds healed enough to join her in the garage. He approached with silent steps, taking in the fluid way Emma shaped her work with her bare hands. He paused in the doorway and watched without interrupting.

Finally, she glanced up. "I wondered where you had gone."

"I was restless."

"More than restless, I suspect. You're all beat up."

He shrugged. "Comes with the territory."

He walked deeper into the garage. "You're making a wolf?"

"Yes."

She stepped back admiring the piece. "I think it's like the one you already have."

He nodded, pleased that she remembered his art collection. Folding his arms, he leaned against a workbench set off to the side. "How did it go with your dad?"

She shrugged. "Better. We didn't argue, at least. Not really. He still hasn't given in to the fact that Grams is gone, but I think I made progress."

"These things take time."

Her mouth pulled to the side in a sad smile, and she returned to manipulating the wire. He enjoyed keeping her company. Seeing her talent and the way her hands squeezed and formed her work was so sensual. What would she make him feel if she touched him like that? She stopped, wiping her hands on a damp towel.

When their eyes met, it was like sparks from her welder, smoldering heat igniting between them. She moved toward him, and he met her halfway.

With a sense of urgency, he slid his hand into her hair, cupped her head, and drew her into a hungry kiss. She wrapped her arms about his neck, holding him so close not even air separated them as her mouth explored his, warm, demanding, and devouring. A floodgate of emotion seemed to be released from within her, which given everything she'd been through lately, was understandable. Venn wanted to absorb her pain and give her something, maybe even pleasure, to replace it.

Locked mouth to mouth, they moved and turned, sidling back to the bare stretch of wood-planked wall in the shop, next to the workbench. Her arm caught a stack of pint-sized paint cans and sent them tumbling, but that didn't stop their powerful whirl of desire. He pressed her up against the wall and kissed her more deeply, his tongue tangling with hers.

When he broke the kiss, she started stripping off her clothes in near desperation, peeling her shirt over her head. He strolled to the side and closed the garage door, shutting the world out. As he walked back to her, he followed her lead, shedding his own shirt, flipping it off to the side as he went. When he stopped in front of her, he helped undo her bra.

"I want you to touch me," she whispered with need. She slid her hands up to hold her breasts to him. "Start here."

Tense, sensitive, and aware of the raw hunger

consuming both of them, Venn dipped his head and nuzzled his face between her breasts. He kissed the warm flesh of her sweet curves and licked her fair areola. He circled his tongue around her nipple until it peaked, then drew it into his mouth.

She moaned and tugged him closer. "More."

He moved to the other breast, suckling harder. And that was the end of nice and easy. In a fury like wildfire, she pushed him back and unzipped her jeans. The sound had every molecule within him aching for the next move. His erection kicked and his balls grew heavy. While she wiggled out of her pants, he dropped his to his ankles.

He leaned into the hot searing kiss they shared. He slid his fingers between her legs and into her slick wetness and thrust his tongue deep into her mouth. Her nails clutched his back, drawing him closer as she raised one leg high, wrapping it around him, right with him on how this would go. He cradled her bottom and held her while she positioned him and slid down his length. "Oh, God. So good."

But this was not slow, languid sex. No, she wanted a wild, flyaway, take-me-to-another-realm, make-me-forget-everything experience. Venn sensed it just as he knew his own thudding heartbeat. So he set a hard rhythm, hammering into her, using the wall to hold her to him as he drove deep inside her, expending full glides over her sweet, damp core. She bit down on his shoulder and moaned, long and intense. His breaths came harsh as he inhaled her scent and felt the early spasms of her climax. And then she exploded, her tightness milking him in rapturous pulses and pulls.

"Venn," she cried, and he exploded so hard inside her that his body shook, every muscle straining and tightening with his release.

As Emma's breathing returned to normal, she collapsed against his chest and circled her arms around him, holding on to him and this moment, not wanting to let go and return to reality. Eventually, she brushed her lips along his jaw until she reached his lips and kissed him, a raw outpouring of emotion.

She let her legs relax, and he set her on her feet. She threw her head back until it rested against the wall and breathed. "Mmm, that's just what I needed."

He looked at her with those hot, smoldering eyes and said in a husky voice, "Anytime."

She could have melted into him all over again. Instead, she got dressed, as did he. She was terribly disappointed when his shirt slid over his broad shoulders.

Once they were clothed, he straightened the cans they'd knocked over. Resting his hand on the final one, he peered at her. "Emma, we need to talk."

Now what? "Okay," she said, hesitantly.

"The reason you came to Tyler was because of the statue and participating in the park ceremony."

"Yes, and to visit Grams as she arranged the entire thing."

He shook his head. "No, I don't think that's the case. Io set this entire event up. He used your grandmother to get to you."

"The project is overseen by a committee," she reasoned.

"Which is head up by Jacob Price."

"Grams was so excited by this project. I…I have to honor my commitment."

"I promised your grandmother I'd keep you safe." He clenched his fist, feeling helpless to convince her. "I think there's something dangerous there. Jacob isn't who he seems."

He hesitated, a darkness entering his eyes. She didn't understand what force was holding him but sensed something was. "Who is he, then? You keep saying that, but you've given me no explanation."

"He's...someone dangerous. The ultimate con artist. And he's deadly. He's killed before."

She gasped. "Killed? Who?"

Venn evaded her gaze and shoved his hands into his pockets. He couldn't lie to her, but he still couldn't tell her the whole truth. "That doesn't matter right now. But you need to trust me. Jacob is out to destroy the Divine Tree, or me, and hurt you in the process. That much I'm certain. And you can stop him by not participating in his plan."

A sense of disbelief nipped at her. What he said seemed too farfetched. And yet, wasn't a shape-shifting Guardian just as implausible? She placed her hand on her stomach to stop from gagging. The indecision and uncertainty were stressing her out even more. "I'll think about it. But first I need to get through what we need to do for Grams."

27

Venn walked along side Emma as the automatic doors that led into the hospice center opened. In the lobby, they paused. She leaned her forehead against his, and let her frustrations seep out of her and into him. He was ready to absorb her tension. He'd gladly take all of her pain away if he could. Last night she'd slept fitfully, tossing and turning, and whenever she'd let him, he cradled he up against him and attempted to sooth her doubts.

"I'm so sorry you have to go through this," he said, pressing his lips to her forehead.

She gave him a small, forced smile. "I know. Thanks."

She blew out a nervous breath and straightened as they turned and walked through the entrance. The center was a gorgeous, state-of-the-art facility, nothing like what it represented. Rough-hewn stone covered the outer walls and the interior, carrying the natural theme into the halls. In the lobby, a fountain gurgled a rhythmic tune. To Emma, it was just extraneous noise she couldn't grab hold of, eclipsed by the erratic beating of her heart.

A few minutes later, they entered a spacious, private room that had a sofa with a seating area and small dining table. French doors opened onto a small patio filled with greenery.

Emma hugged her arms to her chest as she peered across the room at her unresponsive grandmother. The ventilator whooshed, and with it, she noticed the abnormally steady rise and fall of Grams's chest.

"I'm glad there's a view," Emma said. "Grams would have liked that."

She moved to the bedside and tried to control her own breathing. It was so sad to see her lively, vivacious grandmother like this. She smoothed back the auburn hair along Grams's temple. Today was Friday, her usual weekly salon day when she would get her hair fixed for the weekend.

Emma picked up her grandmother's hand and smoothed the back of it with her own. "She was in great shape for eighty-five."

Venn moved closer to stand behind Emma. "Yes, she was."

"Active in the community, too." Emma swallowed. "I have to see the statue placed in the park. She was so excited about that project."

Venn's hands tightened on her shoulders. "Do you think your father will show up?"

"I don't know. I told him nine o'clock and that your lawyer had obtained a copy of the living will. And that we were going to honor it and disconnect the life support whether he wanted it or not."

―――――――――

Venn didn't need to check the clock to know the time. That sort of thing was intrinsic to his nature. It was quarter to nine. The clap of shoes on tile grew louder as they came down the corridor toward him. But he could tell by the sound and tempo of the steps that it wasn't Emma's father. No, it was Kianso, delivering their copy of the paperwork.

Venn left Emma and met his friend near the door. "Thanks, man," he said, taking the packet the lawyer passed to him.

"Is there anything else I can do?" Kianso asked.

"I don't think so," Venn said, then faced the bed. "Emma, would you like me to deliver these to the staff?"

She padded over to him and held her hand out for the folder. When he gave it to her, she pulled out the copy of the living will. "I know what she wanted. But I just need to see the directive with my own eyes."

Venn nodded. "Understandable."

Emma perused the paper, then glanced between the two men. "This is indeed my grandmother's signature. Will you give it to the staff and make the arrangements to honor this?"

"Of course," Venn answered. "As your lawyer, Kianso will speak to them now." He looked to his friend. "If you don't mind?"

Kianso shook his head. "Not at all."

"Thank you," she replied, and returned to her grandmother's side.

Venn and Kianso stepped out of the room, took care of the business with the staff, and then Kianso left after again offering his condolences. When Venn reentered the hospice room, Emma was speaking in soft tones to her grandmother, saying her good-byes.

Look at that. My gray hair is already showing. Claire Grant's spirit hovered off to the right.

Venn smiled at the woman. *Hello, Claire,* he voiced through his mind.

I'm going to miss that girl, the old woman said.

Can I tell her you're here?

I don't know. What do you think? She pursed her wrinkled lips. *I don't want to cause her any more grief.*

Venn lifted his shoulders and let them fall. *She's been*

dealing with some form of the supernatural her entire life. My guess is she'd approve.

Claire nodded. *Right. Right.*

"Emma," he said quietly. "Your grandmother is here to say good-bye."

Emma whipped her head around to stare at him. "What was that?"

With a knowing lift of his brow, he smiled. "She's perched on the far side of the bed next to the pillow."

Tell her I'm proud of her and that I know she'll be fine.

"She says you'll be fine and that she's proud of you."

Emma put her palm to her chest and searched the corner of the bed. "Oh, I'm going to miss you, Grams." Her eyes watered and her voice caught.

Don't cry, Claire sputtered.

"She doesn't want to upset you, doesn't want you to cry."

Emma bit her lips and shook her head. "It's okay. I'm okay."

Let's get this show on the road.

Venn chuckled.

"What'd she say?" Emma asked.

He repeated it for her.

Emma rose and walked over to Venn. He took hold of her hand and squeezed it.

"How long do you think we should wait for my dad?" she asked.

"Let's give him a bit of time."

Hey, it's not like I have a Parcheesi game to play here, Claire grumbled.

His mouth pulled up.

"What did she say now?"

"Talking about Parcheesi."

"Oh, Grams. I love you so much!"

Venn tipped his head and put his lips to her hair. "She loves you, too."

Hey, don't get cocky, Romeo.

Venn straightened, then, hearing heavy footfalls coming through the hospice center. "Your dad's here."

Claire didn't budge, but she smiled as her son entered the room. *He won't understand this, but maybe one day you can tell him, that no matter how much of a pain in the ass he can be at times . . . I love him.*

Venn felt himself choke up as he said, "Of course."

When he glanced at Mr. Grant, the man looked like he'd been up all night. His usual crisp appearance was in disarray and his hair looked like it had been finger-combed a few too many times.

"I found it," he said as he walked by them, raising a book into the air titled *Forever My Child*. He eased into the chair beside the bed.

Venn didn't know what Grant was referring to, but the man carried a book in his hand. Venn shot a questioning glance to Emma.

"It's a book about love and how life changes but family is always family. We used to read it when I was a little girl." She let go of his hand and slipped her arm behind his back, pulling herself more securely into his embrace.

What truly surprised him was Grant's lack of explanation. He gave no indication whether he accepted the implementation of the living will or planned to continue fighting it. However, given his nonconfrontational behavior, Venn was presuming the former.

Carl Grant opened the book and read the story about a family tree and a mother who would put a heart-shaped leaf on the branches each day, claiming that no matter what happened in life, the love of a mother to her child never failed. And when the child grew up, it was his turn to fill the branches of the tree with never-ending love. Venn watched Mrs. Grant's expression change from sadness to one of pleasure as she looked on, her eyes crinkling and mouth softening.

The tale epitomized the love and bond of a mother and exposed a longing in Venn he hadn't felt or thought about for a long, long time. It reminded him how lonely the life he'd been given actually was. To be immortal meant everyone else moved on and he remained. Alone.

His chest tightened at the memory of his own parents, of his long-ago youth, of years and years living a solitary existence. He glanced down at Emma, and the bond between father and daughter and grandmother swirled energy about the room. It brought home just how important it was for him to have Emma in his life, to have someone to love and love him in return.

He took a deliberate, controlled breath.

When the reading was finished, Mr. Grant sniffed mightily. "I love you, Mom. I wish I hadn't wasted so much time. You were right: I had my priorities all wrong."

Mrs. Grant straightened. *Hmph. Did you hear that? I'm right. Imagine that. I don't think I've been right since he was eight years old.*

Dabbing a handkerchief to his eyes, Mr. Grant rose from the chair and crossed to where Emma waited. He hugged her. "I love you, too."

She patted his back. "I know."

As he pulled away, he said, "I'll go get a staff member."

While he was gone, Emma plucked a few tissues from the box on the nightstand. Several minutes later, her father returned with a young doctor.

The woman's voice was calm and informative as she explained, "Since you've elected to honor her living will, we're going to remove the life support systems. If you will step into the waiting room for a few minutes, we'll call you when we're finished."

They filed out of the room to the waiting room across the hall. No one sat, though. At one end of the room, Mr. Grant got a cup of coffee, took a couple of sips, then set it down and stared out the window. Emma clasped her arms about herself, and Venn hugged her and spoke into her ear. "Your grandmother is okay with this, you know."

"I wish I could see her, too."

"Yeah."

"I wish you could use some of your powers to bring her back."

"Unfortunately, it doesn't work that way. Even I will have a time to die."

She gazed at him with a quizzical brow, and whispered, "What do you mean? You're immortal."

"For the most part, yes. But if the tree dies, so do I."

Emma blinked. Any response was cut off before it began as a nurse came in and said they were ready.

In her grandmother's room, they took up posts around the bed.

The nurse remained off to the side. "Many times the patient breathes on her own for a short while, even days sometimes. Eventually the body stops functioning and the patient passes on peacefully. You are welcome to remain in the room as long as you wish."

Venn wrapped his arm about Emma's shoulders. He felt her stand taller, perhaps fortifying herself, as Mrs. Grant's breaths grew markedly more labored and further apart.

Emma took up her hand and held it. "It's all right to go, Grams," Emma whispered.

It doesn't hurt. It's actually quite freeing, she responded to Venn.

He shared that piece of info with Emma. Then Mrs. Grant's corporeal self began to rise and grow larger. *I almost forgot! What about Io? Are you keeping my Emma safe?*

Don't worry. I will take care of her, Venn promised the departing woman.

With that, she vanished into the beyond.

When the nurse pronounced her gone, Emma's body shuddered in his arms as she tried to control the crying heaves that threatened to wrack her body. She straightened her spine and pulled away from Venn with a resolve that worried him.

He didn't want her to shut herself off from him in her grief. He feared his Emma was going in the wrong direction.

28

Her grandmother's passing propelled Emma into overdrive. The statue's dedication was scheduled for tomorrow morning, and she looked forward to honoring Grams in that way, recalling how excited she'd been about the project upon Emma's arrival. To Emma, this was her grandmother's personal memorial. But at the same time, it felt like it was too soon.

She had sent Venn home, and her father was busy making cremation arrangements. Thankfully, he had stepped up after it was all over and had taken charge. They'd decided to have a celebration of life next Tuesday. She wished they could postpone the statue ceremony until after she laid her grandmother to rest. It felt like the right course to take.

She stared at the clothes she'd laid out on the bed for the dedication ceremony, focusing on what she actually had control over. Izzy came over from where he was curled up on the bed and snuggled down on top of a pink floral dress, then looked at Emma with his big, brown eyes. "Yes, I think you're right. That is the best choice."

She tugged the dress from beneath the dog and held it up in front of her to inspect it in the mirror. It was a flowing nylon piece that traveled well and almost never needed ironing. She hung it over the closet door.

Grabbing her cell phone, she intended to call Jacob Price to confirm the details for tomorrow's ceremony in the park, get it checked off her list. But the doorbell chimed before she could dial.

Wondering if one of her grandmother's friends had already learned of her passing, she hurried downstairs to see who it was. No, not a friend. Jacob himself stood there, leaning with his hip propped against the railing.

"Good afternoon. I'm sorry to hear about your grandmother."

"Mr. Price," she said, surprised. "How . . . how did you know so quickly?"

"I just stopped by to confirm the details about tomorrow," he went on, ignoring her question.

She stepped out onto the porch, allowing the door to shut behind her. For some reason, she didn't feel right inviting him inside. "I've been thinking. Perhaps it's the wrong time for the dedication. Given the circumstances, I would really prefer to wait until after Grams's funeral."

"No," he said firmly. "Everything is set. We can't postpone things."

She shook her head. "I really—"

Mr. Price shot her a glare. "Listen up, you little vixen. We will proceed as planned. Who do you think led your grandmother into the well in the first place?"

Emma slapped her hand over her mouth to hold in the scream that threatened to rip her apart. No. That couldn't be.

"Yes, mindless girl. Just as Venn has control of certain things, so do I. Arrows, wells, I can do it all."

Emma bit her lip, beyond confused as her brain worked frantically to piece together what he was saying. Only one arrow came to mind. And it had killed her in her past life.

She shuffled backward.

"Don't be silly. You can't escape me. And I'm not out to harm you this time." He pushed off the rail and pulled himself taller. "But if you want your dear Grams to see her just reward in the lovely hereafter, then you better follow through with our plan. Otherwise, her soul is mine in hell."

She shook her head again.

"Or else . . ." He shrugged, flashing his hand through the air as if throwing something. A ball of fire hurled from his fingertips and slammed into the earth in the front yard.

Emma's chest constricted and her palms grew moist. Her eyes darted about. Where was Venn?

"Do as I say and your grandmother goes to heaven. Don't do as I say . . . Well, you know what happens. It's up to you."

Emma swallowed hard. "Okay."

"Good choice," he said, smirking. "Everything is set. All you have to do is show up. Quarter to ten tomorrow." And with that, he disappeared in a puff of black smoke.

Chills came over Emma, and she trembled violently. Oh, God. What was she going to do? That horrible man, or whatever he was, had killed Grams, and now he was threatening to send her to hell. Could he even do that?

Yes. She couldn't explain how, but she knew full well he could . . . and would. She inhaled a breath down to her toes.

Venn had been right to warn her.

The sun illuminated the proud, ancient Divine Tree, casting Venn and Seth in deep shadows. Venn paced about, stepping over roots that snaked above the earth. Seth pushed his hands into the pockets of his jeans. The officiating guests had not arrived yet.

His gaze shot to the heavy sword leaning against the tree. He didn't know how things would go down, but he'd stocked himself from his arsenal and come prepared, armed with a variety of weapons, from knives to guns to crossbow. Custos's words echoed in his head. *How do you capture the wind? Or kill the rain? How do you control the tornado? Or harness a hurricane?* Did that mean Io couldn't be stopped? Oh, he knew there were reasons he *shouldn't* destroy the demon, but that wasn't the same thing at all.

Absently, he considered the good citizens of Tyler who might attend today's event. They could be in for quite a shock.

The quandary over what to do about Emma and the dedication was eating him up.

"We know Io is going to use Emma in some way," Seth declared as if saying it one more time would give them a solution.

"No shit, Renaissance Man," Venn bit out. He didn't have to check his watch to know time was running out. Emma would arrive any minute. He had wanted to drive her, but she'd insisted on riding with her dad since he was attending the ceremony.

She was in such a vulnerable state after losing her grandmother and with everything that had happened, Venn didn't push it. Besides, it didn't seem Io was as intent on killing Emma as Venn had thought.

Yes. She would be safe from Io, and she was the most important thing in the world to him. Then again, how would she ever be truly safe if the demon was alive?

Custos was his duty. Seth his friend. Emma his love for all time.

Seth snapped his head in Venn's direction, his eyes hard and piercing. "Don't even think about it, Guardian."

Venn straightened. "Reading my thoughts again, angel?"

"You are in such a state of discontentment; your thoughts are dancing on energy and whirling about you. I don't have to dig to read them. You are shouting to the universe."

Venn continued to pace as he growled low in his throat. His beasts joined in his tormenting chorus, adding more snarls and cries.

The wind shifted then, carrying with it a stench, an odor so nauseating that Venn wrinkled his nose and coughed. He'd know that smell anywhere.

The earth shook as the barghest thundered toward them, then stopped, transforming into Io's human form. Every muscle within Venn tightened, from the base of his neck to the curl and flex of his fingers, ready to do damage to that ugly puss. The hair on the back of his neck stood on end. Io had to have a reason for showing himself, and past experience indicated the demon thought he had the upper hand.

Io laughed haughtily. "Having a meeting and you didn't call me?"

Venn made certain to mask his thoughts from both Seth and Io. "Return to your hellhole, demon. There is nothing for you here."

"Ah, but there is. How about giving me a tour into the ancient catacombs of the Divine Tree?"

"When hell freezes over," Seth said with ancient authority.

"Don't be so sure, brother." Io advanced on Venn, his gaze darting between angel and Guardian. "There's a plan in motion that you cannot stop. And if you dare to try . . . well, it will cost dear Emma's life."

Venn clenched his hands into fists. "I'll kill you before I let you harm her."

"Will you now?" Io smirked. "That's not what your angel says. Isn't that right?"

The demon was so smug as he glanced at Seth, and Venn longed to rip his head off right then and there. The debate within him whirled in an angry maelstrom, pitting duty against desire, loyalty against love, friend against soul mate. The blood within his veins began to bubble and the branches of every tree, with the exception of Custos, shook violently.

"You assume too much," Venn spat. "Come on. Let's have this out right now. I'm ready to go to my maker." He'd do anything to spare Emma.

With a vicious growl, Venn changed into his wolf form. He dove at Io, who in a matter of seconds also transformed into beast.

"Oh, geez. A brawl," Seth said, his voice laced with sarcasm. "I haven't had a front-row seat to one of these in ages." Then the angel stepped back out of harm's way.

Venn's wolf increased in mass until he equaled the barghest in size and bulk and strength. He launched for the soft underside of Io's neck, opening his jaw and sinking sharp teeth deep into the demon, ripping away flesh.

Io roared and shook Venn off as yellow blood slung in all directions and sizzled when it struck the ground. Then he swiped his vicious claws at the wolf, catching fur and skin, like a pitchfork scoring bark.

Hot knives of pain caused Venn to buckle. He rolled and stood once more, off to the side beyond Io's reach. He heaved shallow, ragged breaths while his vision cleared. Then he struck again with the singular thought of killing the beast.

In a flail of claws and teeth, they locked on to each other, tumbling over the earth until a powerful force blasted them yards apart, dropping them to the dirt.

"Enough," Seth shouted.

As the wolf altered into man, Venn drew himself up, his ribs expanding with every breath, he faced Seth. "Thanks for stopping me."

Seth clasped Venn's shoulder. "Do what you must, Guardian. I'm willing to take his place in the Dark Realm."

Io reformed with a nasty laugh. "Huh, no need to worry, Brother. He won't kill me." The demon scowled at Venn. "I can take your Emma whenever I want. The only thing you can do to save her is stay the hell out of my business and not interfere with the task I have given her. It's ceremonial, really." As if he knew he was holding all the cards, Io straightened and disappeared.

Venn grabbed hold of his stomach, physically ill at being tied to his obligation to the Divine Tree. As sure as if chains bound him, he couldn't save her. At least not her and his oak. And to consider the havoc the death of Custos would inflict on the world, most likely create another shift of the earth, definitely release more evil, and cause the deaths of untold mothers, fathers, children, and brothers was beyond imaginable. Inconceivable.

And Emma was his Achilles' heel.

Seth stretched his wings in an exhausted expand and retract. "You must stop whatever Io has planned. At any cost."

Venn stood and nodded grudgingly. What if that meant Emma's life? Something inside Venn cracked open. He couldn't go through the agony of her dying again. He just couldn't.

Cloaking his thoughts, he pursued the most difficult decision of his life. If he sent her away then would Io let her alone? No. He still believed that killing Emma was Io's end game. Now that the demon had stirred things up, it was just a question of when and how.

———

Up the drive, he saw her grandmother's car approaching. A nervous energy bounced inside of him. She hadn't stayed with him last night, the first time in four nights he'd slept alone. And he didn't like it, not one bit. His Emma was stunningly beautiful as she strolled across the park in a floral dress. The snow had finally melted, leaving the ground brown and distressed. She lit up the whole dreary place. From across the way, she smiled at him. His heart kicked in his chest.

"Go tell her not to do this, Guardian," Seth ordered.

"It's not that simple. We don't even know what 'this' is, exactly." Venn singled out her scent and breathed it in. "I think we have to play along until we have the whole picture."

Emma walked over and joined them. She kissed Venn on the mouth, a sad brush of her lips that tasted of tears. She drew back with a frown. Dark circles lined her eyes.

"What's wrong?" he asked her.

"Nothing." She sighed. "I just wish Grams were here."

He gave her a hug. "I'm sorry."

Seth cleared his throat. "Emma, Venn won't tell you, so I will."

"Do not," Venn growled.

"You mustn't do this, dear. Let Jacob do whatever he must but do not participate. He is the reason your grandmother is dead. He is the one—"

Venn shoved his palm against the angel's chest and forced him back a step. "No."

Emma inhaled sharply. "Then it's true?"

"Ignore him," Venn told her. "He doesn't know. Pure speculation."

But Seth nodded. "What you're about to do will somehow harm the Divine Tree, and in turn, harm Venn."

"Seth," he growled.

"Venn, I know," she said sadly, with a bitter smile. "Jacob is totally evil."

"Then you understand you mustn't do whatever he's asked." Venn set his jaw.

Emma's eyes closed slowly, squeezed tighter as her breathing increased, then opened to look straight at him. Tears coursed down her face. "I'm sorry."

"Emma. You can't. This is bigger than you, or me, or Seth, or even Io...Jacob." He stepped forward to take her hand and try to convince her not to listen to the demon.

She evaded his touch and sidestepped around him.

Io swaggered over, glaring at Venn and Seth. "Are you ready, Emma? It's time."

Her troubled gaze swept over the three men before her. "I . . . guess so."

Venn's rage exploded within him. The veins in his temple throbbed. He opened and closed his fists. But with every bit of strength he possessed, he held it together for Emma's sake.

"Don't be pissed off," Io jeered. "I always told you I'd win."

29

Io guided Emma to her spot by the statue's base, and as he did so, he could taste the satisfaction of success. A crowd had gathered and filled the transportable bleachers that had been prepared. He held out the three two-foot-long metal spikes for her to take. "All you have to do is place the stakes into the holes and ceremonially hammer them in. That's it."

The process appeared incredibly simple compared to the historic catalyst he believed the act to be. As she wrapped her alchemist's fingers around the metal a stream of heat immediately flowed into his hand. A normal man would have had to drop the scorching stakes. Fortunately, demons were accustomed to far more blistering temperatures.

Excitement nudged him. He peered over at Venn and Seth, a sneer touching his lips. Finally, after all these centuries, he had the means to get rid of a Guardian. He puffed out his chest.

Emma looked at him, and her eyes narrowed. Had he showed his hand? Had he gotten ahead of himself with his gloating? He considered how many times his weaknesses had gotten the better of him.

Then she glanced at Venn. He felt her doubt and concern and pain. *How sweet.*

"Your grandmother would be so proud of you," he purred. "And she'll never know how close she came to spending all eternity in hell."

She jerked her attention back to him. Yes, that's as it should be. *He* was the one with the power this time. *And look at them!* Venn and Seth, and even Custos, did absolutely nothing to stop him.

The glow of the metal stakes changed from red to a bluish white.

Venn and Seth walked in a steady rhythm closer. Venn held a sword tight against his leg. It had been eons since Io had seen such a fine weapon.

"They're making the announcement, dear," he said to Emma. "Go ahead and drop the stakes into place."

Just steps away, Venn stopped, and in a voice thick with emotion declared to Emma, "I love you. No matter what happens. I love you...for all of time."

Woefully, her lips parted. Somewhat in a daze, she knelt and followed the directions he'd given her. *Good girl.* He passed the hammer to her. "Drive them in."

And she obeyed.

As Emma drove the fourth and final stake into the ground, Venn doubled over in pain, grabbing his gut.

Io was ecstatic. That would teach them to play favorites.

———

The pain in Venn's abdomen was excruciating, and every muscle in his body vibrated with tension. He felt shackled, tied as if anticipating being drawn and quartered like in the days of old. His hand tightened on his sword.

Custos, do you know what's happening?

A violent rustle of leaves came to him, the oaks voice rumbling in a sturdy, coarse tone. "We've entered the one thousand days before the Age of Atonement. The Dark

Realm has issued a ransom in exchange for the secrets of the universe."

Venn's gaze met Io's and the evil one smiled in wicked satisfaction.

Fuck. The rush of malevolent forces would go berserk now with every evil act deemed justified in an effort to protect the Dark Realm from extinction.

Emma faced him, her eyes wide, searching, pleading. "He was going to take Grams's soul. She doesn't deserve hell." She pressed her fingers to her lips, as if holding herself together. "I had to…"

Venn threw back his head and howled, closing his eyes. He marshaled his temper. Scenarios flickered through his thoughts. Of him snatching the stakes from her hot hands. Of Io snapping her neck with one twist. Of the people scattering in terror. Of Io abducting Emma and torturing her. Of Emma dying with an arrow through her heart.

His eyes opened, filling with the beautiful sight of his mate as he made a decision.

If the tree dies, he's a dead man anyway. Whether he's able to kill Io or not, the demon needed to suffer.

Venn raised his sword and turned on Io, trying to shield Emma from the view.

In the blink of an eye, everyone in the audience collapsed, tipping over onto one another, dropping in a collective unconscious heap. Seth's handiwork, he thought.

Putting all his strength into the movement, all his anger, Venn slashed the sword across Io's left arm, severing it just above the elbow. The demon screamed and cursed. He whirled on Venn, drawing a long blade from beneath his coat.

"Get her out of here," Venn ordered.

He was vaguely aware of Seth moving to Emma and of the two arguing, of the angel guiding her away. The chink of metal clashing against metal echoed throughout the park. Venn parried and thrust, moving with great speed. They were both strong and both fueled by hatred.

Io's blade came down on Venn's shoulder, cutting a deep gash. Blood gushed from the wound along with a thick, fibrous liquid from where the tree tattoo had been split open. Venn dropped to the ground and rolled in a way that took him closer to the demon, jumping up right in his face. Io growled and transformed into a barghest. The beast launched himself at Venn, flattening him on the ground, the impact knocking his sword from his hand.

Emma yelled his name. With his muscles bulging, he tried to hold off the demon's horrible claws. Off to the side, the clap of running feet came at him. From the corner of his eye, he witnessed Emma, his brave, foolish mate, lift the heavy sword and thrust it hard into the heart of the barghest.

The beast fell heavily to the ground, inches from landing on him. With a shot of black smoke, Io vanished. Emma's knees seemed to buckle, and she landed hard on the ground.

"Emma," he cried. He stood and stumbled over to her. Venn stared at the angel, his heart pounding as he lifted her, cradling her in his arms.

She glanced back to where the barghest had dropped. "Is he…is he dead?"

Seth exhaled loudly. "Afraid not."

. 30 .

Emma hadn't seen Venn since the park dedication, and she missed him dreadfully. The good thing was the past few days had given her a chance to check in with her roommate in Paris. The fire had been fairly destructive, but her savable belongings had been boxed and were being stored in a new apartment Becky had acquired. Emma agreed to send money to cover her share of the expenses. What she didn't tell Becky was that she may not be returning. Her grandmother's place belonged to her now, as her father had no interest in it. And there was Venn. She couldn't fathom what would happen with him.

Funny, she didn't feel a thing after ending it with Todd, but even a day without seeing Venn or hearing his rich baritone voice made her heart ache something fierce. She'd texted him about Grams's memorial and had received only two brief responses that sounded cold and distant. His withdrawn reaction worried her. Had the ordeal with the tree driven a division between them that couldn't be mended?

She'd also been able to get reacquainted with her father. They had reminisced as they'd gathered materials to display at Grams's celebration of life. Her mother had flown in yesterday, making it the first time they'd all been together in the same house in several years.

It wasn't until the conclusion of the memorial service for her grandmother, that Emma saw Venn again. He stood at the back, leaning against the doorframe, and he looked absolutely horrible. His coloring was ashen, his eyes bloodshot, his hair lifeless.

Emma inhaled a sharp breath. So that's why he hadn't come to see her. He was sick. But then she recalled that he had self-healing abilities. Why weren't they working? Each step she took toward him hitched her anxiety higher. His face appeared gaunt. Had he lost forty pounds in three days? Impossible.

"Your grandmother would have enjoyed all this," he said with a sluggish wave of his hand and a lifeless smile.

"You're ill."

"Yes."

She placed a palm to his burning cheek. "Where's Seth? We need to speak to him."

He gave a sad smile. "That will not help."

She grabbed hold of his hand and tugged him along behind her. She paused to speak briefly to her father and let him know she was leaving. Venn needed her.

"Why didn't you call me?" she asked over her shoulder.

"Emma, there is nothing you can do," Venn said, stopping her and placing a kiss on her forehead. "Stay here."

She enveloped him in her arms, holding on for dear life. Something wasn't right here. "No. I'm taking you home. Where's Seth?" she asked again.

"He left."

"At a time like this?" She ushered him out to Grams's car, which was now hers. "Stupid angel."

As she drove him to his mansion, they passed by the park. Her heart caved in on itself when she saw Venn's Divine Tree. She pulled into the lot. "Oh, my God. It's dying."

But Venn eyes were shut.

She opened the car door and stood, peering around its

frame. The tree's spring leaves were completely gone, the limbs had turned a brownish-black color and had the brittle appearance of death, and the trunk was dull gray. The park even emitted a musty odor that hadn't been there a few days before.

She hurried back into the car and drove the rest of the way to Venn's place, a growing lump forming in her throat with each mile that passed. Venn had to pull out of this.

Henry helped her get him settled into bed. Then she pulled up a chair, placing it close-by and took up a vigil. Glen and Loch ambled over and assumed a post beside her. She laced her fingers in Glen's thick fur, savoring its comforting rich texture. Watching the rise and fall of Venn's chest, she prayed for a miracle.

Emma paced in Venn's suite. He had not budged from the bed in twenty-four hours. She was extremely distraught. As was Henry.

"Madam, what is it I should do?" Henry asked.

She looked at his pinched, worried features and sighed heavily. "Make some soup. Cook Venn's favorite meal." She shrugged, sadly. "I don't know."

As the assistant left, she wrung her hands, stared at them. They were simply the utensils necessary to get by every day, yet also the instruments that had wrought all these problems. Could her touch really have changed the spikes into something that would kill the Divine Tree and Venn, as Seth had said?

She lifted her gaze skyward and yelled, "Seth. Seth! Get your ass down here this minute."

She had no way of knowing if she could actually summon the angel or not. She sat curled up on the sofa and waited while Venn slept in the bed across the room. Absently she fingered the wolf statue on the coffee table.

She realized too late how much she loved him. She should have listened to him. She should have trusted him. A tear trailed down her cheek. Vaguely she comprehended that the wolf statue had distorted beneath her fingers. She swallowed hard.

Io had used her.

But she refused to be defeated.

With the heat in her hands, she reshaped the wolf and set it back on the table, thinking. It was imperative to undo her mistake. If the stakes were gone then there would be nothing to leach into the ground and poison the tree. As for the statue, she'd have that moved, too, anything to make certain whatever was killing the tree was gone.

Would that be enough to make things right? She pushed out a frantic exhale, ignoring the ache beneath her diaphragm. There was only one way to find out. Now. Not another second could be wasted. She'd kiss Venn goodbye and pray it wasn't for the last time.

She traveled into the other room, crawled up onto the bed, snuggled up next to Venn, and rested his head on her lap. He opened his eyes just barely and tried to look up. "Hi there," her voice caught as she dipped down and put her mouth to his dry lips.

Her hands shook as she stroked Venn's dark hair, recalling the way it felt when she entwined her fingers in it when she kissed him. Then he rolled onto his side and her vision filled with the tree artwork on his back. Her stomach knotted in shock. The wound on his shoulder had not healed and the image of the magnificent tree had altered into one of shriveled, drooping twigs. She brushed over the thick fluid seeping from the tattooed branches, rolling it between her fingers. Liquid sawdust. The tattoo was filled with bits and fibers of the tree, she realized. And like Venn, it was dying.

"Don't worry. I have a plan," she said.

"A good one, I hope."

"Only time will tell." She grabbed the phone, dialed her

father and told him to meet her at the park project.

When she placed the phone on the receiver, her hand began to shake. This had to work. She poured a cool glass of water from the pitcher on the tray and got Venn to drink a few sips. And seeing how even that slight task took such enormous effort, her eyes misted all over again.

With the slightest of smiles, he murmured, "Don't cry. It's okay."

She shook her head, and the tears flowed more profusely, running down onto his face, wetting his cheeks, his eyes, his mouth. She leaned down and kissed him, memorizing the feel of his lips. "You were right. I didn't know."

He seemed to gather some strength. "You are safe. That's all the matters."

She tipped her head back until it collided with the wooden bed frame. What had she done? God, she didn't want him to die.

Seth appeared then, as if he'd walked straight through the window from outside the house.

"It's about time," she bit out.

"There's nothing I can do," Seth replied.

"He's your friend. You can stay with him." She caressed Venn's cheek.

Seth pursed his lips and slouched, folding his tall form into the recliner.

Leaving Venn curled up in bed, she rose. "I'm going to the park."

"And do what?" the angel said sarcastically.

"Move the statue and prevent any more poison from the stakes from leaching into the soil."

———————

The essence of the grounds had entirely changed. Before it had felt like spring, despite the cold. Now it felt like death.

She took a shaky breath. The tree hung wilted, its branches lifeless. It made her heart ache to look upon the decaying oak. For the hundredth time she wondered what she had done.

Her father approached on silent feet. He sat next to her on the bench. "Do you know what happened?"

He was looking at the tree, his face filled with sorrow. A fortunate thing, she thought, that he seemed to care.

"My touch changed the metal into an element that is killing the tree," she said, appealing to him. If ever there was a time she needed him to get on board with her abilities, it was now. She twisted in her seat to watch his reaction. "We must move the statue. You still have friends in this town. Can you get them to help?"

Her father was slow to react, most likely wondering if she was nuts. *Don't refuse*, she begged in her head as if her will would prevail. "I'll do anything you ask. Please just help me."

"All right." He glanced back to the oak. "Though I fear it might be too late." He pulled his cell phone from his pocket and placed a call. "Fred, meet me at the park. Bring the equipment you used on that statue."

Shocked that he agreed so easily, she asked, "Why are you doing this?"

"Because I fix my wrongs. And I love you." He reached out, and she fell into his hug.

"Oh, Daddy." She hadn't called him that in so many years. "I love you, too. Thank you."

He stood. "So where are we going to move it to?"

Emma considered the grounds. "To the farthest point in the park."

"The men will arrive shortly. I'm going to scout out another location." He nodded and trotted off, his lanky legs taking brisk steps.

Emma treaded in the opposite direction, over to the tree. She sighed and sat by its trunk, tucking her thighs to her chest. She placed her hand on the black dried wood as if her touch would give it comfort. "It will be okay. I'm . . . I'm so sorry. Forgive me."

As she rested there, waiting, she called out to Seth. "Angel, I need you. Get back here and help me fix this."

The air was silent and still. Nothing.

"Seth," she yelled.

Then, from behind her, "All right, already. You don't have to shout."

She scrambled to her feet and faced him.

"Thank God." She brushed her hair from her face. "I did this, so there has to be a way I can undo it."

"It doesn't always work that way," he said sadly.

"Explain to me again my connection with the Divine Tree." She lowered her head and peered at him through her lashes. "And don't leave parts out this time."

After an indignant tightening of his lips, he began and went through her entire connection with Venn and the tree. Emma listened, walked around the ancient oak, and thought.

Then an idea settled in her mind. "I . . . I think I know how to save them!" She met Seth's doubtful blue eyes. "You must go fetch Venn and bring him here. Now."

If anyone was capable of getting Venn back here in an outrageously fast timeframe, it was Seth.

She leaped up and jogged to the car to retrieve her purse. When she returned to the oak, Seth stood holding her mate in his beefy angelic arms.

"Put him down here." She knelt and dumped the contents of her purse onto the ground. Among them was a pocketknife—a multi-tool, to be precise. She flipped the blade free of the tool group and poised it over her hand.

"What are you doing?" Seth inquired.

She lifted a shoulder. "From what you've told me, my blood had something to do with a connection to the tree. It's a farfetched guess, but I'm hoping it will be able to heal it, too."

Seth's brows shot up, and Venn moaned.

Without hesitation, she drew the cutting edge across her palm. Blood welled crimson, and she stared at red liquid as it seeped out of the wound, creating a pool in the bowl of her hand. When the hollow was filled, she made a fist and tipped her hand sideways over the largest tree roots.

"Benison," she whispered, copying the ritual she'd witnessed when Venn had taken her inside the tree.

But she didn't stop there. She dripped her blood over Venn's pulse points, too, and then moved to a dozen other thick roots and repeated the anointing process. It couldn't hurt.

When she'd done all she could do, she stood and faced Seth. Her arms hung limp at her sides, she was beyond exhausted. The archangel offered a sad smile. "I pray that it works." He stepped toward her and wrapped her in a consoling hug.

"So do I." She glanced at Venn passed out, resting on the Divine Tree's roots. "Let's take him home."

Two days after the statue was moved, Venn rose from bed and stretched. "What did you do?"

"You don't remember?"

"No."

"Come. I'll show you. I've planned a picnic. Henry packed a fabulous lunch." She seemed anxious for him to dress and hovered over him in the process, as if he wasn't progressing fast enough to her liking.

"Here." She presented him with his shoes. "I'm so relieved your strength is returning." Her voice caught, and he glanced up at her. Her eyes brimmed with tears, and she fought to regain control. "I thought you were going to die."

Driving his foot into his deck shoe, he stood and

gathered her in his arms. "Shh, it's okay. I'm okay."

"I wouldn't have been able to deal with losing you. And the oak . . . Oh, the tree is awful."

He smoothed a hand along her back and nudged her toward the door. "Well, let's go visit, then."

―――――――――

She helped him out of the car and through the park. With every step closer to the tree, another ten-pound weight was added to his chest. This was not the look of a tree bare during winter's icy passion. No, the Divine Tree appeared to have been scourged by fire and disfigurement. Venn choked back the bile that rose in his throat.

The pain he experienced at the sight equaled what he'd felt when Emma had died before. An all-consuming, gut-wrenching need to scream at the heavens engulfed him.

I'm sorry, my friend, he mentally intoned to Custos.

He glanced over at Emma, and his mood was lightened somewhat by the spring in her step.

Thank God he didn't lose her.

She ran on ahead and spread the blanket. He eyed her long legs and the curve of her bottom as she bent over. Yes, he was healing well, and his body displayed just how much he longed to make love to her.

When she stood, she brandished two mini bottles of wine. "We did this in another life, but it didn't turn out so well. Let's try again." She held up her bottle for a toast. "To new beginnings."

"New beginnings." They both took a sip from their bottles, then Venn threaded his fingers through her hair at the back of her neck, drawing her closer. "I love you. For all time. I love you." His lips took hers in a long, possessive kiss.

"And I love you."

When he finally let her go, she looked up with a

breathless smile. "Mmm, it gets even better."

"Better?"

"Yes, look." She pointed, and he reluctantly slid his gaze from her lovely face to look where she directed him.

There, reaching skyward from a root of the Divine Tree, was fresh shoot of green.

Emma clutched his hand, giving it a squeeze that complemented the warmth filling his heart.

"The oak lives," his voice was thick, filled with awe and wonder and gratitude. "But how?"

"I'll tell you what I did later," she said, a smile on her lips. "Right now, I want another one of those toe-curling kisses."

He was happy to oblige.

EPILOGUE

In Venn's backyard, near the bubbling brook that cut through the property, Seth and Claire Grant shared a new arbor swing fashioned from the dead Divine Tree branches. Venn had given the oak a "haircut," as the guardian called it, taking it down to its trunk. He had brought every scrap of wood onto his property. In a matter of a few weeks, the revived tree had gained eight feet of new growth. And so far, Seth hadn't noticed any repercussions, any flood of evil in the world. However, darkness could hide, lying dormant, lurking just beneath the surface, infecting the minds and hearts of humanity. The slight reprieve might be because Io had been confined to hell. Seth wasn't sure, and only time would give him those answers.

Seth regarded the laughter Venn and Emma shared as they entertained Venn's wolves and Izzy on the lawn. A new era was coming for the Guardians, he mused. He hoped the tree's encouraging conclusion was a favorable sign.

"It does my heart good to see them so happy," Claire said with a wide, bubbly smile and crinkling eyes. Wiggling, she adjusted her posture in the seat. "The wind tickles my wings."

Seth snorted. "That will pass."

"I don't know that I want it to." She grinned and poked him in the ribs with her finger. "Lighten up, will you?"

He heaved a long, dramatic sigh. Easy for her to say. Since she'd died because of Io, and on his watch, she'd immediately earned an advanced angel status. Plus she'd been assigned to him as his assistant. Talk about punishment.

On a positive note, Claire had used the option to knock years off her appearance, and he had to admit, she was quite a looker. He was glad she hadn't gone really young, back to her twenties or anything. She'd taken off thirty years or so, saying she'd earned every one of her life lines and was proud of them. But still, she had a fine curvy body and lovely smile.

"So, have you given my suggestion any consideration?" she asked.

"Which suggestion would that be?"

She gave an exasperated chuckle. "Let's hang around here and watch over the Divine Tree and allow Venn and Emma to have a real honeymoon."

"They're not married," he pointed out.

"Mated then. A vacation. Whatever you want to call it." She pursed her lips.

"That's never been done in the past."

"But you can do that, right? You're every bit as powerful as a Guardian. Even more so. Just because it hasn't been done doesn't mean it can't be."

"That's not my job."

"Oh, please. No more excuses." She stood, putting her hands on her hips. "Look on the bright side. Henry will cook anything you want."

He straightened and licked his lips.

"Come on," Claire said "Let's go tell Venn and Emma."

Izzy romped over to Claire, drawing Venn and Emma's

attention to them. Claire lifted the dog into her arms. He proceeded to enthusiastically lick her face.

"Oh my goodness," Emma exclaimed the moment she saw her grandmother. Venn's gaze followed. They met half way across the yard, and Emma threw her arms around her grandmother's neck. "I can't believe this," she said, her voice growing thick with emotion.

"Well, look at you," Venn chimed in.

Claire stepped back and twirled around. "Not bad, huh?"

"Grams, you look fantastic." Emma swiped her fingers beneath her eyes. "Does this mean...does it mean I'll get to see you sometimes?"

"We'll see," Seth said.

"I'm his assistant," she chortled, clearly pleased.

"Congratulations," Venn said with mischief in his eyes. He raised a brow at Seth. "Have you seen the tree?"

"Yes. It's doing better than I'd thought."

"Okay," Claire said, guiding them all in the direction of the house, completely taking charge. "Here's the deal. Seth and I are going to guard the tree while you two go on a honeymoon."

"Vacation," Seth chimed in.

"Whatever. So go pack your bags!"

Venn shot Seth an incredulous glance. "Really?"

"I've been told change is good."

Venn turned to Emma, "Where would you like to go?"

"How about France?"

He pulled her into a tight hug and kissed her soundly on the mouth. "France it is."

―――――――――

The battered owl perched high in a tall pine tree, overlooking the saccharine scene below. Io ruffled his feathers as hatred rolled off him like brownish steam rising from the dirtiest city.

He wouldn't be able to chase them down himself due to an unpleasant punishment for his failure. But he'd already recruited support for his cause. Io gave a wicked snicker. Before he was done, everyone would learn to fear the Reaper.

Thank you for reading *Awakening Fire*. If you enjoyed this story and want to stay up to date on Larissa's next book and release dates then sign up for my newsletter. (I promise your email address will never be shared and you can unsubscribe at any time.)

https://larissaemerald.wordpress.com/contact/

Stay tuned for the next book in the
Divine Tree Guardian Series

AWAKENING TOUCH

to be released in November 2015.
Get a glimpse of the book at www.larissaemerald.com
Check out the Awakening Series Excerpt Book available
on Amazon.

Larissa Emerald also writes steamy,
contemporary romantic romance.
Read on for a sneak peek of *Winter Heat*.

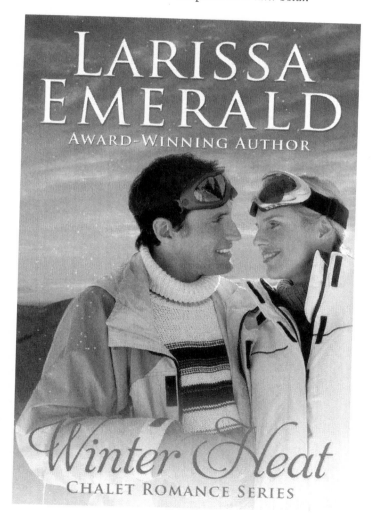

LARISSA EMERALD

AWARD-WINNING AUTHOR

Winter Heat

CHALET ROMANCE SERIES

Secrets. Everyone had one.

Kelsey cranked up the radio with an outstretched pinky, careful not to dip the paintbrush onto nearby papers. Tucked in her office within calling distance from the resort's front desk, she blended a flare of red onto the canvas as last night's dream lingered in her mind. The same weird fantasy she'd been having since she was a teenager.

Good thing her family didn't know about her wicked imagination. They'd disown her.

Though, the dream definitely explained her restless mood.

Her mother would have popped something to calm down, but Kelsey just sighed and swirled her brush in the paint. Funny how, Mama and *disquiet* usually occupied her thoughts simultaneously.

No, she wasn't going to be like Mama, looking for answers in a pill bottle.

But as much as she longed to blame her mom, or the dream, or even the inches of snow that nature dumped on her little chalet ski resort this morning—which now required lots of shoveling and slope grooming—the real reason she was edgy had yet to walk through the lobby door.

Dr. Jared Michaels.

Online research revealed he was a thirty-four year old man of diverse interests, a savvy dermatologist whose Michaels Corporation included real estate development and film production among its many enterprises. He had money and clout, which equaled highly paid lawyers who could destroy Chalet Romance and the safety net Kelsey was trying so hard to build should he decide to sue the resort.

She stared blankly at the painting, tuning out a commercial jingle on the radio.

She hadn't personally spoken with Dr. Michaels when he'd called. The inn's receptionist—and her good friend—Amy conveyed the message, and she'd said he'd made it perfectly clear his visit was on behalf of his injured sister.

What did the universe have in store for Kelsey *now?* In the six months since she'd taken responsibility of the resort, there had been one mishap after another. First a fire in the restaurant, then a ski lift chair derailed and fell—without passengers, thank God—and finally resort guest Tiffani Michaels nearly died on the slope in a horrible ski accident. Wasn't bad luck supposed to end with three?

She hoped so. Because she couldn't deal with a brother's revenge on top of everything else she had on her plate.

Kelsey rotated her stiff shoulders and forced that worry to the back of her mind with a vow: she would fight with everything she had to keep Chalet Romance. Her dad would be well enough soon to take control of the resort again and then she could get back to her own life, the one she'd put on hold when he'd had a stroke six months ago.

She would never abandon her dad, though. No, she knew how that felt too well.

She dabbed her brush vigorously on the pallet, blending blue onto her red brush. Too much of it. But one

of her favorite songs resonated from the radio, and Kelsey
tossed back her hair and allowed the music to inspire her,
raising her confidence almost instantly.

Let it go. Mustn't live in fear.

Jared Michaels dropped his luggage on the floor as he
glanced around the empty lobby of the Colorado mom-
and-pop ski resort. Someone had gone through a helluva-
lot of trouble to turn the average chalet into the hot, image
of a "love nest" that had lured in his sister.

The vase of long-stemmed red roses on the counter
gave the place a classy touch. Not bad. Then again,
Valentine's Day was last week. He almost wished he
weren't here on personal business and that he actually had
a woman in his life.

"Hello. Anybody here?" he called.

No response.

When no one came to greet him after another few
minutes, he impatiently whacked the old-fashioned bell
parked on the counter. The sharp, dinging jingle made him
wince. But as the tinny sound evaporated another replaced
it. From some obscure room, a sultry voice belted out that
Shania Twain song about feeling like—a woman.

The rich tone ran wild fingers over his entire body.

Woman.

Jared chomped down on the wad of gum in his
mouth—he'd been aggressively chewing gum for days in
an effort to quit smoking—and he listened. Each word
packed a punch—drawn out, dynamic, sexy.

He scanned the edges of the room stopping on the
open bar in the far corner—no one. But he knew he had
to meet the woman whose voice warmed him like a
bonfire. And he was a man who trusted his instincts and

knew a good thing when he saw it—or heard it. He'd positioned his dermatology practice so it would appeal to the Denver elite, and he'd also hired the medical professionals and staff who eventually took it over from him. He'd ventured into real estate deals that would generate a tidy profit, resulting in more than enough money to finance his vast and diverse interests. Which meant the movie production company he'd founded two years ago was nearly ready to show off its first project. Yes, he accomplished what he set out to do every time.

He smiled, listening again.

The sultry voice drifted to him with a deep, throaty rumble. He angled his ear toward the song, distinguishing the live sounds of this mystery woman from those of the background music. His gaze shot to a short hallway on his right. Still no sign of the receptionist. He didn't really care anymore, though. He was far more interested in that voice.

He drew in a long breath. What he needed was a real vacation.

But that wasn't going to happen. Come Monday he'd be back in Denver, negotiating the terms of a hotel complex he was acquiring, followed by overseeing the release of his first small feature film at the end of the week.

Leaving his luggage behind, he skirted the counter to pursue the sound of the voice. He unfastened his winter coat as he went, taking long strides to a U-shaped dead-end, where there was a cluster of office doors.

The music was coming from behind one partially opened door.

"Hello?" he said.

No response. Again.

He dipped his head through the crack to look inside the room.

A young woman with wavy, shoulder-length blond hair stood, bobbing her head and doing a damn fine karaoke skit to the audience of—a painting.

She faced an easel and canvas, giving him the full view of her firm backside. Apparently lost in her own world, she balanced a paintbrush in delicate fingers and zipped the tip of the brush through the air in time with the beat, then dabbed a few strokes onto the canvas. Light poured through a set of three tall windows, washing her body in a sunny late-afternoon glow while giving perfect illumination to her painting. She worked in oils, and the pungent odor of paint and turpentine drifted out the door and into his nostrils. Offhandedly, he noted the picture's abstract, brash strokes and bold hues. Rather like her, from what he could tell.

Jared rolled his gum around in his mouth with his tongue, mesmerized. She rocked her hips, bouncing them in a two-beat rhythm from side to side. Jeez, watching her heated his blood more than a shot of Jack Daniels. Forget that he'd just stepped inside from twenty-five-degree weather.

As he swallowed and rapped a knuckle on the door, she performed a little two-footed jump-stomp move, shooting her arms up into a victory stance, all attitude. "I feel like a—"

She glanced over her shoulder, spotted him, and froze, her eyes narrowing.

Woman, he thought.

Oh, yes. She wore low-riding, chocolate-brown corduroy, a clingy off-white sweater that didn't quite meet the waistline—*make that hipline*—of her pants, revealing a scant half-inch of pale skin.

With the toe of his Oakley hiking-boot, he nudged the door open a bit more.

She turned to face him, and he was struck by the eye-catching impact of pert, full breasts that rose and fell with each inhalation.

"Very nice," he said in a voice loud enough for her to hear over the music.

Lowering her chin, she peered at him from beneath

long, dark lashes. "Which? The singing, painting, or dancing?"

"All of it." His lazy gaze ran down to her slender waist and shapely hips, and that morsel of flat, bare skin that taunted him so. Her sweater puckered in a tiny tuft over her navel. *A belly piercing?* He looked up to her heart-shaped face, dying to find out.

But she was busy giving him the once-over, as well. He crossed his arms over his chest, and noticed her nipples were peaked, showing their delicious outline against her sweater.

She blushed, laughed, then lifted one shoulder in a little shrug. "I always paint to music." Leaning sideways, she punched the OFF button on the outdated radio. The room grew silent, and she smiled. "Now, how can I help you?"

Jared hesitated a moment, trying to take in the total package—the singer, the dancer, the painter. Wide hazel eyes blinked at him as she tilted her head and showed him the five-carat dimple in her right cheek. Mid-twenties, he'd say, and that killer smile—She was meant for the stage.

"Ahem," she said while she cleaned a brush.

Mmm. The throat-clearing *sound* was deep, vibrating, and down-right sexy.

He worked his gum. "Yes, I'd like to register."

"Oh, yeah, Right. I'm watching the desk."

"Really?" he snorted, feeling his lips twist upward.

She turned back toward the easel, unflustered, placed the paintbrush near a pallet, then wiped her hands on a towel.

Jared directed another prolonged glance at her body-hugging sweater as she flipped the towel over her shoulder to land on the table.

"Amy had to take her poodle to the vet," she explained as she walked toward him. "An emergency." She paused, looked him in the eye, and continued. "The poor thing was attacked by a larger dog. Part wolf, I think."

By the inflection in her voice, he felt like there was some double meaning there that he was supposed to get.

"That's too bad," he said, puzzled. He stepped back to allow her to pass and lead the way back to the front. The tropical scent of her hair caught him off guard as she eased by him. He breathed in a second deep whiff.

She moved into the bathroom across the way instead of toward the lobby. Everything about her made him smile, it seemed.

"Give me a second to wash my hands and get rid of this paint cleaner," she called over her shoulder.

With the door wide open, she bent over the sink. He waited across the hall and leaned a shoulder into the doorframe, appreciating the view of her bottom. The theme of the song she'd been singing surged through his head. *Woman. Womanly.*

Damn fine.

He forced himself to focus on the reason he was there—business. It wasn't hard to make a few snap judgments about her in that regard, though. She was indeed fresh and sexy as hell, but appeared unprofessional, undisciplined, and irreverent. The carefree, artsy-fartsy type. The sort he was accustomed to dealing with in Denver at the night-club.

This all added up to someone who might spill the details surrounding his sister's terrible ski accident with only the slightest encouragement. If she knew anything, that was.

Maybe his visit would be quick and easy after all.

He mentally sighed. Since when had his life ever been easy?

When she finished washing up, he followed her to the front desk where they separated as he stepped to the foyer side and the dancing artist sauntered to the business side.

As soon as she glanced down at the desk, her relaxed demeanor changed dramatically. Her body—what he could see from her waist up, at least—tensed, and she lifted a slip of paper, holding it between her fingers as if it reeked of urine. Her breathing stuttered as she read what appeared to be some sort of disturbing note. All the while her brow crinkled in a perplexed frown.

"Is everything okay?" Jared asked.

She crumpled the paper. "Yes...Yes, sorry."

She immediately began to punch computer keys with a fervor that surprised him, and he reached for his wallet in his back pocket.

"Okay, Dr. Michaels. Do you have a charge card you'd like to put this on?" she asked a little too pleasantly.

He jerked his head up, blindsided that she'd used his name even though he'd intentionally omitted introductions. His phone call yesterday had been hasty and upon consideration he'd hoped to assume a low profile. Too late. Obviously, he hadn't been thinking clearly. "You know who I am?"

Her earlier vivacious glow had completely faded, replaced by a creased brow. A shadow dulled the sparkle in her eyes as she looked at him. "I visited your sister at the hospital. A nurse told me you were Tiffani's brother. Plus, you called, remember? My name is Kelsey Moore."

"Any relation to James Moore?" The resort-owner bastard who didn't even have the correct medical support lined up to handle on-slope emergencies like his sister's. There were numerous things about the accident that didn't add up. Jared was here to personally do some digging.

"He's my father," she said.

"I see." Every muscle in his back stiffened. Even so, one uncontrollable thought threaded past his hostility—*She said* father, *not* husband. He ignored the purely male instinct to imagine what a date with this gorgeous woman would be like. "And yet you didn't seek me out at the hospital?" he asked, getting back on track.

"Let's just say you weren't in the mood to receive my sympathy."

"Sympathy?" He narrowed his eyes and pinched his card between his fingers. Well, jeez, what did she expect? His baby sister was in friggin' traction for heaven's sake, and all because of something that happened on Chalet Romance's turf. Recalling his mama's old axiom about catching more flies with honey, he breathed deeply, presented her with his card, and adopted a more amiable tone. "Okay. It was nice of you to stop by."

She took the card and held his gaze for a gaping, silent moment, as her fingers brushed against his ever so slightly, the touch almost electric. He snatched his hand away. *Save it for the movies.*

As he considered her again, an inner voice urged him to get this task over ASAP. Forget about her sultry voice, her gorgeous body, her dynamite smile.

"How's Tiffani doing?" she asked.

"They're not sure if she'll walk again," he muttered, praying it wasn't so.

The click of keys stopped. And he thought he heard her swallow, hard. Her reaction gave him pause. Perhaps she did care.

But either way, it was damn heartbreaking to see Tiffani confined, lying in a hospital bed like that. She'd been athletic and had talent as a marathon runner. She was fast, too, and had often chased him down, he thought sadly as he recalled their childhood romps in the backyard.

"I'm very sorry to hear that." She slid his card, keycard, and a resort map over the counter to him.

He gazed into her alluring hazel eyes, thinking she sounded sincere and recalling the performance he'd observed earlier. A knee-jerk response pressed him to get to know her. This was, after all, a resort for romance. But unfortunately, he kept his promises, which meant the sort of amorous adventures the resort advertised weren't for him.

He needed to face the facts. *Reliable answers required objectivity*, he reminded himself.

Opening the map, she pointed out his chalet. "It's a tricky layout, and it's getting dark. I'll show you where the chalet is and you can bring your car around later."

"And the desk?"

She shrugged, grabbed a red parka from behind the counter, and slipped it on. "It's Friday. We're full, and everyone else has already checked in."

He picked up his bag. What did it matter to him? It was her problem.

They were halfway through the lobby when a young man entered. He looked as though he belonged on the slopes, and his ancestry could have been Norwegian given his fair complexion and light-blond hair. "Hiya, Kels," he said.

"How's the snow?"

"Excellent."

"That's what I like to hear." She paused as if with an afterthought, turning back. "Hey, Taylor, you mind hanging out at the desk for a few minutes until I get back?"

"No problem."

"Thanks." She resumed walking, indicating with an outstretched hand that they were changing directions, then she led him down a hall to a side exit. "Your chalet is one of the ones set apart from the main lodge. It's worth the short hike, though, because the view is awesome."

Outside, a cold, clean burst of air washed his face. He followed her as she proceeded along the snow-covered walkway that took them up the mountainside. Without glancing over her shoulder, she moved forward as if she couldn't get away from him fast enough.

When they reached a replica of a quaint Swiss chalet, she halted. A stand of giant pines spread wide, looming limbs overhead.

"You should find everything you need, but if not, please call the office," she said, pushing a clump of snow around with her shoe.

Hiking boots, he noticed. He hadn't caught that earlier. Cute. "Thank you," he said.

"At the side of your chalet there's a pile of firewood."

"Got it." Was she stalling?

She pulled herself straighter, her gaze direct and unwavering. A show of spunk returned as a warm puff of air wisped past her pink lips. She advanced on him, moving close enough that he could touch her, if he wanted to. He pushed his hands in his pockets.

She hesitated, then said, "I suspect you're here to check out the resort's liability concerning your sister's accident. I'll be glad to answer any of your questions."

He admired her guts and straightforwardness. "Then we'll be talking."

"We did all that we could," she added.

He gave a reluctant nod.

A sudden gust whipped through the pines, shaking loose a clump of snow that landed on him, breaking the building tension.

She brushed snow off his shoulder and laughed softly. He couldn't miss her stunning dimple. Then his gaze was drawn to her lovely eyes.

"Where do I find you if I have questions?"

She jerked her head a little to the left. "Hiya, neighbor."

Past another stand of pines, there were two more chalets identical to his. "You're right next door?"

She nodded.

He tossed around the fact that thanks to his reservation, she'd known he was coming and placed him precisely under her nose. She'd been prepared for him. On his mental list next to *artsy-fartsy* and *unbelievably sexy,* he added *smart.*

The two-way radio clipped to her jeans beeped. She unfastened it. "See you around, Dr. Michaels."

As she stepped away, he thought again that it was too bad she was affiliated with the resort. Too bad, indeed.

ABOUT THE AUTHOR

Larissa Emerald has always had a powerful creative streak whether it's altering sewing patterns, or the need to make some minor change in recipes, or frequently rearranging her home furnishings, she relishes those little walks on the wild side to offset her otherwise quite ordinary life. Her eclectic taste in books cover numerous genres, and she writes sexy contemporary romance, paranormal romance, and futuristic romantic thrillers. But no matter the genre or time period, she likes strong women in dire situations who find the one man who will adore her beyond reason and give up everything for true love.

Larissa is happy to connect with her readers. Stop by and say hello at her website, Facebook, Twitter, or send her an email: larissaemerald@gmail.com.

Made in the USA
Lexington, KY
07 October 2015